What Readers Are Saying About

ANGELA BENSON

"I have just loved all of your books. They are all on my keeper shelf."
> —Alabama

"I am so happy you are continuing to write, and I'm even happier that you have chosen to write inspirational romance. Keep up the good work!"
> —Mississippi

"I always recommend your books to anyone looking for a good romance."

"Anticipating your millennial release with Tyndale House. Thank you, thank you, *thank you* for keeping the faith and opening the door for inspiration fiction writers of color."
> —Michigan

"I love your stories!"
> —California

"I have read all of your books to date. I look forward to reading [more]. You're a talented lady."
> —Tennessee

"You are truly a greater writer, and I've enjoyed all of your books! It's hard to put them down. Thanks for making your characters true to life!"

romance the way it's meant to be

HeartQuest brings you romantic fiction
with a foundation of biblical truth.
Adventure, mystery, intrigue, and suspense
mingle in these heartwarming stories of
men and women of faith striving to build
a love that will last a lifetime.

May HeartQuest books sweep you
into the arms of God, who longs for you
and pursues you always.

Awakening Mercy

ANGELA BENSON

Romance fiction from
Tyndale House Publishers, Inc., Wheaton, Illinois
www.heartquest.com

Visit Tyndale's exciting Web site at www.tyndale.com

Check out the latest about HeartQuest Books at www.heartquest.com

HeartQuest is a registered trademark of Tyndale House Publishers, Inc.

Edited by Diane Eble

Designed by Jackie Noe

Scripture quotations are taken from the *Holy Bible,* New Living Translation, copyright
© 1996. Used by permission of Tyndale House Publishers, Inc., Wheaton, Illinois 60189.
All rights reserved.

This novel is a work of fiction. Names, characters, places, and incidents either are the
product of the author's imagination or are used fictitiously. Any resemblance to actual
events, locales, organizations, or persons living or dead is entirely coincidental and
beyond the intent of either the author or publisher.

Library of Congress Cataloging-in-Publication Data

Benson, Angela.
   Awakening mercy / Angela Benson.
     p. cm. — (HeartQuest)
   ISBN 0-8423-1939-5
     1. Women real estate agents—Fiction.   2. Single mothers—Fiction.   I. Title.
   II. Series.

   PS3552.E5476585 A98 2000
   813'.54—dc21   00-026866

Printed in the United States of America

06   05   04   03   02   01
9   8   7   6   5   4   3   2

I'm always grateful to God for the people he places in our lives just at the time that we need them. One such person for me has been my personal Gertrude Brinson. Though she's not the character in the book, the character's care for CeCe is very similar to the care my Mrs. Brinson has shown to me. Over the last twenty-plus years, she's prayed for me and with me, when we were together and when we were apart. She prayed for me and loved me during a time when I couldn't pray for myself and when I found it difficult to believe that God still loved me. This book is for her.

PROLOGUE
Alabama; Five Years Ago

CeCe stood alone on the back porch of the house where she'd grown up. The late November evening was cool, and she rubbed her hands up and down her arms to ward off the chill she felt. "It's all going to work out," she murmured to herself. "He'll come around. He loves me, after all. I know he does."

"CeCe?"

She turned around at the sound of the masculine voice she'd come to love. A voice whose very timbre caressed her skin like a kiss. It had been a long time since she'd felt the loving caress of his voice. Their last meeting had been anything but loving. He'd told her that he was still in love with his old girlfriend and planned to marry her, and she'd told him that their past relationship was soon to bear fruit. "Eric?"

"It's me," he said, coming around the house and up the steps. She moved back and sat on their old green glider, hoping he would join her as he often had in the past. He chose, instead, to remain standing. "Have you thought about what we talked about last time?" he asked.

The strident tone of his voice made her skin crawl. Why was he so distant? Why didn't he hold her? He used to hold her. Why didn't he hold her now, when she so needed to be held? She turned away from him and focused her attention on the bare muscadine vine. Her fondest childhood memories were of sneaking out with her father on warm August nights to pick the first berries of the season. Those had been such good, happy times. Not like tonight. She rubbed her hands on her arms again. *I should have worn a sweater,* she thought. Instead, she had chosen a light sheath that had been one of Eric's favorites. But what had been the point? He no longer loved her, and he couldn't care less what she wore or how she looked.

"CeCe," came the strident tone again.

"I can't do it, Eric. I won't do it."

He grabbed her by her shoulders and turned her around to face him. The emptiness she saw in his brown eyes confirmed that he had no feelings left for her. There was no trace of love in the dark eyes now condemning her. She wondered if there ever had been. "We have to be mature about this, CeCe." His voice calmed. "Look, we have our whole lives ahead of us. What about your plans to go to law school?"

She pulled herself away from him. "You mean *your* plans to get married, don't you?" She and Eric had spent many nights together talking about their future. He'd go to med school at Howard, and she'd join him there for law school next year. When she graduated, they'd get married. But that was before. She knew he and Yolanda were planning to get married at Christmas. Apparently they were so *in love* they couldn't wait until they graduated.

"I'm doing the best I can here, CeCe." He stuffed his hands in the pockets of his light wool pants and rocked back on the heels of his loafers. "I don't know what you want from me."

I want you to love me the way you said you did, she thought, but she couldn't bring herself to say the words aloud. She'd given up everything she believed in because of some girlish notion that she and Eric were soul mates, but she wouldn't give up the last vestiges of her pride. "Does Yolanda know?"

He flinched and she was glad. Bull's-eye! "This doesn't concern her."

CeCe had known he wouldn't tell Yolanda. She didn't think Miss Perfect Yolanda would go for marrying a guy who had gotten some other girl pregnant. "Maybe Yolanda needs to make that decision."

"This is between you and me, CeCe. Yolanda's not a part of it."

CeCe heard the fear in his voice, and the sound made her feel more in control of her life than she'd felt since learning she was pregnant. She shook her head and dropped her hands to her side. She was no longer cold. She hadn't wanted it to come to this, but what choice did she have? She was twenty-one years old, pregnant, and a senior in college. What real choice did she have? "I'd say it's between you, me, Yolanda, and our baby."

His eyes flashed anger, and he moved closer to her. "Leave Yolanda out of this."

CeCe wondered if he wanted to hurt her as much as she wanted to hurt him. She would have laughed if her tears weren't so close to the surface. Didn't he know there was no way he could hurt her more than he already had?

"Did you hear me, CeCe? I said to leave Yolanda out of this."

CeCe looked at him—really looked at him. How she'd loved this man! The dreams she'd had of life with him still burned in her heart, and she guessed the baby inside her guaranteed that the embers would always flicker. But she had more than her feelings for him—or his lack of feelings for her—to consider. She had to think about her unborn child. Placing her hands across her stomach in a protective gesture, she told Eric exactly how things were going to be. "I'm going to have this baby, Eric, whether you want me to or not. If my telling Yolanda is the only way to make you accept your responsibilities, then so be it. I'll do whatever it takes to protect my—no, *our* child."

ONE
Atlanta; The Present

Cecelia "CeCe" Williams clicked her left mouse button with fervor. She still couldn't believe she had to do one hundred and fifty hours of community service. One hundred and fifty hours! That crazy judge. Why hadn't he just let her pay the fine and be done with it? After all, it was only a few measly parking tickets.

As she finished running the numbers for her client's monthly audit report, CeCe considered how she could repay the esteemed judge for his Solomon-esque wisdom. She ought to send a letter to the mayor. And the governor. Murderers and drug dealers were getting off scot-free. Embezzlers and swindlers did no time. And here she was, getting one hundred and fifty hours of community service for a few measly parking tickets!

How many parking tickets, CeCe? came the voice of conscience she sometimes wished she could silence.

"OK, OK," she muttered aloud. "Maybe it was more than a few."

"Talking to yourself, CeCe? Now I don't know why you're doing that, when the two of us could be lunching in a quiet booth someplace making plans for our next date."

CeCe didn't have to turn around to know the words came from Larry Meadows, God's gift to women—or so *he* thought. "I'm busy, Larry," she said, her eyes fixed on her computer monitor. The Excel spreadsheet displayed before her held more interest than her unexpected and uninvited guest.

1

"But you've got to have lunch sometime," Larry said in the exaggerated drawl that he turned on and off at will. "How about having it with me today? We can go to the Ritz."

CeCe turned to look at the tall, lean, brown-skinned guy standing in the doorway of the cubicle that was her home for at least eight hours of each day. He was handsome, she had to admit. Most of the women in the office considered his aristocratic profile and boyish charm a lethal combination. Too bad they only served to remind her of someone she'd much rather forget. "That's not a good idea, Larry."

Larry looked over his shoulder as if to see whether anyone else was around. He turned back to her. "Look, CeCe," he said, his voice tight and minus the drawl now, his hands stuffed in the pockets of his tan slacks. "I've apologized a thousand times for that first date. I just got carried away. I promise you I'm not that kind of guy. I really would like to take you out again."

CeCe actually believed he was sincere. "I'm sorry, Larry, but I don't think so."

"Why not? Do you think you're too good for me?"

CeCe shook her head. A child in a man's body. She bet David, her four-year-old son, was more mature than this thirty-something man. "I don't want to go out with you again. Can't we just leave it at that?"

"Look, I'm not used to begging women to go out with me. I just thought I'd give you a second chance to see what you were missing. I guess you've lost out, though, because I'm not giving you any more chances."

CeCe stared after him as he stalked away. A few years ago, if someone had told her that most men were variations of Eric, she wouldn't have believed them. But she knew the truth now from experience. She seemed to attract two types of men: those who wanted nothing to do with a woman with a child, and those who expected a single mother to be sexually available. The first kind she understood, so she always made it clear up front that she had a son.

The second kind were still a mystery to her. They came in all shapes and sizes, and they had assorted modes of operation. Some, like Larry, went at you on the first date, assuming you were open for anything. Others were more subtle. They were willing to cultivate the relationship a little, but with the expectation that once it was established, sex would become a regular part of it. Even Christian, or so-called Christian, men seemed to have this expectation. She'd quickly grown tired of it and made her celibacy part of the initial conversations. Better they knew that up front, too.

Enough, she chided herself. She didn't need to think about men today. No, she'd made a pact with herself, and she refused to allow men to worry her. She'd been in love once, and once was definitely enough to last a lifetime. Besides, she had more important things on her mind. Like a four-year-old son who was more a little man than a little boy. Like a full-time accounting job that paid part-time wages. Like a part-time job selling real estate that seemed to need full-time hours to be profitable. Like an overzealous judge and a hundred and fifty hours of community service time.

She glanced up at the Mickey Mouse clock on the wall of her cubicle. As always, looking at David's contribution to making her office feel more homey caused a warmth to settle around her heart. She could still remember him standing on her upholstered guest chair, trying valiantly to help her position his gift in just the right spot.

This time, though, she couldn't luxuriate in the good feelings the memory evoked. It was quarter to twelve, and she knew she was going to be late for her noon community service appointment at Genesis House. The drive from her Buckhead office to Genesis House's downtown location would take a minimum of twenty minutes, and finding a legal parking space nearby would take an additional fifteen, if she was lucky. She took a bit of pleasure at the thought of Nathaniel Richardson waiting for *her* this time, though. It would serve him right for standing her up on Saturday after she'd canceled two promising appointments to show houses. Selling even one of those properties would have put her three thousand dollars closer to paying off the debts that hung over her head like a dark cloud threatening to break into a ferocious thunderstorm at any moment. If she missed another appointment because of Nathaniel Richardson's inability to keep to his schedule, the two of them were going to have serious problems working together.

"CeCe, do you want to go to lunch? We're going to Mick's."

Pushing thoughts of her debts to the back of her mind for the time being, CeCe looked around and saw two members of her work group, Debra and Cathy, standing at the entrance to her cube. "Not today," she told them. "I've got an appointment, but I'll walk out with you." CeCe grabbed her purse and followed her coworkers out of the building.

Twenty-five minutes later, after circling a two-block radius surrounding Genesis House four times, praying all the while for a surface parking space to open, CeCe pulled her blue, four-year-old-but-new-to-her Maxima into the first open space in a parking deck about four blocks away. If Nathaniel Richardson missed this meeting, she decided as she got out of her car, she'd have to go back to Judge Solomon and see what kind of sentence his wisdom would mete out for the guilty Mr. Richardson.

Thirty-three-year-old Nathaniel "Nate" Richardson stood in front of the paint-splattered windows of his Genesis House office and looked out on downtown Atlanta without really seeing it. He thought about Cecelia Williams, or more specifically, he thought about the Saturday appointment with her that he'd had to cancel. In his eighteen months as director of Genesis House, Saturday had been the first time he'd allowed his personal problems to interfere with his work. And he didn't like it. He didn't like it one bit. He was a man who believed in commitments, and he prided himself on keeping the ones he made.

A humorless chuckle escaped his lips. Here he was, bemoaning a missed interview with a community service volunteer, when his real concern was for another broken commitment. Not that he'd wanted to break that one. No, that choice had been Naomi's, but he'd participated in it just the same.

He thought it ironic that his only appointment this past Saturday had been at three o'clock, the same time as Naomi's wedding. Had it been divine Providence? Had God given him the appointment with Ms. Williams to help keep his mind off the wedding? Well, if he had, then Nate had certainly messed up that plan. The appointment served as a minor distraction, at best. He had thought of nothing but Naomi's wedding—not the one on Saturday, but the one five and a half years ago when she'd married him. The thoughts had become so oppressive that he had started to feel as though the office walls were closing in on him. He'd had no choice but to cancel the meeting with Cecelia so he could get out of here.

He and Naomi had been married only eighteen months when she told him she was leaving him. Not leaving him to return to her family and her home in Richmond, but leaving him to start a new life in Atlanta. *Shocked* didn't adequately capture his surprise at hearing her words. He'd been happy and had thought she was, too. Evidently she hadn't been, because she'd packed up and moved just as she'd said she would do. Knowing they had no chance for a reconciliation if they lived in separate cities—especially since her city of choice was the home of the guy she was engaged to before she met him—Nate sold his budding Chicago law practice and the home they'd shared and followed her here to Atlanta.

In the four years since his arrival, he'd done nothing but pursue the reconciliation that he believed God wanted for them. Even when Naomi immediately started seeing her ex-fiancé, he didn't lose hope that reconciliation would someday happen for them. He'd talked to Naomi until he'd run out of words. He'd prayed until his prayers became a soulful hum from his heart to God's ears. But by the end of their first year of separation, she'd divorced him anyway.

He still hadn't allowed himself to give up, though. Whatever he and Naomi had lost, he believed God would restore. But his hope had died on Saturday. On Saturday his marriage had finally and irrevocably ended. Naomi had become another man's wife.

The sound of the buzzer on the front door of the outer office alerted Nate to what he suspected was the arrival of Cecelia Williams. He turned away from the windows and went back to his desk, gathering the papers he would need for their meeting. As his family, his friends, his pastor—everybody, it seemed—had told him, he'd done all he could do. It was now time to put off his "sackcloth and ashes" and get on with the life that lay before him. He was blessed with a job that made a difference in people's lives, a loving and supportive church family, and parents and sisters who loved him enough to refrain from saying, "I told you so." He hadn't been able to make right the mistakes of his past—his marriage to Naomi was forever in the failure column of his life—but he could do as his loved ones counseled and accept the forgiveness that God offered him and move forward. Comforted by their advice and now believing he could heed it, he took a deep breath, said a silent prayer, and pulled open the door to the outer office.

"Cecelia Williams?" he called to the conservatively dressed, statuesque woman whose back was to him.

CeCe turned her attention from the announcement-covered bulletin board that dominated the wall of the outer office and looked up into the clear, brown eyes of the man whose face she'd just seen on one of the flyers tacked on the board, the man who was the director of Genesis House, the man who'd cost her three thousand dollars in lost real estate commissions. She knew it was the same man, even though in the picture he sported a full head of closely cropped hair and now he was as bald as Michael Jordan. It was his eyes. There were an honesty and an innocence in those eyes that attracted her and made her feel safe, while at the same time stirring up a primal need for self-protection. It wasn't a physical need for self-protection, though given his size—broad shoulders, muscular, and about six inches taller than her five-foot-seven-inch frame—such a reaction would not have been surprising. No, it was more a need to protect her emotions, maybe even her heart, which made no sense at all. She pushed those thoughts aside and tried to conjure up the anger she'd felt in response to what she considered his unprofessional behavior on Saturday. That effort failed miserably when his face broke into the biggest, stupidest, kindest smile she'd seen on an adult face in a long time.

His extended his hand. "I'm Nate Richardson, and I want to apologize for missing our meeting on Saturday. Personal problem. I hope I didn't inconvenience you too much."

"No," CeCe said, shaking his offered hand. "Everything worked out. And call me CeCe; everyone does." *Way to go, CeCe*, she chided herself. *You really told him off.* She'd wanted to tell him off, but that stupid smile of his reminded her of the one David sometimes wore when he was sitting in the middle of the floor playing with one of his toys—an open, honest smile that came out of a contented and happy heart. How could she stay angry with anybody—man, woman, or child—who wore a smile like that?

"Well, I'm still sorry, CeCe," he said again, placing the file of papers in his hands on the faded green receptionist's desk that looked as though it had seen better days. In fact, all the furniture in the room did. Surprisingly, the eclectic mix of worn furnishings gave the office a lived-in feeling that was both comfortable and full of vitality. "I want you to know right now," he continued, "that we'll count Saturday as a full eight hours worked. It's not your fault I had to leave before you got here. Sound fair?"

CeCe smiled, mentally deducting the eight hours from her required hundred and fifty. "More than fair."

"Good. Now, have you eaten lunch?"

She waved her hand, dismissing his question. "I really wanted to meet with you so I skipped lunch today."

"Well, we can't have that. What say I buy you lunch? I think I owe you one anyway."

"But you don't have to—"

He cut her off with a disarming half grin. "I know I don't have to. I want to. If I don't eat lunch, I get grouchy, and believe me, you don't want to see me grouchy. How about it? We can talk while we eat."

Her lips curved upwards at his playful words and the expression that accompanied them. "When you put it like that, I guess I don't have a choice."

After taking the file from the desk and tucking it under his arm, he opened the door for her. "Come on, then. My stomach is growling."

Laughing, CeCe preceded Nate Richardson out of the building.

"Do you feel like walking?" he asked once they were outside. He looked up at the clear June sky. "I don't think we're going to get any rain today."

She smiled as she fell into step with him and walked in the opposite direction of the path she'd taken from the parking deck. "Walking is fine."

They walked down about four blocks that were bustling with downtown workers on lunch break before Nate stopped at a street vendor's cart. "How do you feel about a hot dog or two?"

She smiled at him again. She was turning into a regular Cheshire cat around this guy. "Don't go all out on my account," she said, at ease with him enough to tease him.

He jingled the coins in the pocket of his olive slacks. "Hey, remember that Genesis House is nonprofit. Two hot dogs *is* going all out."

She laughed. "OK, I'll take a hot dog and a soda, if it fits in the budget."

"Only because I need to make up for my bad manners on Saturday," he said, his voice light with laughter, as he turned to speak to the vendor.

CeCe watched and listened as he ordered three hot dogs—one for her and two for himself—and two Cokes. As she did so, she realized that it had been a very long time since she'd been as relaxed and at ease with a man as she was with Nate Richardson.

She'd just met the man, and they were joking around as though they'd known each other for a long time. Given her track record with men, she wasn't sure this was a good thing. "Better safe than sorry" was her motto. She silently repeated it now as a reminder to protect herself around this man as she would around any other male.

"I'm impressed," he said once they were seated on a just-vacated concrete bench in Woodruff Park right across the street. The park was full of Yuppies and Buppies out on break, the city police having rid the area of the homeless during the year leading up to the Atlanta Olympic Games.

CeCe took a bite of her hot dog, then wiped the mustard from around her lips. "Impressed with what?"

He inclined his head toward her can of Coke. "You went for the caffeine and the sugar. I think we're going to get along well."

If I don't smile myself to death first, CeCe thought. "I think I'll reserve judgment until you tell me what the remaining one hundred and forty-two hours of my community service are going to be."

"One hundred and forty-two hours, huh?" Nate laughed again, and CeCe decided that she liked the sound. "You don't have to tell me, but I have to ask. What did you do to get a hundred and fifty hours?"

CeCe chomped down on her hot dog. "You wouldn't believe me if I told you."

He nodded. "Yes, I would. Stuart, your judge, is a big supporter of Genesis House, not to mention a close friend. I know he'd never send us a hardened criminal without first making me aware, and I also know he has a weird sense of humor. He's fair, though."

CeCe peered up at him over her hot dog. "Well, I'm not sure about the *fair* part." She wasn't sure if she liked the idea of this man's being friends with the judge who'd sentenced her.

"So what did you do?"

Taking another bite of her hot dog, CeCe mumbled, "Unpaid parking tickets."

He leaned toward her. "What? I couldn't understand you."

Realizing that he wasn't going to give up until he had an answer, she looked directly at him and said clearly, "Unpaid parking tickets."

"Stuart gave you a hundred and fifty hours for a few unpaid parking tickets?" Nate whistled. "You must have said something to upset him. That sentence seems stiff even for him. What did you do, mouth off to him or something?"

CeCe shook her head. "All I did was tell him how ridiculous the sentence was."

"One hundred and fifty hours." He studied her, and his probing brown eyes made her nervous. "Just how many tickets did you have?"

CeCe put the last bite of her hot dog in her mouth and answered with a full mouth.

"How many? I couldn't understand you."

What was the point in trying to evade his question? "Forty-something."

Nate's eyes widened, and his hands froze with his hot dog three-quarters of the way to his lips. "Forty-something? You mean you had more than forty unpaid parking tickets? How did you get so many?"

"I've been asking myself that same question." She lifted her shoulders in a shrug. She knew she'd gotten the tickets because she was always in a hurry and it seemed that she was never able to find a legal parking space when she needed one. It didn't matter if she was trying to get into the courthouse on her lunch break to look up the title to some property, or if she was trying to make a quick run to the pharmacy. It never failed; if she parked illegally, she got a ticket. "They just added up over the four years I've been in Atlanta. You know how you get them and toss them in the glove compartment?" He gave an affirmative nod. "Well, I guess I tossed them and promptly forgot about them."

The probing brown eyes seemed to assess her again.

"What are you thinking?" she asked.

He chuckled. "I'm thinking I'd better check my glove compartment. I probably have a few tickets in there that I haven't paid."

Surprised and pleased that he sought to identify with her on this point rather than tease her, CeCe acknowledged that her new boss was a charmer. It occurred to her again that she needed to protect herself emotionally from this man. She found him much too appealing for her own good. His smiles, his self-deprecating humor, his easy manner, and those probing eyes of his could prove dangerous to her if she didn't watch out. Her best strategy was to keep the focus of their interactions on their work. "So," she asked him in her most professional tone of voice, "you've got me for a hundred and forty-two more hours. What are you going to do with me?"

Once more his intense eyes zeroed in on her. Then he asked, "What do you want to do?"

She took a swallow of her Coke and then placed the can on the bench in the space between them. "I haven't really thought about it," she said, recalling her conversation with the receptionist when she'd come in on Saturday. CeCe had taken an immediate liking to the woman, who seemed as upset with Nate for canceling their appointment as she was. "As I told Shay on Saturday, I already have two jobs, and I'd like to keep both of them while I'm doing my community service. So I'd appreciate it if I didn't have to work all day every Saturday."

Nate nodded. "Shay mentioned that to me. I don't think it will be a problem. Any other requests?"

"Not really. If you're willing to work with me on the schedule, I'm pretty open about the work. I confess that I didn't know much about Genesis House before Saturday. Shay gave me the rundown on your programs and services, and I admit that I'm impressed with all you're doing and all you're trying to do." She didn't see a need to add that she thought some of the goals were a bit ambitious. She couldn't fault them too much for that, anyway. As one of the few Christian-based organizations run by blacks that served the poor and underserved in downtown Atlanta, Genesis House had worked miracles given what they had to work with. She was especially impressed with their community self-governance efforts in the Robinwood area, an eclectic section of the city that consisted of families ranging from the lowest socioeconomic level to the high-middle socioeconomic level. The idea of empowering neighborhoods to manage their own interests appealed to her on a very basic level. "Just tell me how I can help."

His scrutiny this time seemed to take on a greater intensity. She wondered what she'd said or done to trigger it. Just when she'd decided to ask him, his inspection ceased. He finished his second hot dog and tossed the wrapper into a can about five feet from them. Then he opened the file he had brought with him and handed her a red folder and a yellow folder. "I've been thinking of two different projects. Right now, the key concerns facing us are unemployment and teen pregnancy."

"Teen pregnancy?" CeCe took the folders as her antennae of suspicion immediately shot up. She wondered what, if anything, Nate Richardson knew about her past. Had this teen pregnancy idea just come out of the air, or was it chosen because of her unique qualifications?

"That's right, teen pregnancy. People rarely think of it in the context of the family. There's usually this picture of the pregnant teenager, all alone, but most times that teenager is a member of a family unit, and that entire unit is affected by the pregnancy."

He was right, of course, and she had the scars to prove it. "What would you want to do about it?"

"I'm not sure of the details," he said, stretching his long legs out in front of him and resting his folded arms across his stomach. "All my ideas are in the red folder. I was thinking we could start with small group sessions for the teens and their parents and see where it went from there. What do you think?"

"I'm not sure," CeCe said. What she thought was that the teen pregnancy issue hit too close to home. "What's the other idea about unemployment?"

"That's much easier. Check out the yellow folder. I was thinking we could help the unemployed and the underemployed seek new or better positions. You know, give them pointers on presenting themselves professionally in an interview, conducting an effective job search, updating their basic skills—those kinds of things. Some small group sessions where family members discuss how their job situation affects them might be a good idea, too. As you can see, I have ideas, but again, no solid plans. Do you think you can work within parameters that general?"

CeCe answered with a slow nod of her head. "I think I work best that way. I kind of understand what you're looking for, but there's still room for me to be creative in how it's accomplished. Or at least that's the way I'm reading you."

"You're reading me right."

"The people we're planning these projects for—who are they, and do they know what we're planning?"

He finished his soda and flattened the can with his hands. "They're everybody. Some people come in off the street; others are directed to us from Social Services. We've adopted the Robinwood area, so everything we offer is targeted specifically to them."

CeCe thought the continued focus on the inner-city Robinwood neighborhood was a wise and commendable choice. It showed Genesis House's long-term commitment to the neighborhood and its people. She felt a bit guilty that her personal knowledge of the area was limited to an occasional drivethrough en route to some destination in southeast Atlanta. "Does that mean I get to talk to the residents as I build the programs to make sure I incorporate what they need?"

"That's exactly what it means. You'll spend some time in the office, but your real work will be in the community. This job takes a lot out of you, but you get a lot back. I can promise you that."

CeCe believed him. She could hear the satisfaction in his voice. "So how long have you been with Genesis House?" she asked, wanting to know more about the man and what made him tick. She told herself she only wanted the information because it would help her to work with him more effectively.

"I started as a volunteer four years ago."

"A community service volunteer or a regular one?"

He laughed, and the gleam in his eyes told her that he appreciated her wit. "A regular one. The founders, Shay and Marvin Taylor, are friends of mine. You met Shay on Saturday."

"Now I'm embarrassed," CeCe said. "I thought Shay was the receptionist. She didn't say anything about being the founder."

"No need to be embarrassed," he said. The light in his eyes seemed to dim, and she wondered what had caused it. "She and Marvin haven't been around much since I took over the directorship about eighteen months ago. Shay has recently started coming in to help around the office. I hope we'll be seeing more and more of them."

CeCe knew there was a lot that Nate wasn't telling her, but she didn't feel it was her place to inquire further. She, perhaps more than most people, understood a person's right to privacy.

"So which assignment appeals to you most—teen pregnancy or unemployment?" he asked, turning her attention back to the work.

CeCe looked at the two folders. "I'd say unemployment." There was no way she was ready to lead any workshop or any discussion on teen pregnancy.

He extended his hand to her again. "Welcome to Genesis House, CeCe Williams. We're glad to have you."

As CeCe took his hand, she searched his face for some clue as to what he knew about her past and what conclusions he'd drawn about her based on that knowledge. All she saw were his bright eyes and kind smile, and maybe a tinge of the pain from a few moments ago. Having no other choice, she did what she'd done since first meeting him—she returned his smile. "Believe it or not, I'm looking forward to the experience, Nate Richardson. Maybe a hundred and fifty hours of community service won't be as bad as I had expected." As she made the statement, the thought that she should protect her heart from this man pressed against the forefront of her mind.

TWO

"Stop it, CeCe," she told herself as she turned her car into the Apple Lakes subdivision in the South DeKalb suburb where she lived. The community was so named because of the copse of apple trees the developers had planted near the entrance, not because of any lakes on the property. CeCe had been thinking about Nate Richardson and Genesis House all afternoon. She was amazed that she'd been able to get any work done, which was definitely a new experience for her. At twenty-six, she was too old and too experienced to go crazy over some guy, even a nice guy. She'd had enough of men, of that she was sure. Besides, she'd been through nice guys before. And always with bad results.

She sighed as she pulled into the paved driveway of the rambling two-story colonial that she shared with her son, David, and Miss Brinson, her dorm director from college. David was the only man in her life now, and she was sure of him. She smiled as she thought about her son and wondered where he was. Unless it was raining or he was away, he always ran to the car to meet her.

CeCe got out of the car and walked around to the back of the house. She liked coming in by way of the deck and through the den. The smell of Miss Brinson's cooking usually greeted her, and she felt good about coming home to her family. For that's what David and Miss Brinson had become. They were her family—the people she could count on. Miss Gertrude "B.B."

Brinson had been her advocate since the first day they'd met in Laura Spelman Hall during her freshman year at Spelman College. The older woman had quietly and quickly let all the girls know that she was a believer. And she'd always had an ear to listen and a heart to pray. CeCe couldn't count the number of times she'd come to Miss Brinson with some seemingly insurmountable problem, only to have her pray it into right perspective. Unfortunately, she also remembered a time when she'd shunned Miss Brinson's counsel, along with the counsel of others who'd only had her best interests at heart.

Miss Brinson hadn't held her willfulness against her, though. Rather, the woman had embraced her with open arms when CeCe had told her she was pregnant. She'd gone on to tell CeCe that she was retiring early from Spelman and had suggested that the two of them move in together. CeCe hadn't been able to find the words to express how much the offer meant to her then, and she still wasn't able to now.

Though the two of them had started out looking for a rental to share, when they'd heard about the house in Apple Lakes, they'd known it was perfect for them and the baby CeCe was going to have. Between the two of them, they had been able to come up with the down payment, and in short order, they were homeowners. The house-hunting experience had triggered CeCe's interest in becoming a real estate agent. After David was born and she'd gotten her job in Buckhead, she started to look into real estate as a part-time venture. When she learned that she could take the courses required for licensing on-line without leaving home, she decided to go for it.

"There you are," Miss Brinson said with a smile as she pushed open the screen door so CeCe could enter the house. "I thought I heard you pull in." As always, the older woman was dressed in the height of fashion. Today she wore a multicolored peasant blouse and skirt ensemble, set off with a Native American necklace and matching earrings. The total effect, including her graying, closely cropped Afro, made her look much younger than her sixty-five years.

CeCe smiled. "You didn't hear me. You must have seen me."

"Don't be smart, missy. My ears are as good now as they were when I heard you girls trying to sneak in after curfew."

CeCe followed Miss Brinson to the stove. "Well, I wasn't one of those girls," she said, lifting the cover off one of the pots. "Where's David?"

"He went with Timmy and his grandfather to the mall. Timmy needed new sneakers, and he wanted David to go with him. They should be back in a little bit."

CeCe nodded as she dipped the serving spoon into the pot of chili. Nobody made chili like Miss Brinson. Spicy and delicious. She knew chili meant that Mr. Towers, Timmy's grandfather, was staying for dinner. She liked Richard Towers and considered him a good friend. Not all grandfathers would be generous enough to share the time they spent with their grandchildren. But then Mr. Towers wasn't like all grandfathers. They had met him about three years ago when he'd helped his son move in next door. To welcome the newcomers, Miss Brinson had cooked one of her famous sweet potato pies, and the three of them had trooped over to their new neighbor's house with the welcome gift. That night she and Miss Brinson made a new friend, and eighteen-month-old David found a surrogate grandfather. Last year Mr. Towers's son had moved to Alpharetta, a suburb about thirty minutes away, but Mr. Towers still found the time to visit the "old neighborhood" whenever he made the trip down from his Virginia home, which he did at least four or five times a year. And he always made a point of including David in at least one, most times more, of his outings with Timmy.

Miss Brinson slapped the back of CeCe's hand with another wooden serving spoon. "Get out of my pot, young lady," she said in her strictest dorm director voice.

"One taste," CeCe pleaded, "just one."

Miss Brinson frowned, but there was no starch in it. CeCe giggled. "You always were a pushover."

Miss Brinson playfully pushed the younger woman aside.

"And you always were a smart aleck. Now get out of my way." She inclined her head toward the counter. "Why don't you do something useful like read your mail?"

CeCe brushed a soft kiss on Miss Brinson's forehead and then gave her a private's salute. "Yes, ma'am," she said, marching over to the counter. "Nothing but bills," she muttered to herself as she went through the short stack of mail. "I've got to get this real estate business in hand if I'm ever going to get out of debt, or we're never going to be able to start a day-care center."

"We've already started one," Miss Brinson said.

CeCe looked over at the older woman. Miss Brinson currently kept five children, including David, in their home each day. The parents were from their church, and Miss Brinson was doing it more as a friendly favor than as a business proposition. "You know what I mean. We're no closer to forming a business this year than we were last year."

"Stop worrying, CeCe. All in the Lord's timing. All in the Lord's timing."

CeCe took comfort in those words, as always. They were Miss Brinson's favorite words. Over the years, CeCe had learned personally just how true they were. She knew she'd come a long way since David's birth, and she knew she had no one to thank for that but the Lord. There were times when she had doubted she'd make it, times when she'd wanted to give up, but she hadn't. The Lord had been there for her, had brought her through. She'd attended church all her life, but it wasn't until after David's birth that she came to know the living Christ and to bask in his loving care. When people—all but Miss Brinson—had let her down, the Lord had remained true. He'd been there in her darkest moments. He knew every awful thing she'd done, and he loved her still. Not just loved her, but blessed her as well.

"Thank you, Lord," she whispered softly. "Thank you so much." She blinked quickly to stop the tears that always came to her eyes when she thought about the past, the terrible mistakes she'd made, and how much she'd endured and survived. "'Forgetting the past,'" she recited from the book of Philippians, "'and looking forward to what lies ahead.'" The truth of those words had kept her going then, and they'd keep her going now. She took a deep breath and turned her attention back to the mail. Bill. Bill. Bill. Junk mail. Junk mail. Junk mail. Bill. Junk mail.

She paused as she picked up the next envelope. Not a bill, but definitely junk mail. Without opening it, she tore the envelope in half and tossed it in the wastebasket at the end of the counter. Nothing but junk mail.

She stared at the torn envelope in the wastebasket until the tug of Miss Brinson's eyes made her give the older woman her attention. She didn't want to look at her friend because she knew what she would see. Disappointment. She sighed and forced herself to meet Miss Brinson's gaze.

The older woman didn't open her mouth; she didn't have to. CeCe heard her as if she'd been screaming. *You have to forgive them, CeCe,"* Miss Brinson had told her a hundred times, if she'd told her once.

"I have forgiven them. I'm just not ready to talk to them yet," she feebly protested her friend's unspoken reprimand. The words sounded hollow even to her own ears.

"I know, but sometimes we have to *get* ready even when we don't want to," Miss Brinson said. "Think about David, CeCe."

"I *am* thinking about David," she said, her eyes closed to stop her tears. "Who else am I thinking about? How will I explain to David that he has grandparents but that he doesn't have a father? I won't have my son in an environment with a man who doesn't want him. I won't do it, B.B. I can't do it. Not yet. Maybe when he's older."

The tears CeCe had fought finally fell from her eyes. She'd come so far, but every time she got one of those letters, she felt as though the clock turned back five years. The pain was as real as it had been then. All she'd done—and all she'd suffered because of what she'd done—weighed on her like a pile of cement pressed against her chest.

Miss Brinson came over to her and took her in her arms. "CeCe, I love you and the Lord loves you. If you give him this burden, he'll take it. He wants to take it, but you have to give it over."

"I'm trying," CeCe said between her tears. "But I can't see them. I can't. I'm just not ready yet. It still hurts too much."

Miss Brinson patted CeCe on her back. "I know it hurts, sweetheart, and it's going to keep hurting until you do something about it." She continued to hold CeCe until her tears subsided. Then she stepped back and wiped at CeCe's tears with her fingers. "I love you, CeCe; you know that, don't you?" After CeCe nodded, Miss Brinson turned her toward the downstairs powder room. "Now go wash your face before your son gets home and you scare him half to death."

CeCe gave a weak smile and moved to do as Miss Brinson directed. When she reached the entrance to the hallway, she turned and said, "I love you, too, B.B."

"And then Timmy—"

"Don't talk with your mouth full, David," CeCe said to her four-year-old son. They were having dinner with Mr. Towers in the dining room. When it was just the three of them, they normally ate in the breakfast area directly off the kitchen. The dining room gave them the extra space they needed when they had a guest. "We're not going anywhere. You have plenty of time to tell your story."

"But, Mama—"

"No *buts*. Eat."

"All right," he said, lowering his eyes to his plate. CeCe had to fight a grin when he lifted a brow to see if his meek act was working with her. Biting back the smile that always came to her face when she thought about how precious her son was, she turned her attention to Mr. Towers. "How did you put up with the two of them today?"

The older man grinned, and his eyes twinkled in his wrinkled face. Mr. Towers looked every year of his sixty-seven years—

receding hairline and all—but he was still an attractive man. "We had fun, didn't we, Davy boy?"

David opened his mouth to speak, then looked at his mother. He chewed quickly, swallowed, and then said, "We sure did, Mama. You should have been there." Now that his mouth was empty, David could tell the entire story, and he did. In detail.

When he wound down, CeCe looked at the half-eaten food on his plate and asked, "Are you finished?" David nodded. "Well, you're excused. Why don't you go get ready for bed? You've had a long day."

CeCe could tell he wanted to protest, but he must have been more tired than she guessed, because he mumbled, "Excuse me," and left the table.

"You've done a good job with him, CeCe." At Mr. Towers's words, CeCe turned to him. He nodded. "David's a good boy."

"Well, I should be thanking you for some of that, shouldn't I? You're good for him. Thank you for making time for him when you visit."

Miss Brinson stood and looked from one of them to the other. "If you two are going to start a mutual admiration society, I guess I'll clear the table."

Mr. Towers winked at CeCe. "Jealous, Gert?"

"Of what?" Miss Brinson said with a bit of sauce in her walk as she left the table with her plate in her hand.

CeCe giggled, and Mr. Towers shook his head. "That woman is going to be the death of me yet."

"I don't know about that. I think you enjoy teasing her as much as she enjoys being teased."

CeCe didn't miss the twinkle in the older man's eyes. "You're right about that, girlie, but I think I'll let her stew awhile before I give her any more. Tell me about you. How did it go at your new job?"

CeCe couldn't help it. She rolled her eyes. "New job? Don't you mean jail sentence?"

"Well, it was your decision to be a felon."

"I'm not a felon. I just had a few parking tickets."

Mr. Towers pushed back from the table, clearly enjoying CeCe's discomfort. "I know I'm an old man, but I think fifty is more than a few, even for you young people."

CeCe slapped his wrist with her open palm, not hard enough for it to hurt. "All right, you're right. Anyway, it went OK. The director seems nice enough. The work doesn't seem that hard. In fact, it seems interesting. And I think I'll still have some time for my real estate business, though, as usual, not enough."

"I don't know why you and that stubborn woman back there—" he inclined his head toward the kitchen, where Miss Brinson had disappeared—"won't let me help you out. I could loan you the money to open your day-care center, CeCe. I've told you that."

CeCe shook her head. "I couldn't let you do that. This is something I want to do on my own."

He raised his hands to stop her. "Well, don't get started. Between you and my son, I'm about to start thinking there's something wrong with my money. You two need to stop playing that same old tune."

"It's not a tune," she said. She appreciated Mr. Towers's offer more than he would ever know, but making the money to pay off her debts and free herself to start the day-care center was something she needed to do on her own. No matter how hard it was.

"Don't get all upset. You know what I meant. Look, I don't like to get both your feathers ruffled in the same night, and tonight's her night. You'll have to wait until tomorrow to get your dander up."

CeCe smiled. "You're a mess. You know that, don't you?"

The old man grinned. "I try."

"Try what?" Miss Brinson asked when she came back for the rest of the dishes.

"To be a gentlemen, of course." Mr. Towers pushed back his chair and began to help Miss Brinson clear the table. "Let me help you with the dishes."

"You don't have to do that," Miss Brinson said.

"I know I don't have to, Gert. I want to." He gave CeCe another wink.

"Well, suit yourself."

CeCe watched the two of them as they left the room. Mr. Towers was courting Miss Brinson, and CeCe didn't think the older woman even realized it. *Courting.* Now where had that word come from? But that's what they were doing. They weren't dating. They weren't a couple, but Mr. Towers was letting Miss Brinson know, in the ways that counted, that she could rely on him. That he'd be her friend whenever she needed a friend. CeCe wouldn't be surprised if he relocated to Atlanta within the next year or so, just to be close to her.

A bit of envy bubbled in CeCe's stomach. She didn't need a man, and she didn't want one, she told herself. A picture of Nate Richardson's smile flashed in her mind, and it was as if his probing eyes forced the truth from her. Sometimes—just sometimes—she did wonder if the Lord was preparing someone special for her. She had even gone so far as to paint a mental portrait of him. She knew he'd love the Lord, and David, and Miss Brinson, and her. He'd be a good husband, father, and friend. Best of all, he'd know everything about her and love her still. Her heart would be safe with him because he'd never hurt her. She'd be free to love him without fear of that love being rejected or used against her in—

"I'm ready, Mama," came David's voice from behind her. She'd been so wrapped up in her thoughts that she hadn't heard him enter the room. She pushed Nate and her fanciful thoughts from her mind and directed her attention to the realities of the present and the male who mattered in her life: her son.

"Way to go, Marcus!" Nate yelled from his seat at the scorer's table. He raised his hand to give his little pal a high five. "You're on a roll tonight. What's that, strike number three?"

The eight-year-old smiled at Nate. "Number four."

Nate whistled. "Hey, I'm going to have to watch out for you."

"How many strikes do you have, Mr. Nate?" Stephan, another eight-year-old, asked.

"I'm not telling. I think I'm going to have to start practicing before I bowl with you guys again." He glanced over at his best friend, Stuart Rogers. "What do you say, Stuart? How about you and I get together every month before we bring these guys out? They're killing us."

Stuart peered at Nate over the top of his glasses as the two men stood up. "I didn't do so badly myself. Maybe you need the practice."

Nate staggered back at his friend's words, and all ten of the eight-year-old boys who comprised their combination Bible study and big brother–little brother group laughed. "I guess that's my cue to say, 'Let's eat.'"

Nate stood back and watched the ten youngsters rush past him and down to the snack bar.

Stuart shook his head and laughed. "Sometimes I think they're more interested in the food than the bowling."

As Nate gathered the belongings the boys had left behind, his thoughts turned to his friend Marvin, who had started the group and recruited him and Stuart to colead with him. His thoughts remained with Marvin as he fell into step with Stuart and they made their way to join their charges. They were in no rush. Their monthly bowling outings put them on a first-name basis with the staff in the snack bar, who automatically gave the boys their pizza order.

"Have you talked to him this week?"

He didn't have to ask who Stuart was talking about. "I went by their house the other Saturday. The day of Naomi's wedding. I think Shay invited me because she was worried about me. I saw him. No change. How about you?"

"I went by yesterday. He's still feeling sorry for himself. I pray for them all the time, but Marvin seems to be drifting further away."

"I know what you mean. We all have our crosses to bear, and

losing a kid has to be right up there." Marvin and his wife, Shay, had lost their only child in a tragic car accident almost two years earlier, and neither was coping very well. "I think Shay is coming around. She was really worried about me last week. That's a good sign, don't you think?"

Stuart nodded. When they reached the snack bar, they placed their belongings on a table next to the one their charges had taken. They had settled into a routine that seated the adults at one table and the kids at another. Nate didn't know quite how that had happened, but he didn't have a problem with it. The time had become a very valuable sharing time for him, Stuart, and Marvin, and remained so for him and Stuart in Marvin's absence.

After he and Stuart made the rounds of the kids' table to make sure everybody was settled, they went to the counter and picked up their already prepared orders—one of the benefits of being creatures of habit as well as regular and well-paying customers.

"Thanks, Roy," both men said to the cook-cashier for the night. Then they headed back to their table.

"I do think Shay is coming around," Stuart said, continuing the conversation as if they had not been interrupted. "We can only pray that the change in her will have a positive impact on Marvin."

"Amen to that."

"So how are you?" Stuart asked, taking a bite of his Philly cheese steak.

Nate washed down a bite of club sandwich with a swallow of Sprite. "I'm good. Very good, in fact." Nate caught a movement out of the corner of his eye and turned his attention to the boys. He made eye contact with Warren Thomas, who'd gotten out of his chair and was poised to give Jerome Mims a solid thump on the head, and silently bade the boy to take his seat. With an embarrassed smile, the child did so. "The pain has eased," he said, completing his answer to Stuart's question. "It no longer hurts."

"What's the *it?*"

"What do you mean?"

"You said, 'It no longer hurts.' What doesn't hurt?"

Nate gave a rueful smile. "Remind me to find some friends who haven't passed the bar. What kind of question is that?"

Stuart wiped his lips with a paper napkin. "You know what I mean. Now answer the question."

"Well, your honor, the *it* is everything. My whole situation reminds me of David and the child he had with Bathsheba. When the child was alive, David fasted and prayed, but after the child died, he ate. The people didn't understand his actions until he explained to them that while the child was alive he prayed and fasted that God might spare him, but after he was dead there was no need to continue. That's the way I feel. For the four years of our estrangement, I could pray for and work toward reconciliation, but now that Naomi's remarried, I can no longer pray that prayer. Now I have to pray that she and her new husband find happiness together and that they make their peace with God." He paused for a moment to collect the rest of his thoughts. "I had to let my marriage go, and when I let it go, in a way, I set myself free. It's as though God prepared my heart for reconciliation or final separation, so that whichever came I would be able to deal with it. That's what I mean when I say the pain has eased."

Stuart nodded and Nate was sure his friend understood. "Enough of that," Nate said after a few quiet moments. "With friends like me and Marvin, you may never jump the broom."

Stuart finished off his sandwich and leaned back in his chair. "That's one thing you don't have to worry about. Believe me, if the woman for me came my way, I'd snap her up in a minute and say later for you fellows."

Nate laughed, just as he knew Stuart wanted him to. That's one reason he liked being around Stuart. Stuart was solid, but he never took himself too seriously. "Are you even looking for this paragon of marital bliss?"

"Never. If I looked, I'm sure I'd look up on the wrong thing. I'm just taking things as they come. I'm in no rush, but neither am I running away. How about you?"

"What about me, your honor?"

"Are you running away?"

Nate knew what Stuart was talking about, and he really didn't want to get into it because the idea was too new to him. His finding love again was now possible, but he didn't know how probable it was. If he met somebody, it would have to be because the Lord brought them together. He surely didn't see himself changing his lifestyle to seek out a possible mate, the way he had done with Naomi. He'd burned up the airways, highways, and telephone lines with trips and calls between Chicago and Richmond, and look where that had gotten him. "I guess I'm like you," he finally answered. "I'm definitely not looking, but I don't think I'm running away either."

Stuart grinned. "I sorta hoped you would say that. I have two tickets here for the Annual Fourth of July Black Tie Gala, and you have to bring a date. The good news is that you have a month to find one." Stuart leaned forward, reached in the back pocket of his jeans, and pulled out two tickets. He slid them across the table to Nate. "Complimentary tickets, of course, in deference to your nonprofit status."

"Of course," Nate said, taking one of the tickets and pushing the other one back toward Stuart. "I'll be there. You know me; I'm always ready to make a pitch for the cause."

Stuart leaned forward. "Come on, Nate. I think you need to do this. The evening doesn't have to be a romantic one. Invite one of the sisters from church. It'll do you some good to have the company of a nice female for an evening. I don't want you to forget how to appreciate the opposite sex." He pushed the second ticket back toward Nate. "All women aren't like Naomi, and all marriages don't end in divorce. I think you need to reaffirm that in your mind—and in your heart."

Nate didn't know if he agreed with Stuart's conclusion that he needed to go out, but he knew his friend well enough to know that he'd nag him to death until Nate followed the suggestion.

"Look," Stuart said, building on the case he'd already laid. "If you're uncomfortable asking somebody, though I don't know why you would be, I could set something up for you and we could go together."

"A blind date?" Nate shook his head. "I don't think so. This is something I could handle on my own if I wanted to handle it."

"You need to handle it, Nate. Do it for me. I promise you if you bring somebody to this thing, I'll get off your back."

Nate picked up the ticket, and CeCe's face flashed through his mind. She was somebody he'd like to get to know. As a friend, of course. He wondered if she'd be interested in going with him. She'd really impressed him during their meeting, and he'd been thinking about her a lot since then. They'd clicked immediately, he thought, as evidenced by the easy and natural way they had teased each other. Not a flirtatious teasing, but two friends enjoying each other's company. Then when he'd asked her what she wanted to do at Genesis House and she'd said, "Just tell me how I can help"—well, that had sealed it for him. CeCe wasn't his first community service volunteer, not by a long shot, but with that statement she'd separated herself from the others. God bless her, she wanted to help. Most people just wanted to get their hours in, and he'd assumed she'd be no different. He was happy he'd been wrong about her.

He'd noticed other things about her that day as well. Of course, he'd noticed her packaging—he was a man, after all—but he'd also gotten a glimpse of the person inside, and what he saw, he liked very much. As he'd studied her closely, he realized that her expressive face held no secrets. With CeCe, what you saw was what you got. He still remembered how she'd shyly lowered her eyes when she'd caught him observing her. He'd found her embarrassment endearing, and it had taken all of his self-control not to tease her about it.

"Do you have any idea who you're going to bring with you?" Stuart asked, interrupting his thoughts.

"I have an idea," he said evasively, "but I don't know if it's a good one." Nate didn't want to give Stuart a name, because Stuart would be like a dog with a bone. His friend could be relentless when he needed or wanted to be. A good trait in a prayer partner, but trying in certain other situations.

"What do you mean? Is it somebody from church?"

Nate shook his head. "I wouldn't feel comfortable asking a sister from church. I think too much significance would be placed on it. Right now I'm not any closer to one woman than I am to another, and asking one to go out with me might signal more than I'm ready to signal. You know what I mean?"

Stuart nodded. "That's the same reason I don't go out with women from the church. It makes life a lot less complicated. Have you thought about asking my parking ticket volunteer?"

"Cecelia Williams?" Sometimes Nate wondered if Stuart was holding back when asked about his spiritual gifts. His friend had the uncanny ability to know what Nate was thinking most of the time.

"You remember her name," Stuart said, with a knowing grin. "I take that as a good sign. Of course, she's hard to forget with those big, brown eyes of hers. How are you two getting along?"

"We're getting along. I don't know her that well." *But I'd like to.*

"Then she's perfect. Invite her to go with you. It would be a chance for you two to get to know each other. Besides, she works for Genesis House, so she's a reasonable choice. You can call it a professional appearance. That is, if she's willing to go out with a guy with a mug like yours."

Nate ignored Stuart's jab. "What do you know about her?" he asked in what he hoped was an offhanded manner. He didn't want to show interest, because doing so would only pique Stuart's curiosity, but he wanted information about CeCe, if his friend had any. "Did you know her before the case?"

Stuart shook his head. "I didn't know her, but one of the clerks in the court knew of her. She's a Christian, so there's no chance of an unequal yoke thing happening. Anyway, a friend of this clerk goes to the same church she goes to. I got the impression that she's pretty selective." He chuckled. "Actually, the guy said that she had shot down so many men at their church that they've stopped asking."

A crash sounded next to them, and they looked over at the

table of boys and saw an overturned chair. "The natives are getting restless," Stuart said. "I think we'd better shove off."

Nate got up and rounded up their group, all the while thinking about CeCe. He was glad to know she was a believer, but he wasn't really surprised. Their shared faith would explain the connection he'd felt with her. As he followed the last boy out of the bowling alley, he wondered if CeCe would shoot him down as she'd done the others and how he'd feel if she did.

THREE

"I'll be around to see you again, Mrs. Vines," CeCe said, as she and Anna Mae Wilson readied themselves to leave the elderly woman's small but immaculate two-bedroom frame home in the Robinwood section of Atlanta. After seeing David off for a day of fishing with Mr. Towers and Timmy, CeCe had met Nate at the Robinwood Recreation Center so that he could introduce her to the neighborhood and its people. Anna Mae, a resident of the neighborhood, had arrived just as CeCe and Nate were about to start their trek, and she had volunteered to take over the task. Nate had agreed, though CeCe thought he seemed reluctant— she wasn't sure what to make of that, if anything—and she'd enjoyed Anna Mae's lively companionship. In the short time the two women had been together, they had become fast friends. "Thanks so much for the peach pie," CeCe told Mrs. Vines. Then she leaned down and kissed the older woman's soft cheek.

"Next time you girls drop by," Mrs. Vines said, "I'll have you a potato custard ready. Anna Mae just loves my potato custard, don't you, Anna Mae?"

Anna Mae smiled at CeCe over Mrs. Vines's head. "I sure do, Miz Vines. I'll have to make sure CeCe gets back down here real soon if you're going to cook her my favorite."

"You do that, Anna Mae," the older woman said, taking her hand. "You just do that. I can tell that this girl has a good head on her shoulders, just like you. We need more of y'all down here to keep these young heads straight. They think they know everything, but they don't know nothing. I try to tell 'em something, but they ain't listening to me. Maybe they'll listen to y'all."

CeCe placed a hand on the woman's shoulder. "We'll just have to listen to you and then tell them what you have to say because I'm sure you can teach all of us a lot."

The older woman waved CeCe away, but CeCe could tell by her soft expression that she appreciated the praise. CeCe followed Anna Mae out of the house and back onto the street that was Robinwood. As the two of them strolled back toward the Rec Center, CeCe soaked in the neighborhood's charm. The laughter of children, the muted sounds of televisions and radios, even the husky voices of the men huddled near the corner stop sign were pleasant to her ears. Though CeCe had lived in Atlanta eight years, counting the four that she had spent in school at Spelman, she'd never spent any time in the Robinwood area. Now she knew the choice had been her loss. Robinwood was an old neighborhood with the feel of yesteryear, even the pockets with the new homes made possible by funds from the Federal Empowerment Zone program. Though some parts were still in need of renovation, on the whole, the neighborhood had a bright and sunny feel about it. Sure, some of the families were poor, but they didn't seem to be poor in spirit. Those needing help lived very close to those who could provide help. People of different socioeconomic levels shared many of the same concerns and problems. Robinwood was definitely a unique segment of Atlanta.

A child's cry followed by a mother's soothing voice turned CeCe's thoughts to David. She glanced at her watch. "It's almost four. I had no idea that much time had passed. You know, I've really enjoyed myself today," she said to Anna Mae. "Thanks so much for taking me around and introducing me to everybody. I sure didn't mean to take up your whole Saturday."

"Don't worry about it. I wanted to do it," Anna Mae said as they turned the corner and headed back to the Rec Center parking lot, where CeCe had left her car. "When Nate told me he had another volunteer, I wanted to meet you and see if I could be of any help since you're going to be helping us. Nate needs you and we need you."

The thought of Nate needing her took CeCe aback. She couldn't imagine that man needing anybody. He seemed so . . . so complete. But she knew what Anna Mae meant. "I guess another pair of hands can go a long way."

Anna Mae laughed. "Further than you've ever imagined. You'll know what I mean after you've worked with Nate for a while. He'll have you doing more work than you ever thought you'd be doing, and you'll find that *you* asked *him* for the work, not the other way around."

"Is he that bad?" CeCe asked.

Anna Mae cut a sidelong glance at her. "How long did you plan to be out here today?"

CeCe pursed her lips together. "Hmm, I think I get your point. The people here are just so nice. The time went really fast for me. It's like everybody down here is one big family. Did you grow up here?"

Anna Mae gave CeCe a brief history of her life in Atlanta and Robinwood as they continued their stroll. As CeCe listened to her and watched her expressive gesturing, she thought again how pretty Anna Mae was. Skin the color of a perfect Nabisco Nilla wafer was matched by reddish-brown hair, which she wore in twisted braids that looked like crinkles. She learned that Anna Mae had grown up in East Atlanta, but her husband's family had lived in Robinwood. After they married they'd moved here too. They had moved to New York right after the birth of their daughter, Danita, and had lived there until her husband's death a few years back. After that, Anna Mae had wanted to come home. Home to her was Robinwood.

"I could have moved somewhere else, I guess," Anna Mae was saying, "but I didn't want to. Every neighborhood has its problems and we have ours, but I still think this is a good place. And we're working to make it better. What about you? Have you always lived in Atlanta?"

CeCe didn't feel the tenseness she usually felt when she was asked about herself. She wasn't sure if that was due to Anna Mae or Robinwood or the combination. "No, I'm originally from a small town in Alabama. I came here to go to Spelman, and I'm still here."

Anna Mae stopped in her tracks. Then she stepped ahead of CeCe and turned to stare at her with widened eyes, as if she were in awe. The reaction did not surprise CeCe. It was a common one when she told people she had gone to Spelman, one of the premier historically black colleges in the country. In fact, Spelman was ranked among the top colleges in the Southeast, not just the black ones.

"I didn't know you went to Spelman," Anna Mae said after she recovered from her initial surprise. She hadn't started walking again, but her eyes were back to their normal size. "That's where I want my daughter to go. She's a junior in high school. Excellent student. Boy crazy, but a good kid. You'll have to meet her. She's excited about going since her current boyfriend—he just gradu- ated—is going to Morehouse in the fall. Sometimes I wish he wasn't. I think they're too young to be as serious as they seem to be, but what can I tell her. I'm just boring old Mama." After that long spiel Anna Mae took a deep breath, moved back to CeCe's side, and resumed walking. Then she asked, "So, did you have yourself a Morehouse man?"

CeCe fell into step with her friend and shook her head. Some- times she wished she had fallen for one of the guys she'd met at Morehouse College, the all-male counterpart to the all-female Spelman. "He went to Morehouse, but he was a boy I knew from back home. Somebody I'd grown up with. I thought the sun rose and set on that guy."

"I guess it didn't work out."

"I guess you could say that. I got pregnant, and the guy got lost. So I'm probably not a good person for your daughter to talk to."

"Are you still in love with him?" Anna Mae asked, concern in her voice.

"No," CeCe said, and meant it. "Now I don't even think I was at the time, though back then I was so infatuated that I was ready to spend the rest of my life with him. Had I not felt those feelings myself, I don't know if I could believe that anybody could feel that strongly about a person."

"All the more reason I want you to meet Danita," Anna Mae said. "She's now where you were. The boy goes to our church, and he's a good kid, but they're just so young. I'm afraid they're going to take chances that they're later going to regret. Once kids start talking about love and marriage, I think things get harder for them. They tell themselves that it's all right since they're going to be married." She shook her head, a gesture CeCe recognized as one of bewilderment. "I tell you, teenagers keep you on your knees."

"I can't even imagine. My little boy is four, going on fifty, and I want to keep him a baby for as long as possible."

"Spoken like a wise mother. Danita's gone on a field trip with her Sunday school class, or I'd introduce you to her today."

"I'll have plenty of time to meet her since we're going to be working together on these workshops. She'll probably get tired of seeing me." CeCe wasn't in a hurry to meet the young woman. She was uncomfortable casting herself as a role model.

"Maybe not. You're not her mother. It's me she gets tired of. You, she might tolerate for a month or so." Both women laughed. "I'm really glad I met you, CeCe. And I do think you're going to be good for us. You know Nate's unattached, right?"

It was CeCe's turn to stop walking and stare. "Where did that come from?" she asked, completely surprised by the question.

Anna Mae raised both hands, but she didn't break her stride. "Just passing on some information. A person can never have too much information."

CeCe forced her feet to start moving again, but she didn't respond to Anna Mae's comment. She wanted to know more about Nate, but she knew she couldn't ask without showing more interest than she wanted to show. Exactly what did *unattached* mean, anyway? Was he single, divorced, widowed? Did he have kids? For someone who thought a person could never have too much information, Anna Mae sure didn't give a lot.

"So what are you thinking about?" Anna Mae prodded.

"Oh, nothing much. Just letting my mind roam." *Roam to Nate Richardson, that is.*

They strolled on in silence, which was broken by Anna Mae's laughter just as the Rec Center came in to view. "He's divorced and his ex-wife is remarried, so I guess you could say he's free as a bird," she said as if she'd guessed CeCe's thoughts. CeCe could have hit her.

Nate tried to keep his attention on Mr. Hood's complaints about the Braves, but his eyes kept going to CeCe, who spoke animatedly with Anna Mae Wilson as they walked up the street to the Center. He hadn't intended to spend the day down here, but, as usual, the time had gotten away from him. He'd stopped to talk to one person, and then to another, and then another. And now it was after four.

He glanced in the direction of CeCe and Anna Mae again. He'd thought a lot about CeCe since Stuart had given him the tickets to the Gala. She was the first woman he'd thought about this way since Naomi, and he wasn't sure yet if the attraction was a good thing or not. First, he didn't know her very well, and second, he wasn't ready for anything romantic. But, he admitted, he found the idea of getting to know CeCe very appealing. Since she wore her emotions so close to the surface, he found her familiar and comfortable, as though he'd known her a long time. He smiled to himself. *Familiar and comfortable* sounded more like a description of a pair of old house shoes than the description of a woman.

So how was he going to ask her to go to the Gala, if he decided to ask her? He couldn't remember the last time he'd asked a woman to go somewhere with him. He could give her the ticket, he supposed, and tell her she was welcome to attend as a guest of Genesis House. In which case, they would meet at the Westin Peachtree Plaza. Or he could ask her if she'd like to go with him to represent Genesis House. In that case, he'd pick her up.

He nodded at Mr. Hood's next complaint and tried to keep his attention focused on the older man, but it was no use. When Mr. Hood stopped to take a breath, Nate made his excuses and went to meet Anna Mae and CeCe.

"It's about time you got some new blood around here, Nate," Anna Mae teased as he approached them. "I think I like this one."

Nate pulled on one of her braids and grinned at her. "What's new about that? You like everybody, Anna Mae."

"Well, not quite," Anna Mae said, her eyes directly on him. At times like this, Nate knew the church he attended was much too small. Too many people knew your business. Too many people cared.

"Anna Mae is going to help me with the workshops," CeCe said. "She has some great ideas."

Anna Mae shrugged off the praise. "Not really. I just know what I wish somebody had told me. I think this job series is a really good idea. I'm just sorry that it's taken us so long to do it."

"All in God's timing," CeCe said.

"Well, yeah, maybe, but sometimes I get the feeling God is waiting around for us to make a move." Anna Mae turned away when someone called her name. When she turned back to CeCe and Nate, a frown marred her lovely face. "That's my girl, Danita. Apparently, they got back early from the field trip. You'll have to meet her the next time you're down here," she said to CeCe. "I think you'd be a good influence on her. That girl makes me wonder how my mother survived my teenage years. Well, let me go. I'll see you next week, CeCe. And I'll see you tomorrow, Nate."

"I look forward to it, Anna Mae," CeCe called after her.

Nate noticed CeCe was quiet as she turned and followed him over to their cars. He wished for the animation she'd shown with Anna Mae or the teasing banter she'd displayed on their first meeting. "So you and Anna Mae hit it off," he said.

"Definitely. She's a really nice woman. Thank you for introducing me to her. Now you won't have to squire me around the neighborhood. Anna Mae said she'd do it."

He kicked away a stone that was in their path. "Sounds like Anna Mae. She's the best. I've known her a long time. We go to the same church."

CeCe's eyes twinkled with what he suspected was mischief. "She didn't mention that you went to the same church, but I did get the impression that she knew you well. She said that I should watch out for you because you're a slave driver."

The teasing in her voice made him smile. "That's Anna Mae. She calls them like she sees them. Of course, in this case, she's overstating the situation. I'm not a slave driver. At least I don't think I am. Am I?"

CeCe laughed, a melodious sound to his ears. "I don't know. I do know that I had only planned to be out here for four hours, and I've been here almost eight. We just finished an early dinner with Mrs. Vines."

They stopped walking when they reached CeCe's car. Now that the mood between them was light, Nate was reluctant to end their time together. "Let me guess. She gave you potato custard for dessert."

CeCe shook her head and licked her lips together in an exaggerated fashion. "That's for my next visit. I got peach pie this time. The woman could sell the recipe and become the next Famous Amos."

He raised a brow. "I guess you told her all this, right?"

CeCe nodded and leaned back against the door of her Maxima, making Nate wonder if she was as reluctant to end the conversation as he was.

"You were too easy. Anna Mae should have told you to hold back a little on the praise. You would have come away with enough food to last you a week."

She tapped the toe of her shoe against his. "You're so bad. I know you don't do that."

"I plead the fifth." He raised his right hand. "You have to

remember that members of my sex don't tend to be that strong with baking. Now we can grill up a side of beef in a minute, but a pie—forget it."

"Sounds just like a modern man," she chided.

"True because, above all, the modern man is honest."

"Touché," CeCe conceded.

Their conversation had about run its course, but Nate still didn't want her to leave. "So you think this job is going to work out for you?" he asked, when he could think of nothing else to say.

"Maybe too well," CeCe said in a way that made him think she'd seriously considered the matter. "I have a feeling that working for a slave driver like you is going to take all my energy, and I won't have time for my real estate business or anything else for that matter." She studied him for a long moment before continuing. He wasn't sure what she was looking for or whether she found it. "How do you keep the work from consuming all of your life?" she asked.

He thought about her question because he sensed his answer was important to her. "I haven't really considered my work at Genesis House as consuming my whole life. I've had a lot of time to give." For Nate the job had been a godsend. It had given him something productive and worthwhile to do while he waited for the reconciliation that he prayed for and dealt with the guilt he felt for the role he'd played in the failure of his marriage. "Actually, I think the time requirement has been a positive aspect of the job for me. Besides, the job has its benefits. For example, I get invited to all sorts of functions. I have complimentary tickets to this year's Fourth of July Black Tie Gala."

"And those go for about two hundred and fifty dollars each, don't they?" CeCe asked, clearly impressed. Nate considered that response an encouraging sign.

"You got it."

"Well, I guess there are benefits. So why didn't I get a ticket?"

Nate knew she was teasing him, but she'd also just given him the perfect opportunity to invite her to the Gala. Should he, or shouldn't he? Well, it was an open door, he reasoned. He decided to walk through. "I do have two tickets and I'd love to—"

Nate felt a tightness in his chest when she lowered her eyes. The somber expression he'd read in them told him that she knew where he was going, and she didn't want him to go there. The lightness of the afternoon and their time together slipped away as she began to speak. "Nate, you're a very nice man and I think we're going to work very well together, but I try to keep my work life and my personal life separate. I think it's best that way. Nobody gets confused. You know what I mean?"

"Yes," Nate said, her *"you're a very nice man"* still ringing in his ears. "I know what you mean. Maybe that is best." When she moved away from the car and turned to open the door, he held it open for her and closed it after she was seated. As she drove off, he chided himself for even thinking about asking her. What did he know about women, anyway? Not much, as his experience with Naomi made very clear. Besides, he didn't need any complications in his life. If CeCe wanted it strictly professional, he'd keep it strictly professional.

CeCe cut Nate a glance as she started the car and pulled out of the parking lot. She couldn't help but notice the twitch in his cheek. She'd hurt him. She knew she had. But it had been necessary. A little hurt now was better than a lot of hurt later. There was no future for her and Nate. Oh, but how a part of her had wanted him to ask her. She'd never been to an event like the Gala, and the thought of going with someone like Nate was tempting. Too tempting. She just wasn't sure she was ready for the associated risk.

She hadn't been around Nate very much or very long, but she'd known from their first encounter that he was a man who could break her heart. Maybe not intentionally, but break it just the same. She'd been down heartbreak road before, and she couldn't go there again. Clarifying the boundaries of her relationship with him had been the right thing to do. Whoever said it was better to have loved and lost than never to have loved at all must never have lost at love.

FOUR

CeCe was apprehensive as she drove to the Robinwood Recreation Center at nine Saturday morning for the first of the series of employment workshops that she and Anna Mae would be conducting. First, she felt guilty for having to bring David along this morning. It really wasn't fair that he had to be cooped up inside with her on a sunny day like today, but she had no other choice. Miss Brinson and Mr. Towers had gone to Savannah with the Seniors group from church, and the baby-sitter had canceled at the last minute. Second, this would be the first time she'd seen Nate since she'd declined his invitation two weeks ago. Her planning meetings with Anna Mae had occurred at Anna Mae's home or here at the Center, and her one or two trips to Genesis House had occurred when Nate wasn't around. During the two weeks, she'd replayed their conversation over in her mind at least a thousand times. Her conclusion: she'd overreacted. And third, she didn't know how Nate would react when he found out she had a child. He didn't know anything about her, and she knew very little about him. What if he turned out to be as shallow as the Erics and Larrys who'd passed though her life?

"Wow, look at that, Mama!" David called out from behind her, where he was buckled into his booster seat.

CeCe didn't have to ask what her son was looking at. Nate, two boys who looked to be a little older than David, and a mutt about as big as David were playing in the grassy area to the left of the Center's entrance. The dog seemed to belong to Nate, and she wondered if the boys did, too. "When we get out of the car, I don't want you to go near that dog, David," CeCe said, knowing her son's inclinations. She also knew the "I want a puppy" litany she'd be hearing for the next few weeks.

She shut off her car's motor, quickly got out, and proceeded to assist David out. "Come on, sweetie," she encouraged as her son wrestled with his seat belt. "Let Mama help you."

"No, Mama," David said. "I can do it."

CeCe bit her lips together and told herself not to be impatient with her independent young man. She'd been warned that the fearsome fours made the terrible twos look like fun. With no assistance from her, David managed to unbuckle his seat belt and scoot out of the car.

"Wait right there," CeCe said as she reached in after him and grabbed a couple of his books and toys. When she turned to him, he was bouncing from one foot to the other and his eyes were glued to the dog.

"That sure is a big dog," David said, with a tinge of what sounded like fear in his voice.

Good, CeCe thought, as David slipped his small hand into hers. Now she wouldn't have to tie him down to keep him away from the animal.

"Hi," Nate said when the two reached the entrance. He and the dog had left the boys to come and greet her and David. He wore a smile that suggested he wasn't perturbed by their last encounter, but she read the question in his eyes as he looked from her to David.

"Morning, Nate," she said brightly. Not too brightly, she hoped. Tugging on David's hand to bring him forward, she added, "This is David, my son. David, this is Mr. Nate, my boss."

She waited to see the reaction in Nate's eyes. Would she read disappointment or budding excitement? She was pleasantly surprised when she saw neither. He stooped and extended his hand to her son. "Nice to meet you, David."

David shook the offered hand but moved back closer to his mother.

Nate's face smiled when the sheepdog-mutt nuzzled at his back. "No need to be scared of old Shep here," he said to David. "He's nothing but a big baby." He looked back at the other boys, who had moved in closer to the dog. "Isn't that right, fellows? Old Shep is nothing but a big baby." As if to prove him right, the boys jumped on Shep's back. Then the dog turned and sent the boys flying onto the grass in a gale of little-boy laughter.

"I've never seen a dog that big," David said, his eyes wide and his hand holding CeCe's even tighter.

"He's big, and he likes to play. Do you like to play?" Nate asked. His interest in David struck CeCe as genuine.

David nodded but moved even closer to her.

CeCe sighed. She wasn't surprised at David's reserve with Nate. She was used to it, but it always made her wonder how different David's life would have been if Eric had assumed his parental responsibilities. She didn't complain or worry much about her son's skittishness, though, because she trusted God to be the Father her son didn't have, and so far, he hadn't let her down. "We'd better get inside," she said to Nate. "I'm late already and Anna Mae's probably wondering if I'm going to stand her up."

From his crouched position next to her son, Nate looked up at her. "Anna Mae's fine. She's in her element when she's telling people what to do." He said the words fondly, with no trace of malice.

"Well, I'd still better get in there."

"You're taking David with you?" he asked, as she tugged her son's hand to get him moving.

Her back stiffened. "You have a problem with that?"

He grinned, and his probing eyes told her that she was the object of his amusement. "None." Then he rubbed his hand across David's head. "But I bet David isn't looking forward to being cooped up all day, are you, David?"

The boy shook his head and looked up at his mother. She could read the question in his eyes and was about to give him a negative answer when Nate spoke. "Why don't you leave him out here with me, Shep, and the boys? We'll take good care of him." As if the big dog knew Nate was talking about him, he chose that moment to nuzzle again at Nate's back, almost knocking him over.

David giggled and moved a bit away from CeCe, and toward Nate and the dog.

Nate fell to the ground in exaggerated fashion, and Shep jumped on top of him and began licking his face. The play attracted the other boys, and soon they had jumped into the fray as well. They looked so silly and Nate was so obviously faking that CeCe couldn't help but laugh too. David started with a soft giggle and was soon engaged in full-fledged laughter along with the others.

From under the pile of boys and dog, Nate looked over at David. "You're not laughing at me, are you, David? We men have to stick together. It's us against the dogs, don't forget that. You should help the fellows pull this mutt off me."

CeCe looked down at her son, whose eyes had grown wide at Nate's suggestion.

"Fortunately, I have a secret weapon." Nate pulled something from his pocket—a dog biscuit, maybe—and tossed it about fifty feet away from him. As if on cue, the big dog ran after it, the two boys on his heels.

Nate got up and brushed the debris from his jeans. "How'd you like to stay out here and help me, Shep, and the boys wash my truck?" he asked David. "We could even give your Mama's car a good wash." He leaned closer to the child and lowered his voice. "Between you and me, I think the Maxima needs a wash. Badly."

"Mama—"

"You don't have to do this, Nate," CeCe said before her son could pose his question. "David can spend the morning inside with us. I brought along some toys and books."

"It's not a bother, really. If I can handle two of the little rascals—" he pointed toward the other boys—"I can handle one more." At her hesitancy, he added, "We'll be right out here where you can see us from the window. Of course, you can come out and check on us any time you like."

"It's not that I don't trust you—"

"Then go on inside. David and I will be fine."

CeCe looked down at David's eager face and up at Nate's solemn one. Though she hadn't known Nate that long, she didn't doubt he would take good care of her son. His interaction with the other boys assured her of that much. And she had no doubt that David would enjoy himself. She just didn't feel right letting Nate do this personal favor for her, not after she'd gone out of her way to tell him that she wanted to keep her personal life and her professional life separate. She didn't want Nate to think she was sending mixed messages, or worse, that she would accept personal interaction when it benefited her. She looked down at David again, and the excitement in his features made her decision for her. "You do what Mr. Nate tells you to do, David, and don't ask him a million questions, all right? I'll be right inside if you need me." She glanced up at Nate. "He's at that age where everything is a question, but I'm sure you know that."

"No problem. I'm used to it." Nate placed his hand atop David's head again. "Besides, I like questions. Don't worry. We'll get along fine. Go on inside. I promise to keep my eyes on him."

CeCe met and held Nate's glance for a moment; then she nodded and went into the Center.

Nate watched CeCe as she walked away, thinking again that she was a fine figure of a woman.

"Are we gonna wash your truck?" David asked him.

Nate turned to the boy, glad for the distraction. He knew he didn't need to be thinking about CeCe's fine figure. He smiled at David, who looked so much like his mother. They had the same expressive face and the same big brown eyes. "We sure are, but first we have to track down our helpers. Think you're up for it?"

David gave a vigorous nod that made Nate's stomach tighten. Needy kids always got to him. And he could spot the needy ones a mile off. Unless he was wrong, David was one of them. Not unhappy, no, not that. Just needy. With a smile, he took the boy's hand and led him over to the other boys. After brief introductions, he directed his group back to his truck, where he assigned each one a specific task and pointed them to the appropriate supplies.

When he had everything organized and David was hard at work on his task of scrubbing the floor mats, Nate's thoughts returned to CeCe. There were many layers to the woman. He guessed she was raising David alone. That would explain the neediness he saw in the boy as well as CeCe's reluctance to be separated from her son. The thought that she might have gone through a divorce made him sad, for both her and her son. He knew the pain he'd felt, and he didn't wish that on anybody—especially an innocent child like David. Though Nate had wanted children, he was glad now that he and Naomi hadn't had any. Divorce was hard enough on adults. He knew it had to be even harder on children.

He shook off the sad thoughts and the questions, and turned to David. "How you doing, sport?"

By the time CeCe reached the classroom, Anna Mae was already up in front introducing the morning's session. She tried to slip into a seat in the back of the room and let her friend continue without her, but Anna Mae called her to the front, and they coled the session just as they'd planned. About halfway through, she saw Shay enter the room and take a seat in the back. She stayed there until something outside the window caught her attention. Shay gazed out the window for a few minutes, then she eased back out of the room.

The session continued smoothly and ended right on schedule, after ninety minutes. CeCe and Anna Mae chitchatted for about half an hour with those who wanted to hang around. After the students had all gone, the two women began to gather their equipment and belongings.

"You did a great job, Anna Mae," CeCe told her new friend. She wasn't exaggerating, either. "I think you should handle it on your own next week. I'll be here, but I think you can do it."

"I'm not ready yet, CeCe," Anna Mae said as she placed the slides they'd shown back into the carrier. "But give me some time. I had a real good time today. You make it seem so easy."

"We're a good team," CeCe said absently. The sight of Nate, David, and the dog playing together outside had commanded her attention. She wondered where the other boys were.

"He's good with kids, isn't he?" Anna Mae commented from behind her. "He must have guessed some of the parents would bring their children with them. His taking care of them made it easier for the parents to concentrate on the session."

CeCe nodded her head at Anna Mae's words, but she didn't say anything. The workshop had gone well, the participants had left happy, and from what she could see from the window her son had had a great time with Nate and company. Then why did she feel so down?

"Hey, did you hear me?" Anna Mae asked.

CeCe turned around. "I'm sorry, Anna Mae, my mind was somewhere else."

Anna Mae lifted her brows. "You wouldn't be the first."

"What do you mean by that?" CeCe asked, though she could have made a pretty good guess.

"I mean you wouldn't be the first woman to be distracted by Nate Richardson. He's definitely something to look at, isn't he?"

Only if you're into tall, dark, and handsome. "I wasn't looking at Nate," CeCe said. And she wasn't, not really. She had been watching David with Nate.

Anna Mae lifted her shoulders in a skeptical shrug. "Hey, it's nothing to be embarrassed about. I've done my share of looking, too. Besides, Nate's a great guy." She looked out the window. "Your kid seems to think so, too. Nate's good with kids. He and a couple of his friends lead a small group at church for boys a little older than yours."

CeCe looked out the window at the two of them again. She agreed with Anna Mae's assessment that Nate was good with kids. She had kept watch on him and the boys during the workshop and, from what she saw, Nate had handled them effortlessly. It had seemed he was having as much fun as the boys were. "I know you said he was unattached, but were those other two boys his children?" she finally asked, no longer able to keep her curiosity at bay.

Anna Mae frowned. "Your mind really was somewhere else, wasn't it?"

CeCe didn't know what her friend was talking about, and she was sure her eyes reflected her cluelessness.

"No, sad to say," Anna Mae answered, "Nate doesn't have kids. Those two boys belonged to a couple of the parents who were in our session," she explained. "If any man deserved kids, Nate did, but that wife of his—"

"Wife?"

"I mean ex-wife. They've been divorced for a few years now, and she recently remarried and set that man free. It couldn't have been more than a month ago." Anna Mae waved her hand, dismissing the ex-wife and her new marriage. "Whatever. I'm sure if it had been up to him, he would have some kids, but that ex-wife . . ."

"What about her?" CeCe asked, looking out the window again.

"Nate's had some rough breaks, but it's not my place to tell you about them. I've said too much already. Are you interested in him?"

CeCe turned to stare at Anna Mae. "In whom?"

Anna Mae rolled her eyes. "The tooth fairy. Nate. Who else are we talking about?"

CeCe turned away and needlessly began straightening the chairs in the first row. "No, I'm not interested in him. I don't even know him." A fresh thought formed in her mind, and she turned back to Anna Mae. "You and Nate—?"

Anna Mae lifted her hands, palms out. "No way. We're friends. We go to the same church. That's it. Besides, Nate's not my type."

"What type is that?" CeCe asked.

"Older," Anna Mae said. "At least ten years older."

"You're not that old yourself." CeCe guessed Anna Mae was no more than thirty-six, though she could have been off a year or so. "Besides, what does age have to do with it?"

"Nate needs somebody as innocent as he is."

"Innocent? I thought you said the man was divorced."

"Not that kind of innocent," Anna Mae explained, "but somebody who sees the world the way he does. That divorce would have rocked a weaker man, but I think it made Nate stronger. He needs somebody with the same innocent faith that he has. Somebody who continues to believe even when the circumstances have so obviously turned against her. Not just faith in God, but faith in people too. Now that's real faith. And that's what Nate has."

CeCe wasn't so sure if Anna Mae was right that having faith in God and in people was a sign of real faith. Faith in God she could definitely support, but faith in people was something else. Experience told her that people would let you down. It was a lesson she had learned well. "The way I see it," CeCe said, "people are fallible, and your best bet is not to put too much faith in them. You set yourself up to be hurt if you do. And regardless of how much faith you think you have in God and in your ability to know his will, there comes a point when you have to accept that you were wrong, and that even though your intentions were right, and even though you had all the faith in the world, you were just wrong."

"Are we still talking about Nate, or are we talking about you?" Anna Mae asked, her voice soft and caring.

"A little of both, I guess." CeCe turned her gaze away again, a bit embarrassed that she'd been so transparent. She'd been thinking about the past. At one time, she'd convinced herself that Eric was the man she'd spend her life with, the man God had chosen for her. She'd had faith in God, and faith in Eric. How wrong she'd been.

"Do you want to talk about it?"

CeCe tried to shake off the past. "Not really. It's such a beautiful day, and I promised David we would go out for pizza. Let's just keep things on a light note." She touched Anna Mae's shoulder. "I appreciate your asking, though. It means a lot." She and Anna Mae had talked briefly about their pasts in the couple of weeks they'd known each other. As mothers raising children alone, they shared many of the same hurts, many of the same concerns, but CeCe had never discussed the details of her relationship with Eric, and she wasn't sure she ever would.

"What are friends for?" Anna Mae said, then she laughed. "You know, some good came out of those parking tickets, anyway."

CeCe groaned. "Please. I hate to even think about those parking tickets. I still can't get over that judge."

Anna Mae laughed again. "It sounds just like Stuart."

"You know the judge?" It seemed to CeCe that the world was a lot smaller than she'd imagined. She didn't need six degrees of separation to find a person who knew him. It seemed everybody knew Judge Rogers.

Anna Mae went back to the desk and loaded the slide carrier into its case. "Didn't I tell you? He goes to our church too. He's a good guy. You should meet him. I know you two would hit it off."

"There might be some hitting, all right," CeCe murmured. "I'd probably hit him."

Anna Mae laughed again. "Now *that* I'd like to see. The women at church have spoiled him—Nate too, for that matter. Unattached men can about get away with murder in our church."

"I know what you mean. They can do no wrong at my church either."

"And it doesn't help that both of them are so handsome and so blessedly faithful."

CeCe laughed at the pique in her friend's voice. "You're sounding upset?"

"Well, I am. I'm tired of these women fawning all over these men. It makes the men think more highly of themselves than they ought to think, if you ask me. They could actually start believing we're fortunate they give us the time of day, and then where would we be?"

"You don't have to tell me." CeCe thought about Larry from work. "I've met some of those guys before."

Anna Mae's lips twitched in barely contained laughter. "Well, there is one good thing I can say about it."

"What's that?"

"I bet we have the best-dressed, best-groomed women in Atlanta in our church. There's been a noticeable improvement in the personal care department since Nate and Stuart joined."

Both women laughed. "Anna Mae, you ought to be shot for saying that."

Anna Mae stepped back and placed her hands on her hips. "Why? It's the truth and you know it." She looked as though she were about to say something else, but she glanced at her watch instead. "Oh, no, look at the time. I promised that daughter of mine that we'd go shopping for some new clothes for her today, and I'm running late. Just a wonder she hasn't beat a path down here to get me. Are you ready to get out of here?" she asked, lifting the carrier case off the desk.

"Sure," CeCe said, her thoughts returning to Nate, his ex-wife, and his lack of children. She wondered if different opinions about children had led to their breakup, but she couldn't imagine Nate leaving his wife. He didn't seem the type. The wife probably left him, and if that was the case, he was probably still in love with her. CeCe told herself she shouldn't care since she wasn't interested in Nate. But she did care.

"OK, I'm ready," Anna Mae said, pulling CeCe's thoughts back to the task of returning the classroom to its before-workshop state.

"Me, too." CeCe gathered her purse and the toys and books she'd brought for David and followed Anna Mae out of the meeting room.

Both women headed for the doors, but they stopped when they saw Shay standing in the foyer looking out one of the windows at the main entrance. Anna Mae chatted with them for a couple of minutes, then made her excuses and headed for home.

"Take care," CeCe said to Anna Mae. "And tell Danita I said hi. I'll see you next week." CeCe had met the teenager a couple of times now, and she didn't think Anna Mae had anything to worry about. Danita seemed much more mature and grounded in her faith than CeCe had been at her age.

When CeCe turned back to Shay, the tears streaming down the woman's face replaced all thoughts of Danita. Shay had to have been on the verge of tears the entire time they'd been talking with Anna Mae. *Why didn't I notice?* CeCe asked herself.

"What's wrong?" CeCe asked. She looked out the window and guessed that Shay had been watching Nate and David fly a kite. CeCe pulled Shay into her arms and tried to calm her. She chastised herself for not thinking about the effect David would have on her. Anna Mae had told her of the despair Shay and Marvin had fallen into after the death of their son. She should have considered her friend's feelings. Shay had sat in on a couple of CeCe's and Anna Mae's planning meetings, and CeCe suspected she would show up today. She should have planned for that possibility.

"I'm so sorry, Shay," she said. "I wouldn't have brought David if I'd known he'd have this effect on you."

Shay sniffled some more, then said, "No, no, I'm glad you brought him. He's such a wonderful little boy. The two of them out there now remind me so much of Marvin and Marvin Jr. Oh, CeCe, I miss my little boy so much."

CeCe just held her friend. She had no words to give her. As a mother, she knew platitudes would do more harm than good, so she just let her friend cry her way through. When her tears seemed to subside, CeCe asked, "Will you tell me about Marvin Jr., Shay? I want to get to know him."

Shay smiled a trembling smile and began. She told of the joy she and Marvin had experienced when they'd found out she was pregnant, how protective Marvin had been during her pregnancy, and how proud they'd both been that their first-born had been a big, healthy boy. "He was such a bright boy, CeCe, so happy, and so in love with his father. The two were inseparable. Oh, I miss them both so much. It's as though I've lost Marvin too. I don't know if we'll ever get over losing Marvin Jr."

CeCe listened with an almost envious heart. While she couldn't bear to allow herself to even consider the possibility of going through such a tragedy, she was envious of the intimacy Shay and Marvin had shared. Shay's story made her relive the anguish and aloneness she'd felt when she'd learned she was pregnant. How she'd gone through her pregnancy in a state of near depression. The shame she'd felt. And the guilt. Her dreams of pregnancy had always included the doting father and loving husband that Shay had in Marvin. Her reality had been much different.

"Thank you, CeCe," Shay said, gripping her friend's hand tightly. "Thank you for bringing David here today. You know, I haven't really allowed myself to enjoy a child since Marvin Jr.'s death. It was time, and I'm not sure I would have figured that out had you not brought David."

CeCe didn't have a response, so she just pulled Shay into a warm embrace. When they separated, Shay said, "Why don't you go on. I'm going to go freshen up before I go home. Marvin's waiting for me, and I don't want him to know I've been crying. Tell Nate I'll lock up, and he can head home too."

"Are you sure? I can stay with you."

Shay squeezed CeCe's hand. "You've done more than enough. Please go and enjoy your son before I feel even more guilty for crying all over you."

CeCe studied Shay's face, trying to determine if her friend was really OK. Her smile was wobbly but sincere. CeCe nodded. "OK, I'll go, but you call me if you need to talk."

"Mama, Mama," David called to her just as she stepped outside the Center. He ran toward her, his little legs pumping furiously.

"Slow down, David, I'm right here," she called to him. "I'm not going anywhere."

By the time he reached her, he was nearly breathless. "Guess what, Mama? Mr. Nate's taking me to a ball game. He said Timmy could come, too."

CeCe looked from her son to Nate, who'd just walked up behind the little boy. "Is that right?" she asked Nate. She couldn't help but notice that he looked as fresh now in his jeans and polo shirt as he had when she'd first seen him—a true sign that he was experienced with children. An inexperienced person would look a bit worse for the wear after spending the morning with three rambunctious little boys and a huge, playful dog.

"Hold on a minute, sport," Nate said. "Remember I said we had to *ask* your mother, not *tell* her."

"Ask her, Mr. Nate. Ask her."

CeCe grinned at the sheepish expression on Nate's face. Leave it to David to embarrass the man. "That's right. Go ahead, ask me, Nate."

"OK, I'm caught. I admit it. I coach this Little League team at church—the guys are a little older than David—and I thought he might enjoy seeing them play. Of course, you're welcome to come, too."

"Please?" David begged. The hopefulness in his bright eyes told CeCe that Nate had completely won over her son.

She grinned at her child and then at the man who'd brought him such joy. "If you're sure."

"Positive," Nate said.

"Yeah," David said. That battle won, he went for a second one. "I'm hungry, Mama. Can we go get the pizza now?"

CeCe looked down at her son. "We sure can."

"Can Mr. Nate come, too?" David asked.

CeCe's gaze skittered over to Nate, then back down at her son.

"We can't tie Mr. Nate up all day, David. It was nice enough of him to watch you while I taught my workshop. You'll see him again at the ball game."

David looked up at Nate. "But you want to come, don't you, Mr. Nate? You want to see me play the pinball game. You remember, don't you, Mr. Nate? I told you about the pinball."

Nate smiled down at the boy. "Sure I remember, sport. And I am getting a little hungry." He rubbed his stomach as if to prove his point. "I could go for a large pizza about now." He looked over at CeCe. The expression he wore bore a remarkable resemblance to the one David had worn when he was pleading to go to Nate's ball game. "That is, if your mother doesn't mind me tagging along."

She looked at Nate and wondered if thoughts of her personal/professional proclamation were floating around in his mind, but his face gave away nothing. How could she say no? Both of them were giving her puppy-dog looks. After all, Nate had been so nice to David, and David wanted him to come. Besides, what could happen over pizza with a four-year-old chaperone? "Of course, I don't mind," she said in what she hoped was a relaxed tone. Inside, her heart was thumping. She hadn't forgotten her internal warning to guard her heart around this man. "We're going to Kids' Pizza. I hope you're ready for more kids."

Nate grinned at her. "Like I always say, a man can never get enough of kids."

CeCe returned his banter. "And like I always say, spoken like a man who doesn't have kids."

Nate's expression sobered, and he gazed into her eyes. She would have sworn that those probing eyes of his read every thought on her heart. "How would you know whether or not I have kids, Ms. Williams? Been checking up on me?"

CeCe held Nate's gaze, and the dance of flirtation reflected in his eyes made her question the safety of the pizza lunch they were about to share. He was definitely flirting with her. Had he misread her invitation to lunch as something more than it was? She hoped not, but . . . *He meets David and immediately he starts flirting.*

She put the pieces of the puzzle together in her head as she'd done many times in the past. In those cases, she'd been disappointed to find out the men were so shallow. With Nate, she was more than disappointed. She was hurt. She'd wanted him to be different.

FIVE

Good going, Richardson, Nate chided himself as he followed along in his truck behind CeCe and David to the pizza place. *Why'd you have to get all cute with her? The first time you flirt with a woman in over five years and you blow it. CeCe told you she wasn't up for anything personal, and what do you do—you flirt with her.* Her big brown eyes had gone dark at his comment, and he'd been at a loss for how to extricate his foot from his mouth. She probably thought he was a lecher or something. OK, maybe *lecher* was too strong a word, but he could tell that his comment had hurt her. Even though he thought she might have been a bit oversensitive, he didn't want to see her hurt—or to be the one to hurt her.

The thing was, he liked her. Really liked her. Of course he found her attractive. That didn't surprise him. That he liked her did surprise him. He liked her outlook on life, the little that he knew of it. He liked the way she had jumped in with both feet at Genesis House, the loving care and acceptance she'd shown the people of Robinwood, the relationship she had with her son. He even liked her shy smile. And he especially liked how easily embarrassed she was. In fact, there wasn't anything about CeCe Williams that he didn't like. Everything about her, and now her son, tugged at his heart in a way he had not expected.

He'd felt a similar tug when he'd first seen Naomi. That time, he'd gone into full Nate mode and set out to win the heart of the one who'd so easily grabbed a part of his. Of course, he'd told himself that he was only following God's lead. Now he wasn't so sure that's what he'd been doing. Naomi had been elusive, very much a challenge, and he'd never been one to run away from a challenge. One of the many mistakes he'd made with Naomi was to pursue her so relentlessly. He'd gone straight from the chase to the altar with very little time spent getting to know her or allowing her to get to know him.

He didn't want to do that with CeCe. He wanted to get to know her, to be her friend, and to have her as a friend. He knew that going into full Nate mode wouldn't win her friendship. This time he was going to follow the pace she set. "Lord," he prayed, "show me how to walk in this new way. I know how to do things my way, but I want to do them her way, because I believe her way is also your way. I've searched my heart, and I believe that you placed this woman in my life. I'm not sure yet what to expect, but I want to follow you. Please show me how."

By the time they made it to the pizza place, Nate knew he owed CeCe an apology. He made quick work of getting out of his truck and heading for her car. She and David were out before he got there. He gave her what he hoped she'd recognize as an apologetic smile as David slid one small hand into his and the other into CeCe's, and they made their way into the restaurant.

Before Nate could say anything to CeCe, David had dropped his mother's hand and was trying to lead him off to play pinball. "Give the man time to catch his breath, David," CeCe admonished.

"You got your breath already, don't you, Mr. Nate?" David asked, as though his mother had said something ridiculous.

Nate gave CeCe a smile and said, "Who can argue with that logic?"

He was relieved when she returned his smile. "I know I can't. You two go on. I'll get a table and order for us. We tend to keep it simple—just cheese and pepperoni. Does that work for you?"

"Sounds good. Toss in a salad and I'll be good to go."

Nate heard her soft laughter and her murmured, "I'll do it," as David dragged him off to play a challenge match of pinball.

CeCe smiled after the two males as she watched them fold into the crowd in the game area of the restaurant. The drive over here had given her enough time to calm down. For the second time, Nate had made her feel silly. To be honest, the truth was that for the second time, she'd overreacted to something he said, and that overreaction made her feel silly. She'd known, even as she'd walked away from Nate to her car back at the Center, that he hadn't meant anything beyond a harmless flirtation. Had she not been conditioned to think the worst of the men she met, she would have realized that truth before she turned away from him. Any doubts she had about his sincerity had been wiped away when he'd joined her and David in the parking lot. His smile told her that he realized his comments had upset her and that he wanted to make amends.

A waitress finally seated her at a booth big enough for the three of them and took her order. Afterwards, CeCe headed for the game room in search of David and Nate. She knew David's favorite game, so she wasn't surprised to find them at one of the programmable machines that based game difficulty on the age of each player, making competition between an adult and a child relatively fair.

"Not like that, Mr. Nate," she heard her son say. "Let me show you."

David was standing on a platform in front of the machine. Nate stood next to him, the controls in his hand.

CeCe bit back the laughter that bubbled up in her as Nate stepped to the side and proceeded to take instruction from her four-year-old son. As she watched, he nodded appropriately at David's somewhat jumbled instructions. When her son decided that Nate was sufficiently trained, he stepped aside and let Nate at the controls.

David cheered. "That's it, Mr. Nate."

"I think I've got it, David—," Nate began. "Uh-oh, it's gonna get me."

"Get out of the way, Mr. Nate, get out of the way!"

"Oh no, it got me," Nate said in a voice that sounded much too wounded to be entirely for David's benefit. Apparently, Nate was a competitor.

"Well, you'll do better next time," David said, taking the controls. "Watch me and I'll show you again."

"So who's winning?" CeCe asked, deciding the time was right for her entrance. She stood a step behind the two males, peering between them at the screen.

"He is," Nate said, looking back over his shoulder at her. "But I'm going to ask for a rematch after I get in some practice." He placed his hand around David's neck and squeezed affectionately. "How about that, sport? Will you give me a rematch?"

"Sure, Mr. Nate. But you're going to have to practice a lot. I can help you, though."

"Why, thank you." He gave CeCe a private grin.

David looked at his mother. "Do you want to play, Mama?"

Before CeCe could answer, Nate said, "Yeah, how about if you play me, CeCe? I probably stand a better chance against you than against your son."

"But—," David began, but she cut him off with a smile and a wink that Nate missed. Her son got her message and stepped off the platform and out of the way.

"Who's going first?" she asked Nate.

Nate gave an exaggerated bow and slid a secret smile to David. "Ladies first, madam."

David found Nate's antics hilarious, but CeCe just raised her brow and stepped up to the controls. "If you're sure?" she queried before starting the game.

"I wouldn't have it any other way, my lady."

CeCe took the controls without feeling the least bit of guilt. It was Nate's own fault. He'd blithely assumed that she played about as well as—make that as poorly as—he did, but he'd soon find out he was wrong. She felt him as he pressed close to her right side, while David positioned himself at her left.

She was not surprised when, forty-five seconds into the game, a loud groan sounded in her right ear. She grinned.

"I've been scammed," Nate complained. "You're a professional. I bet David's been giving you lessons."

CeCe winked at her son, who was now giggling, before saying to Nate, "Who do you think taught David?" CeCe wanted to laugh at the surprise in Nate's eyes. "Watch it," she said instead. "I'm beginning to think you aren't the modern man that you claimed to be."

Nate leaned behind CeCe and said to David, "Why didn't you tell me she was so good?"

"I was gonna tell you, but Mama made me be quiet, didn't you, Mama?" CeCe nodded, her concentration on the game. She was going to show Nate her best. Then she'd gloat about it while they ate their pizza. "She winked and everything," David continued.

Nate moved back to stand next to CeCe. "A pinball shark. I don't think I've ever met one before."

CeCe turned to him and whispered, "Be careful, Mr. Richardson. I'm teaching my son the importance of being a good sport. You wouldn't want me to use you as an example of how *not* to be a good sport now, would you?"

Nate's grin told her that he knew she was teasing. "Yes, ma'am," he whispered to her. "I'll be on my best behavior from now on." In a louder voice, he said, "Your mama's really good, David. I'm going to have to challenge both of you to a rematch. Before that, though, I'm probably going to need both of you to give me some tips on improving my game."

David moved to Nate's side and begin telling him about the game, just as CeCe was wrapping up. She stepped back and relinquished the controls to Nate. "Not on your life," he mouthed. Louder, he said, "Don't you think our pizza should be ready by now?"

"Yeah, pizza," David chanted.

CeCe shook her head in mock dismay. "Poor sport," she mouthed to Nate. Then she led the two boys to their table.

At the tug on his sleeve, Nate looked down at the picture David was coloring in the book provided by the waitress. The boy had talked more than he'd eaten, starting with the blessing and continuing until CeCe had bidden him to rest his mouth for a while, but Nate had enjoyed him. Now David held up his book for Nate to see his picture.

"Let the man eat, David," CeCe chided.

Nate murmured something to the boy, then looked up at her. "It's not a problem. I'm probably having as much fun as he is."

CeCe lifted a brow at the man seated across from her. "So you like to color, huh?"

"Not every day," he said with a shrug and a straight face. "But sometimes coloring can be the best thing for a man. Relieves stress and all that."

"I think I'll let that one pass. I do have to say again that you're good with kids. Very good."

Nate chuckled. "Thank you. You know, I'm glad you're no longer upset with me. I could have kicked myself for what I said before we left the Center. I just wanted you to know that I didn't mean anything by it. So this is my apology, though it seems I'm giving it after I've been forgiven."

"Not a problem," she said. "It's possible that I may have overreacted. I have it on good authority that I have a tendency to do that."

"Hmm, I haven't noticed."

She quirked a brow at his barely contained grin. "You'd better stop while you're ahead."

He chuckled again before looking down and commenting on David's progress. When he looked back up at her, he said, "So, CeCe Williams, do you think we're going to make it through your hundred and fifty hours of community service?"

"A hundred and twenty-two hours now, but who's counting?" He chuckled, and she continued, "To answer your question, I do think we're going to make it. I'm glad Marvin and

Shay had a friend like you to keep their dream going when they couldn't."

Nate didn't have a response, but he appreciated her words. "Well, it's not the lawyering I was trained to do, but I don't see myself doing anything else."

"You were an attorney?" she asked, her eyes bright with interest.

He finished off the last of his salad and pushed his plate aside. "Sure was. I had a law practice in Chicago, and I joined a firm when I moved here. Working for the firm wasn't the same as being on my own, so coming to Genesis House was good for me. I don't own it, but it feels more mine than the law practice ever did. I have Marvin and Shay to thank for that." As he finished speaking, Nate felt a bit exposed. He knew he owed much to Marvin and Shay for making a place for him at Genesis House, but saying it aloud to CeCe made him realize that his greatest joy had come out of their greatest misery. He could no more repay them than he could take away their loss. He watched as CeCe absorbed his words and waited anxiously for her response.

He held his breath as she pushed her plate away and leaned forward, her arms folded on the table in front of her. "You know, at one time I thought I was going to be a lawyer. I had plans to go to law school and everything."

Relief mixed with gratitude at her change of topic, and he encouraged her effort by asking, "So what happened?"

She glanced at her son, the depth of love there obvious for all to see. "That bundle of joy. I guess I still could have gone, but I couldn't imagine putting in the time that would have been required and still being able to give David the time he needed. Besides, I don't think my heart was in it anymore by then. Or maybe it's a dream deferred."

The wistfulness in her voice struck a chord in Nate's heart. "Do you think you'll go back and get your law degree?"

She shook her head. "No. I can't imagine it now. My goals are a little closer to the ground these days."

"Like what?"

She leaned back against the booth and placed her hands in her lap. "Well, the first thing I need to do is get rid of the mountain of debt I've accumulated over the years." Her eyes clouded briefly as if she'd had a sad thought. "That's why I'm doing the real estate in addition to my regular job. I need the money."

"How's it coming?" he asked, taking one of the last two slices of pizza.

"Slowly," she said. "If I'm going to make the kind of money I need in real estate, I'm going to have to find a different clientele or start working longer hours. I don't see myself doing longer hours because of David, so that leaves finding a different clientele as my only option. Right now, most of my clients are people trying to buy a first home on a tight budget. I almost feel guilty taking the commission."

Nate was touched by her compassion. As if she were aware and made uncomfortable as a result, she glanced at David and then back at Nate. "Don't look so impressed," she said. "I said I *almost* feel guilty."

Nate didn't follow up on her comment, for he knew that doing so would only embarrass her more, but he was pleased that she had such a soft heart. "So what you need are people with money selling houses that cost a lot of money."

"That would be nice, but it's a lot easier said than done. I don't move in those kinds of circles, and I don't have the time to cultivate the necessary relationships to gain entrance."

Nate sat back on the bench seat he occupied with David. "I can see that you don't know the person with whom you've just shared a pizza."

Her eyes widened. "Are you telling me that you have an expensive house that you want to sell?"

"Better than that," he said. "I have access to people who buy and sell expensive houses. For that matter, so do you."

"How's that?"

Nate rubbed his left index finger back and forth over his right one. "Shame, shame, shame. Fortunately for you, a lot of people who own expensive houses are also generous in their charitable giving. As the director of Genesis House, I get to beg in the best circles in Atlanta. Since you're on staff, you have access to those same circles."

The waitress interrupted them when she refilled their glasses. CeCe dumped a couple of packets of sugar in her tea and stirred it. "Well, now I am impressed. I didn't realize I was in such auspicious company. Neither did I realize that my community service job was going to give me a boost in my real estate business." She grinned, lifting her glass to her lips. "Do you think I should call Judge Rogers and thank him?"

Nate couldn't believe the door had opened again for him to ask her out, but it had. *OK, Lord, here goes nothing.* "You can do better than that. Why call him when you can tell him in person?"

CeCe pursed her lips as if she'd just taken a swallow of pure lemon juice. "I'll pass on that suggestion. I don't think I ever want to see the inside of traffic court again."

"Actually, I was thinking of another place."

Her eyes found his. "What exactly are you getting at, Nate? You may as well spell it out. It should be pretty clear to you by now that I'm not going to figure this out without your help."

"Well," Nate said, leaning toward her with a grin on his face. "Stuart gave me two tickets to the Black Tie Gala. I mentioned it to you the other week." He thought but didn't say, *And you shot me down.* "He's going to be there, of course, along with quite a few of the inner-circle group. It would be a great networking opportunity for you. And Stuart would be grateful."

"Grateful? Why?" she asked.

Nate suspected she was stalling for time. Probably trying to determine what it would mean if she went to the Gala with him. "Because he's sick of me attending these events by myself," he answered. "That's why he gave me two tickets. He even offered to fix me up, a blind date, but I was able to talk him out of that idea."

CeCe folded and refolded the clean napkin next to her plate. "I bet you get it worse than I do. The matchmaking attempts, I mean."

He shrugged off her concern. "They mean well, so I try not to let it bother me that much. But Stuart is a hard case. He says that if I bring somebody to this Gala he'll stop worrying about me. So what do you say? You could get Stuart off my back, make a few contacts, and maybe even have a little fun."

"I appreciate it, Nate," she began slowly. "I really do, but—"

"No *buts*," he said, placing one of his hands on top of hers to stop her from folding the napkin. He looked into her eyes, easily reading the uncertainty there. "And no pressure. Just two coworkers who are also working on a friendship. Nothing more." *Yet.* Though he'd only said the word to himself, it hung in the air between them as though he'd spoken it aloud. "So what do you say?"

CeCe drove home amazed that she'd agreed to attend the Gala with Nate, while David chattered on and on about Mr. Nate this and Mr. Nate that. She had a feeling that she'd be hearing Nate's name quite often, especially if he took David to the ball game like he'd promised, and if they got together for more pinball. A part of her wished Nate wouldn't follow through, but the larger part of her, the part that loved her son beyond reason, prayed that he would. David didn't have a lot of men in his life, so the ones who were allowed in had to be stable and good role models. She owed her son that and so much more.

But what do you owe yourself, CeCe? a voice asked. CeCe shook off the question. She didn't have time to think about herself these days. She had no life without David anyway, so any thoughts about him were also thoughts about herself. She hadn't given her son a very auspicious beginning in this world, but she'd give her last breath making sure that the life he lived was the best she could provide.

God had been faithful, and David didn't seem to have suffered overly much because his biological father wasn't present in the home. CeCe had been reluctant to look for substitutes, choosing rather to keep David and herself protected in the love and care of Miss Brinson and Mr. Towers for the most part. She hadn't even allowed the people at her church to breach the barrier she'd erected, not really. She'd been afraid to let people see the real her. Afraid they would reject her once they saw her as she was. But somehow, she realized now, Anna Mae and Shay had sneaked in, almost without her noticing it, and she already cherished the friendships she was forming with them. She wondered if it wasn't time to allow more people in. Nate, for instance. It seemed right, if only because she'd met Anna Mae and Shay through him.

How did she go about making a place for him in their lives? It sounded easy enough, but God knows, she had no idea how she was going to do it. *Lord, please,* she prayed silently, *don't let me make a fool of myself with this man. He's being nice to my son, and he's being nice to me. Don't let me read too much into it. He hasn't shown anything but a friendly interest in me, and so far I've reacted as though he's been stalking me. Show me how to be a friend to him. He wants to be David's friend, so show me how to allow that friendship, in spite of the conflicting feelings I have about him. Thank you for widening my circle of close Christian friends. As usual, you're meeting my needs before I even ask.*

The prayer lightened her thoughts considerably, and she was able to attend more closely to David's queries and comments. By the time she pulled into her driveway, she'd thought of an additional plea. *And Lord,* she added, *if it's your will that something more should come of this friendship with Nate, don't let me scare myself off. Teach me how to have a relationship. I have a child, but I've never had a relationship. I want one, but I'm scared. So, if this one is it, teach me how to make it work.*

SIX

CeCe knew she should have gone to the beauty parlor to get her hair done. As she stared in her bathroom mirror at the frizz that was her hair, she was convinced that she'd been out of her mind to think she could take care of the task herself. "Help!" she yelled. "Miss Brinson, I need you."

Miss Brinson and David came rushing into CeCe's once-large-but-growing-smaller-by-the-minute bathroom. "What is it, CeCe?" Miss Brinson asked. "Why are you screaming?"

CeCe turned around to face her son and her friend. "Look at my hair," she wailed. "What am I going to do? Nobody is going to talk to me with my hair like this!"

"What's wrong, Mama?" David asked, his eyes wide.

CeCe turned around and opened her arms to her son. "Mama's just fine, David. I'm going to a fancy dinner tonight, and I'm a little nervous about it."

"Oh," David said, sliding off her lap. "I thought you were sick or something." With those words, the child eased past Miss Brinson and out of the bathroom.

The older woman watched the child leave the room and shook her head. "He certainly handled that well, didn't he?"

"He's growing up on me, and much too fast." CeCe turned back to her mirror. "What am I going to do with my hair? It's after seven, and Nate's going to be here at eight-thirty. If he sees me looking like this, he's going to withdraw his invitation." She caught Miss Brinson's grin in the mirror. "What's so funny?"

Miss Brinson lowered the lid on the toilet and sat down. She took CeCe's hand. "You're excited about tonight, aren't you?"

CeCe wanted to pull her hand away and say no. Instead, she took courage from her friend's touch. "More nervous than excited."

Miss Brinson squeezed her fingers. "CeCe, this is me you're talking to. I think I know you about as well as anybody. Why can't you admit that you're excited about tonight? There's no sin in it."

CeCe did pull her hand away then. "I just feel so silly. I'm twenty-six years old, and you'd think I was getting ready to go to the prom instead of to a Gala for all the bigwigs in Atlanta."

"What's wrong with that? Stop thinking so much and enjoy yourself. You have a gorgeous dress—"

CeCe twirled a Q-Tip in her fingers and continued to pout. "Thanks to you. Left to myself, I'd be wearing that navy suit that I wear every time I have to dress up."

"That's beside the point. The point is that you have a gorgeous dress. It looks gorgeous on you, and you look gorgeous in it."

"You're biased," CeCe said, but she agreed with Miss Brinson. The off-the-shoulder black dress with thin straps was gorgeous. She looked pretty decent when she put it on, even if she had to say so herself.

"Well, I may be biased," Miss Brinson said, "but it doesn't mean that I'm a liar. Now your dress is gorgeous, and I'm sure I can do something with this hair. I won't bother to remind you that I told you to go to the beauty parlor."

CeCe didn't see a need to respond to that statement. "Do you really think you can do something with it?"

"Of course I can." Miss Brinson got up and stood behind CeCe. "Now hand me that curling iron. You'll see what I can do."

CeCe did as she was told and sent up a silent prayer that her friend could work a miracle. As she sat and watched, a miracle formed right before her eyes. There was hair under all that frizz after all. Not long, flowing hair, but short, coarse hair that she'd inherited from her father's side of the family. When done right—and Miss Brinson was doing it right—it could be curled and feathered around her face to give her a look that had more than once been described as angelic.

Miss Brinson made quick work of it, with few words beyond "turn your head" and "hold your ear." When she was finished, she said, "Now what was all the fuss about?"

CeCe turned and pulled her friend into her arms. "I love you. You know that, don't you?"

"Sure you do," Miss Brinson said gruffly. "Now what else do you have to do if you're going to be ready before your date gets here?"

"I told you," CeCe said, correcting her friend for what seemed like the hundredth time, "he's not my date. We're just going together."

"That's a date, CeCe." Miss Brinson shrugged. "I'm looking forward to meeting this man who's put the household in such an uproar. David talks about him as though he hung the stars in the sky, and you're flitting around here like this nondate is a real date and a really important one, at that."

CeCe concentrated on putting on her makeup and tried not to let Miss Brinson's words make her more nervous than she already was. She was blessed with good skin, so the ritual was brief. Normally she wore moisturizer under a light foundation. Tonight she was going to add a tinge of blush and some lipstick. "The evening is important. I'm going to meet some people who could turn out to be valuable contacts in my real estate business. The better I do with the real estate, the sooner I can pay off my debts and we can get going with our day-care center. So I have a reason to be nervous. A lot is riding on this evening."

"If you say so."

CeCe continued with her makeup under Miss Brinson's watchful eye. Neither woman spoke, which wasn't new for them. They were comfortable with the silences. "Did you see the mail today?" Miss Brinson asked after a while.

That statement made CeCe's hand wobble, and she ruined her lipstick line. After taking care of the error with a damp tissue, she tried again. "Yes, I saw the mail." She'd also seen the letter from Eric's parents. She hadn't opened it, but neither had she ripped it up and thrown it in the wastebasket. She hadn't wanted to give any place to the emotions that thinking about the letter would evoke. She still didn't. "I don't want to talk about it. Not tonight. I have enough on my mind as it is." Her tone was curt, she knew, but sometimes B.B. didn't know when to let a topic rest.

"It's going to be here when you get back," Miss Brinson said. "Ignoring it won't make the situation go away any more than tearing up those letters does."

CeCe stopped with the makeup. What was the use? She wasn't going to get anything done until she finished this conversation. She turned to her friend. "Why are you doing this to me tonight? You know how much those letters upset me, and you know how nervous I am about tonight. Why are you being so cruel?" CeCe felt the tears build in her eyes, but she was determined not to let them fall. Not tonight. Tonight was going to be special. She was going to be nice to Nate and they were going to have a good time. She'd never gone to anything like this Gala, and a part of her was giddy with excitement, though she tried to hide it.

Miss Brinson didn't say anything. She leaned forward and kissed CeCe on her forehead. Then she turned and left the room. The tears that CeCe had been trying to keep at bay began to fall as soon as Miss Brinson closed the bathroom door.

Nate pulled the phone away from his ear so he could adjust his cuff links. The right one done, he put the phone back to his ear. He stood in his second-floor bedroom trying to get ready to pick up CeCe for the Gala. "Look, Stuart, if you keep me on the phone all night, we're both going to be late."

"Wait a minute," came Stuart's voice. "Did you get her flowers?"

Nate frowned and moved the phone away from his ear to take

care of the other cuff link. He put the phone back. "Of course, I got her flowers, Stuart. I'm not a jerk, you know." A part of Nate wanted to hang up on his friend. He was more than a bit annoyed that Stuart had felt the need to call and give him pointers.

"I know you're not a jerk," Stuart said. "But you didn't get her a dozen red roses, did you?"

Nate looked at the box containing a dozen red roses that lay on his bed. "What's wrong with roses?" he asked.

"You can't give her a dozen roses, man. You told her this wasn't a date. You shouldn't give her roses at all."

"Well, you chose a fine time to tell me. Just where do you think I'm going to get something else at this hour?" Nate looked at the roses and felt more and more unprepared for this evening. He didn't think he'd been this nervous on his first date way back in high school.

"OK, it's not that big a problem. Don't give her the dozen. Give her one. She'll like that much better."

"Spoken like a man who's been around," Nate murmured, though he admitted to himself that Stuart's advice was timely. Now that he thought about it, he could well imagine how uncomfortable CeCe would have been had he given her a dozen red roses. His mood was so contrary, though, that he refused to give Stuart the thanks he deserved.

"What did you say?"

"Nothing important. Now if you don't have any more instructions for me, I think I should get off the phone. We're both going to be late picking up our dates—I mean, friends—if we don't get a move on. I'll see you when I get there."

"You bet you will," Stuart said, and Nate could see his friend's grin in his mind's eye. "I can't wait to be introduced to your, ah, friend."

Nate mumbled a good-bye and gladly hung up the phone. He slipped on his shoes and stood in front of the full-length mirror on his closet door to check that nothing was sticking out that wasn't supposed to be sticking out. The black suit was the one he always wore to events like these. He'd spent a lot of money for it, and the quality showed. Besides, it was comfortable. He'd considered getting something new for the occasion, but visions of himself squirming in discomfort all night had changed his mind. He'd opted for comfort over newness.

Satisfied with his attire, he went to the bed and opened the box of roses. Pulling one out, he smelled it and wondered what CeCe's reaction would be when he gave it to her. Then he checked his watch and headed for the door. If he didn't get a move on, he was going to be late.

Nate pulled into CeCe's driveway twenty-five minutes later, his damp palms on the steering wheel the only evidence of his nervousness. He took a deep breath. *OK, Nate, you can do this,* he told himself. He tilted his head upwards. *We can do this, Lord. Give me the wisdom to treat CeCe the way she should be treated. Help me to make this night a fun and relaxing one for both of us.*

Armed with renewed confidence, Nate got out of his Mercury Sable—he'd decided against the truck—and headed for the door, rose in hand. With just the slightest hesitation, he rang the bell. *This is it,* he thought.

The door opened, and the faces he saw belonged to David, who was dressed in his pajamas, and an attractive older woman he hadn't met. The woman was dressed in a tunic and skirt made of Kente cloth. Was this CeCe's mother? He probably should have brought her a flower or some token. Maybe she was the baby-sitter. He didn't have a clue.

"Hi, Mr. Nate," David said, reaching for Nate's hand. "Mama's not ready yet, but you can come in."

Nate smiled at both of them, then took David's hand. "I like a man who gets to the point."

The woman returned his smile. "That's our David. Do come on in, Mr. Richardson." She stood back so that he could enter.

"I'm Nate," he said.

"Well, then, I'm Gert, or B.B.," she said, leading him from the foyer to the living room. She pointed to the sofa upholstered in a muted floral pattern. "Have a seat. You'll hear CeCe call me Miss Brinson sometimes, but that's a carryover from the days when I was her dorm director. Mostly she and David call me B.B., and you're welcome to do the same."

Nate sat down, setting the rose on the table. He felt comfortable with this woman. "Well, thank you, ma'am. I think I'll try B.B." He turned to David, who also had seated himself on the sofa. "What do you say, sport? Do you agree that I should call your—" He looked back at Miss Brinson.

"Oh," she said, "CeCe and I are very good friends, and we share this house."

"We're not just friends, we're family." At the sound of CeCe's voice, Nate looked up and saw her standing in the entranceway. He'd consciously tried to keep his thoughts from dwelling too much on how attractive he found her, but tonight, with her in that dress, he gave up the fight. She was absolutely gorgeous—from her curly hair to the silver slippers on her feet.

Coming to his senses, he stood up. "Hi, CeCe. You look very nice this evening." Talk about understatement. He couldn't tell her what he really thought, of course. No, if he told her how good she looked to him, and how good looking at her made him feel, he'd embarrass them both, not to mention B.B. and David.

CeCe smiled, a real smile that touched her eyes, and he felt his heart turn over. It occurred to him that seeing this woman smile like that could become addictive. "You look very nice yourself, Mr. Richardson. Doesn't Nate look handsome in his suit, David?"

The boy looked at Nate, but he didn't answer. "David's not much on suits," she told Nate. "Sunday mornings are major squirm time for him."

Before Nate could comment, CeCe held out her hand to David. "Tell Nate and B.B. good night, David." After the boy did her bidding, CeCe said to Nate, "I'll be back in a moment. I just want to get him into bed before we leave."

"Can Mr. Nate come, too?" David asked.

"No, David," CeCe began.

The boy's words propelled Nate into action. "No problem. I think I'd like to see my friend off to bed. That is, if you don't mind."

She shook her head. "I don't mind."

He followed CeCe into her son's second-floor bedroom, noticing the shelf filled with stuffed animals above his bed. The boy immediately went down on his knees and said his prayers. He ended with, "And God bless Mama and B.B. and Mr. Nate. Amen." Then he hopped into bed, and CeCe tucked him in, leaning down to press a kiss against his forehead when he was all settled. "I love you, David."

"Love you, too, Mama. Can Mr. Nate read me a story?"

"You've already had your story tonight, David," CeCe said.

"Another night?"

Nate spoke up before CeCe could bite back the pain she felt at her child's obvious need. "Sure, sport. I'll read to you some other time." Then he leaned down and kissed the youngster on his forehead just as he'd seen CeCe do.

The boy smiled, and Nate's heart turned over again. This boy and his mother had quickly made their own places in his heart. He stepped back and exited the room. CeCe followed. As she turned off the light, he heard her say, "Sleep well, sweetheart."

"Sorry about that," she said, once they were in the hallway. "David seems to like you a lot."

"There's nothing to be sorry about. I appreciate your allowing me to be a part of your family time. I'm honored, in fact."

CeCe said nothing, but Nate could sense the wheels turning in her head, and he wondered what she was thinking. She led him back down the stairs, where she took her wrap from the hall closet. Nate finally remembered his rose. "I have something for you," he said. He stepped into the living room and brought back the rose. "For you," he said as he extended it to her.

Her eyes brightened in childish delight. Then she brought the rose to her nose and closed her eyes briefly as she inhaled its fragrance. "Oh, thank you, Nate. This is so sweet."

It was his turn to be speechless. The lump in his throat stopped any words he might have spoken. CeCe's pleasure in his simple gift had almost undone him. Glad for something to do, he helped her on with her wrap. When they were ready to leave, she called out to B.B., who joined them in the foyer. "Enjoy yourselves," the older woman said. "And take good notes, CeCe. I want to hear everything."

Nate and CeCe didn't talk much on the drive to the Peachtree Plaza. CeCe picked out a CD—he was glad to see it was Fred Hammond, a favorite of his—and they contented themselves listening to the music and entertaining their own thoughts.
In short order, though, he was helping her out of the car and leading her into the glass elevator that would take them to the Sundial Restaurant on the hotel's seventy-third floor. Her hand rested lightly on his arm, and he could feel the tension in her as he led her off the elevator and into the throng of the other Gala attendees.

He leaned down to her. "Ready to have some fun and make a few contacts in the process?"

She nodded, and he felt her relax a bit. "I'm game if you are."

En route to their table, Nate spotted Stuart out of the corner of his eye. If there had been a way to delay introducing CeCe to his friend until later in the evening, Nate would have done so. Unfortunately, Stuart was making a beeline directly for them. "Brace yourself," Nate said to CeCe. "Here comes the judge."

Her eyes widened in question. "The judge? *My* judge?"

"One and the same." He felt her tense up again. "Don't let Stuart bother you. He's a good guy—most of the time. Like most good friends, though, sometimes he goes overboard in his teasing. Let's hope he's on his best behavior tonight. OK, here he is."

Nate and CeCe both turned just as Stuart reached them. Nate wondered, as he always did, how Stuart managed to look as relaxed and comfortable in formal settings like this as he did on bowling night with the boys.

"Well, it's about time you got here," Stuart said, all smiles and grace. "I've been looking all over for you." He turned to CeCe, but spoke to Nate. "So are you going to introduce me or not?"

Or not, Nate thought, but of course he didn't say it. "I think you've already met."

Stuart took one of CeCe's hands in both of his. "It's nice to meet you, Ms. Williams. I'm sorry our first meeting couldn't have been under more favorable circumstances. I can only hope that your experience at Genesis House thus far has proven that I'm not an ogre."

CeCe's lips curved sweetly, and Nate knew Stuart had won her over. He had to give his friend credit. He definitely had a way with words.

"Call me CeCe," she said. "As to whether or not you're an ogre, the jury is still out on that one. I'll let you know after a hundred and six more hours."

Stuart chuckled, then turned to look at Nate. "You owe me, my friend," Stuart said, a clear message in his eyes. "And I mean big time."

Nate let that remark go unanswered. "So where's your date?" The question was his subtle way of reminding Stuart to find his own woman and leave his alone.

"Unlucky me," Stuart said with a self-deprecating grin. "She had to cancel at the last minute. I was hoping I could hang out with you and CeCe. You don't mind, do you?" Without waiting for an answer, Stuart turned to CeCe. "Nate tells me that you're in real estate." Before CeCe could nod her response, Stuart continued, "If that's the case, there are some people that you have to meet. Come on, Nate," he said, appropriating CeCe's hand, "let's introduce CeCe around."

Nate found himself following behind CeCe and Stuart, and he felt like a lost puppy dog. What was Stuart trying to prove, anyway? Was he interested in CeCe himself? Nate shook off that thought. Stuart wasn't interested in CeCe. His friend wasn't the type to do something like that. But Stuart did like games, and Nate had a pretty good idea what game he was playing now. His only question was whether he should kill his friend now or later.

CeCe felt awkward with the interplay between Stuart and Nate. Something was going on between them, and she was sure it concerned her. She cast a quick glance up at Stuart. He was charming enough, if you liked the polished type, but she'd come with Nate and she wanted to be with Nate. She couldn't very well tell Stuart that she didn't want him to introduce her around, though, now could she? Maybe Nate had arranged for Stuart to do the duty. He probably knew more of these people than Nate did, anyway.

She rejected that thought as quickly as it had come. Nate had pointedly asked Stuart about his date. She slid her gaze back toward Nate and noticed his jaw had tightened. Was he upset with his friend? with her?

She stopped suddenly, causing Nate to bump into her from the back. Over his muttered "excuse me," she said, "If it's all right, gentlemen, I'd like to leave this wrap at our table before we make our rounds."

"No problem," Nate answered. He stepped closer to her and took her wrap, dislodging her hand from Stuart's and handing him the wrap at the same time. "You'll take it back for her, won't you, Stuart?" he said, to his friend's slack-jawed surprise. "I'd like to introduce CeCe to Mr. Cronin. I know he buys and sells lots of properties in the area."

SEVEN

Nate pretended interest in Mr. Cronin's running monologue of his development projects in southwest Atlanta, but his real interest was CeCe Williams. He was enjoying being with her this evening. After she'd gotten over her initial nervousness, he believed she'd started to enjoy being with him as well. When another couple joined their discussion with Mr. Cronin, Nate deftly took CeCe's arm and led her away from the group. He smiled down to her and asked, "Having a good time?"

The warmth of her smile touched that place inside him that had become hers. "Wonderful. I'm so glad you invited me."

A feeling of total contentment encompassed him, and he grinned. "Not even Mr. Cronin's relentlessness has put a damper on your evening?" The big man had apparently taken a liking to CeCe, for he'd sought them out on several occasions during the evening. He'd been almost as bad as Stuart. Fortunately, Stuart had finally taken the hint and left him and CeCe alone.

She shook her head, an impish grin on her face. "He says that he wants to talk to me about a couple of his Bankhead and Cascade projects."

Nate placed his empty glass on the tray of a passing waiter. "And if you believe that, I should be trying to sell you some swampland in Florida."

"Are you saying that Mr. Cronin has something other than a

professional interest in me?" she asked, studying him over the rim of her glass.

"Nah, I'm not saying that. I'm saying the man is a lecher and you'd better watch out."

CeCe covered her mouth with her hand, almost choking on her iced tea as she tried to stifle her laughter. "You're awful; you know that, don't you?" she said when she recovered.

"Just honest, CeCe. I've told you that before. I'm just an honest man."

CeCe looked into his eyes as if she were measuring the truth in his words. He withstood her scrutiny, feeling it was important to her that he do so. "You know, I'm beginning to think you may be just what you say you are," she concluded.

A man couldn't ask for more, Nate thought, so he moved on to less intense ground. "Do you want to get some air? It's getting a bit stuffy in here." He nodded his head to the left, where he could see Mr. Cronin fast approaching. "Unless you want to get an early start on those Cronin projects."

"I'll need my wrap," she said.

When she would have turned to go get it from their table, he tucked her arm snugly in his and led her toward the door. "We have to make a quick getaway. If you need a wrap, I'll give you my jacket."

CeCe nodded, and Nate led her out of the ballroom. Their trek took them on the same path they'd taken when they'd entered the building about three hours ago. He led her around the circular drive and onto the sidewalk, content to stroll with her, breathing in the fresh air and enjoying the night sounds of downtown Atlanta on the Fourth of July. People dotted the sidewalks and café entrances. Strands of soft jazz mixed with more urban tunes filled the air, as a line of couples formed to wait for rides in a white horse-drawn carriage. Nate didn't need Stuart to tell him that a carriage ride would be inappropriate for his nondate with CeCe, though he found the notion intriguing.

While they were waiting for the light to change at the intersection of Peachtree and International, CeCe said, "Stuart's a nice guy. How long have you two known each other?"

"Too long," Nate quipped. He placed his hand on the small of her back and helped her off the sidewalk and across the street. He certainly didn't want to spend this time talking about Stuart. He hoped she didn't either.

"What's the matter?" she asked. Her soft chuckle told him she had heard the irritation in his voice and found it amusing. "I thought Stuart was cute tonight."

Nate groaned. "Cute? Are we talking about the same Stuart?"

She leaned to her side and bumped him with her shoulder. "Come on, you know what I mean. I admit that he threw me at first with all the attention, but I soon figured out that he was just doing it to rag on you. He was being the typical little brother/best friend."

Nate gave what he knew sounded a lot like a snort. "That's exactly what he is. We've known each other since the first day of law school. Stuart, Marvin, and I quickly became Shadrach, Meshach, and Abednego, or The Three Musketeers, depending on how you want to look at it. There was a lot of pressure in law school—social and academic—and I'm not sure I would have made it through with my faith intact had it not been for those guys. There's no doubt God put us together for that reason."

"And you all three ended up in Atlanta."

He dropped his hand from her back and enclosed her fingers lightly in his. They weren't really holding hands, he reasoned, but they were close. "Marvin went to undergrad at Morehouse, Shay was from here, and so they had always planned to come back. Believe it or not, Stuart was a New Yorker who considered Atlanta much too slow for him. One day I'll tell you the story of how he got here. Not tonight, though. I think Stuart has made enough of an impression on you.

"My story's pretty simple. My family's from the Chicago area, and I always wanted to practice near them. I did for a while." He stopped speaking and considered how much he should tell CeCe. He didn't want to overwhelm her by dumping too much on her at one time, but neither did he want to lie to her. He decided to be vague. For now. "Circumstances brought me here, and I'd like to believe that God has kept me here."

CeCe looked up at him as if she expected him to say more. Before he could decide what more to say, she eased her hand out of his and brushed it needlessly across her hair. Then she said, "You must miss your family. Is the Richardson clan a large one?"

"Fairly." He shrugged, not sure what had changed between them but certain something had. "My mom and dad, and three sisters, though sometimes the three of them seem more like thirty."

"So which kid are you?" she asked, with a twinkle in her eyes that made him think that whatever had concerned her was now all right. "No, don't answer. Let me guess. I'd say you're the oldest."

He seized the moment and joined in her teasing playfulness. "You'd be wrong. I'm the baby."

"You don't act like the baby."

He lifted his eyebrows. "I think that's a compliment, but I'm not sure."

"It's a compliment. I would imagine the baby boy in a family with three girls would certainly be spoiled, while the oldest would be a protector."

He took her hand again, this time giving it an affectionate squeeze. "That was definitely a compliment. Nate, the protector. I like it. It fits."

"Maybe." She looked up into his eyes, and he held her gaze, trying to see what lurked behind those big brown eyes. He wanted to know everything about her. He needed to know that she was the woman he thought she was. A woman he could trust. She didn't look away, either. It was as if she wanted him to search her, to see her, to know her. "You're a tough woman, CeCe," he said finally.

She lowered her eyes and resumed walking. "So I've been told."

"Do you really want to be?" he asked.

"Want to be what?"

He guessed she was stalling for time. Since they had walked a fair distance, he asked her if she'd like to walk back down the other side of the street. After her affirmative nod, he assisted her across the street, and they began the trek back through the downtown revelers to the Peachtree Plaza.

"So, are you really a tough woman?"

She shivered, and he knew it wasn't because of the weather. The July night was just right—not hot, or humid, and certainly not chilly. "I guess it depends on whom you ask."

"I'm asking you."

She seemed to think seriously before answering, and he appreciated the effort. Her answer was very important to him, though he couldn't really explain why. He just knew that it was. "Not with David," she said, "and not with Miss Brinson, but I can imagine that some people just getting to know me might find me tough. I'm probably not the easiest person to get to know." She cast him a sideways glance. "What do *you* think—am I really a tough woman?"

He was pleased with the honesty and openness of her answer. Deciding they both needed a break from the seriousness of the moment, he answered, "I don't think I should answer that one. I like your smiles a lot better than your frowns."

"I'm not that bad, and you do have to answer. You're an honest man, remember?"

"Ah, a woman with a memory. I'll have to remember that. Let's see, are you a tough woman?" There was an outdoor café up ahead, and he said, "Maybe we should sit down for the rest of this discussion. Do you mind?" She didn't, and he led her to the café and secured a table.

"Would you like something? Coffee or dessert?" the waiter asked.

Nate noticed the flicker of interest in CeCe's eyes at the mention of dessert and suggested the waiter bring them a dessert menu. After reviewing the appetizing list of sweets, they settled on the brownie ice cream pie, which they would share.

"I'm being really bad tonight," she said, leaning forward to rest her forearms on the table. "I'll have to exercise for a year to make up for this splurge."

After an admiring glance, he said, "I don't think one night will hurt you. You look pretty good to me."

She shot him a look that said she doubted his words. So she didn't take compliments well, he surmised. He wondered if she knew how appealing she was—toughness and all. Yes, CeCe was a tough woman, but he'd bet his life it was an external toughness that she used to protect the softness of her heart. She'd been hurt, and she wasn't going to be hurt again. He recognized the signs because he fought them in himself. He knew how hard it was to open yourself up to another person after you'd been burned badly.

"You still haven't answered my question," she said.

She'd been honest with him, and he could do no less for her. "You try to be tough, but you're a softie."

Her burst of laughter surprised him. When she would have spoken, the waiter interrupted them with their dessert. Nate moved his chair closer to hers—so close that her shoulder brushed against his arm—and enjoyed the muted sounds around them as they ate from the same bowl.

CeCe broke their silence. "I can't eat another bite." She placed her spoon on the table, sat back in her chair and watched him eat.

"I'm a growing boy," he explained, "so I'll just eat the rest of this."

"You know," she said after a few more minutes of shared silence, "I envy you, in a way. I'm an only child, and I've always wished for a brother or sister."

"And I spent a lot of my childhood dreaming of a world without sisters, or without sisters who took up all the bathroom time."

"So little brother couldn't go to the bathroom, huh?" she asked in a singsong voice usually reserved for little children under the age of two.

He polished off the last of the dessert and sighed. "I think we'd better leave that topic alone. Tell me about you. How did you get to Atlanta?"

The glint in her eyes suggested she'd rather continue teasing him, but when she spoke she honored his request for a change in topic. "I guess I was sort of like your friend Marvin. I went to Spelman and fell in love with Atlanta. I'm originally from a small town in Alabama about two hours from here. I love Atlanta because it's big enough to have all the conveniences of a big city, but its small neighborhoods give it a homey feel. I guess it has the best of both worlds."

He nodded his understanding, though he had the feeling there was a lot she wasn't telling him. He now regretted not being more forthcoming about himself with her. How could he expect her to open up to him when he hadn't done so with her? "Are your parents still in Alabama?" he asked, feeling comfortable exploring this area of her life since he'd shared about his family.

"And still living in the house where I grew up."

He picked up one of her hands for no particular reason and studied her fingers. "It must be great to pick up and drive to see your folks whenever you want," he said, wondering what he could learn about her from her recently manicured hand. "They must love being so close to their only grandson. My parents would probably move to a warmer climate if my sisters and their families weren't in the Chicago area. They could leave my sisters, but I don't think they can leave their grandchildren. I bet David has your parents wrapped around his little finger."

"Not exactly." She eased her hand from his grasp and rested it on the table. "My parents and I aren't very close."

"I'm sorry," he said, responding to the distress in her voice. He wasn't sure if it was his hand-holding or the discussion about her parents that had caused it. Maybe it had been both.

"So am I, but that's the way it is."

He placed his hand atop hers, which was now resting on the table, and squeezed. "But it doesn't have to stay that way. People and situations change."

"Maybe" was her only response.

I don't know what to say to her, Lord. I can see that she's hurting, but I don't know how to help. Show me what to do. Give me something to say. Nothing came, so Nate said nothing. When the waiter came back to clear their table, Nate suggested they head back to the Gala. CeCe agreed and they made their way back, her hand resting on his arm. She seemed lost in her thoughts, and he was wondering why her happiness meant so much to him.

CeCe was filled with apprehension as she walked beside Nate to her front door. She told herself that she was being silly, but she couldn't stop the feelings. The evening had been both wonderful and disappointing. It had been wonderful because Nate had been so attentive, and, for most of the time anyway, she'd been so relaxed in his presence. In spite of that, the evening was not without its disappointments. First, Nate hadn't been as forthcoming as she would have liked about his marriage and subsequent divorce. While she accepted his right to privacy and understood his need for it, she was still disappointed. She wanted to think he felt free to discuss it with her, which she knew was odd since she really didn't know him that well. But that was the point. She was beginning to feel that she knew him very well, and his refusal to discuss such an important part of his life made her wonder if she was reading too much into their budding friendship.

Later, she'd been disappointed when he'd called her a tough woman. She thought she'd let her guard down tonight so that he could see beneath the tough exterior that she'd developed. Obviously, she hadn't. Then there was that business with him counting her fingers. All he'd done was hold her hand and count her fingers, but she'd had to ease her hand from his grasp because his touch felt too intimate. She must be losing her mind. Now they had to go through the ritual of ending their first evening out together. She didn't know whether to expect wonder or disappointment. She would rather not have to deal with either at this point.

"I've enjoyed your company, CeCe," Nate said as they walked up the three steps to the porch. "Do you have to go in now, or can we sit and talk for a while?" She could see his expectant face in the porch light Miss Brinson had left on for her. He pointed to the wooden swing to the left of the door. "Being from the North and all, I don't have much experience with porch swings."

She knew he'd chosen his words to calm her and to convince her to sit with him, but she was still hesitant to do so. "It's late—," she began.

Nate tugged on her hand and led her toward the swing. "It's not that late. Besides, I've been a perfect gentleman all night, and that's not going to change now. I wouldn't want Miss Brinson to come out here with a shotgun."

CeCe laughed and willingly followed his lead. Maybe they would end the evening on a note of wonder. "Do you make a joke out of everything?"

"I try my best to find humor in most situations," he said, sitting down and tugging again on her hand. She sat next to him. "If I took everything seriously, I'd probably be in a padded cell by now."

"Not you. I think you've led a charmed life," she teased.

He didn't immediately respond, but when he did there was no teasing in his voice. "Sure," he said, "I've led a charmed life, all right. That explains why my wife left me after living with me for only eighteen months and went back to her old boyfriend." As if the floodgates of his heart had opened, Nate shared with CeCe the details he had omitted earlier.

As she listened to his story, she realized that he held no bitterness toward his ex-wife. Disappointment, maybe, but not bitterness. She also detected guilt, an emotion with which she was very familiar.

"It's still hard for me to accept the role that I played in the failure of my marriage," he said. "It was easy to lay the blame at Naomi's feet because she was the one to leave and because she never made any attempt at reconciliation, but I've come to see that maybe it seemed to her that I left first. I was new in my solo practice and afraid of failing myself and her. I was so wrapped up in my practice and in having a family like the one I grew up in, that I didn't cherish my wife as I should have. That's a bitter pill to swallow."

"You must have loved her a lot," CeCe said, not expecting a response. She wondered how it would feel to be married to a man who felt about marriage the way Nate did. She couldn't imagine leaving such a man.

He squeezed her hand, and the concern in his eyes told her that his touch was meant to comfort both of them. "Yes, I loved her, but you know something? I don't remember the feeling. When she left me, I hurt all the time. I missed her. I was disappointed in myself, and I felt I had failed God. I can remember all those emotions, but I can't remember what it felt like to love her. Maybe it's because I spent more time with those emotions. We were together only eighteen months, she divorced me within a year after I moved here, and we'd been divorced three years before she remarried." The corners of his mouth turned up in a half smile. "You're the first woman I've been out with since Naomi. So if I'm rusty at this, you have to cut me some slack. That's me and my sob story. Tell me about you."

"What do you want to know?" she asked, though she knew the answer. He wanted to know about David's father. He'd asked her to tell him about herself twice already. Before, she'd held back because he had. She no longer had that excuse.

"What do you want to tell me?"

She breathed deeply. "I didn't expect to enjoy myself as much as I did this evening," she began. "I'm really glad you invited me."

He squeezed her hand. "I guess that means I wasn't that rusty."

She looked down at her hands. "Stop saying that. You weren't rusty at all. If anything, I'm the one who was rusty. I'm not good at this man-woman thing. I haven't been very successful with it."

"Well, that's the past. We're talking about now."

Nate tilted her chin up so he could look into her eyes. A part of him wondered if he was jumping off the deep end much too soon. What if this woman broke his heart? Would he be able to recover? He didn't have the answers to the questions, and right now the answers didn't seem that important. "I know I said this wasn't a date," he told her, "so I won't try to change it into one, but I'd like to see you again, CeCe. I'd like to get to know you and David and Miss Brinson. I don't know what the future holds for us, but there's something about you. . . . My heart has opened to you. I didn't expect it and I didn't plan it, but that's what has happened. I told you about me and Naomi because what happened with her is so much a part of the man I am now. God was true to his word, as he always is, and he used the horror and pain of that situation for my good.

"In some ways," he continued, "Naomi's leaving me worked out as a blessing because it served as a wake-up call. Until then, I'd been walking around like Samson with his hair cut off. I was shaking myself—going through the motions, thinking all was well with me and her, and with me and God—not realizing my ears had become dull to the voice of God. During the four years that Naomi and I were estranged, I learned again the power of prayer and the peace that only God can provide. I learned that nothing is more important than following God and being in his will. They weren't easy lessons, and I wish I could have learned them some other way, but I thank God that I learned them. And I pray that I won't have to learn them the hard way again."

He studied her open face and thought again that he could trust this woman. "If the Lord gives me another woman to love, I don't want to repeat the mistakes of the past. I've been honest and open with you because I want you to know where my heart is. I didn't go looking for you, CeCe Williams; you sorta dropped into my lap, so to speak. I don't want to walk away from you if you're supposed to be mine, but neither do I want to force myself where I don't belong. So before I go any further with this, I need to hear from you. I need to know if there's anybody else. I need to know if you think I'm off my rocker for talking to you this way."

She shook her head. Nate couldn't read the expression that

flashed across her face. Was is relief? "I'm the tough woman, remember? There's nobody else."

"Is that because your heart belongs to somebody who's not around?"

She lowered her eyes and studied their clasped hands. "I haven't seen David's father since before David was born. I'd had a crush on him all my life. We saw each other during my junior year in college. I got pregnant, and he married somebody else. I took my baby and my broken heart and moved on." She raised her eyes to his. "End of story."

Nate pulled her into his arms and held her as a brother comforting a sister. He'd thought she wanted to cry, but as he held her she didn't allow one tear to drop. *No, CeCe,* he thought to himself, *it's not the end of the story. Maybe the end of a chapter but definitely not the end of the story.*

CeCe walked into the house mentally and emotionally exhausted but very, very happy. Nate wanted to see her again. Next Saturday after the employment workshop he was going to take her and David to his ball game. She was confident Nate was like no man she'd ever known. She didn't know any men who would have opened themselves to her the way Nate had done tonight. It had been scary because she'd known he would expect the same level of honesty from her. She wanted to give it—or at least she wanted to try.

She was glad Miss Brinson wasn't up because she didn't want to share the details of her evening yet. She wanted to savor it in her own mind. She tiptoed up the stairs and peered into David's bedroom. He was sleeping peacefully. She walked into the room, a smile on her face, and straightened the bedcovers around him. She kissed his forehead and quietly left the room.

She felt the grin on her face as she made her way to her bedroom, closed the door, and turned on the light. Her eyes went directly to the letter propped prominently on her pillow. She should have torn it up before she left. Why had Miss Brinson done this? Her friend was being very obstinate about this issue, but then so was she.

CeCe picked up the envelope and turned it over in her hands a couple of times. *Open it, CeCe. What harm can it do?* She didn't open it, though. Instead she dropped down on the side of her bed and stared at it. There had been a time before David's birth and even immediately after when she would have welcomed this letter, but coming four years after David's birth was too late. How would she explain it to David? She'd written Eric's parents, told them she was concerned about the effect of their presence on David. She suggested that they wait until he was much older before trying to become a part of his life, but they wouldn't listen. They kept writing. They could continue to write, but she wasn't going to subject David to their whims, and she wasn't going to have him exposed to the biological father who didn't love him or want him. She might give in on a lot of issues, but on this one, she wasn't going to budge.

CeCe admitted that while David was her primary concern, she wasn't in any rush to spend time with Eric's parents herself, either. Being around them would only bring up unpleasant memories of a time in her life that she wanted to forget. She didn't want to go back to the place where she had been with Eric. She didn't like to remember herself that way. She much preferred to remember the girl she was before Eric and the woman she'd become after him. Her life was easily divided into two segments: pre-Eric and post-Eric, with the Eric interval totally wiped out.

She looked at the letter again. This time she shook her head as she ripped it into little pieces. As she threw it into her wastebasket, she remembered that she hadn't told Nate her position on premarital sex. They'd talked about everything else. She'd just have to talk to him about it the next time they were together. She wasn't interested in starting something that would only end in heartbreak because he expected more from her than she was willing to give. While she felt in her heart that Nate would agree with her and support her position, she still needed to discuss it openly so she could put it to rest for good.

"Lord," she said aloud, "I believe you sent Nate into my life. I don't know what role you want him to play, but I do believe you sent him. So help me take it one day at a time. Don't let me start dreaming years into the future. Let me think friendship and not marriage. Nate is a good person; I believe that sincerely. And I think he'd be a good friend, even if we never move beyond that state. Show me how to be a friend to him. Give me the courage to open myself up. I'm scared that I'm going to be hurt again, but I want to try."

CeCe turned off the overhead light, crawled into bed, and turned on her bedside lamp. Then she picked up the worn Bible on her nightstand. She took comfort in the Scriptures and then fell asleep.

EIGHT

Nate felt a growing sense of pride as he walked toward the baseball field with CeCe and David by his side. CeCe was an attractive woman—the pale pink walking shorts and matching T-shirt that she wore today were no less flattering than the knockout dress she'd worn to the Gala. But his pride wasn't based on her looks. No, it was based on the person he'd glimpsed inside—the caring woman with the soft heart that she tried to hide behind her "I'm perfectly fine by myself" mask. It was that woman he wanted to get to know and that woman he believed he could come to love.

Love. A part of Nate wanted to turn and run for the hills at the thought of that word. When he looked at CeCe and David, though, those hills looked awfully bleak and lonely without them.

"He's overcome with excitement," CeCe said, referring to David, who was running ahead of them. Fortunately, his short legs didn't allow him to get too far ahead.

Nate quit his intense thoughts and kicked a pebble that was in his path. "I thought he'd enjoy himself. I'm just sorry his friend Timmy couldn't come today." On the heels of Mr. Towers's departure, Timmy's maternal grandparents had come for a visit, and the boy was spending the day with them. "I'd like to take David into the dugout with me, if you don't mind your menfolk leaving you alone. I think he'd get a kick out of it."

She placed her hand on his arm. "You don't have to do that, Nate. David is so excited that he's bound to get in your way."

He tapped his index finger on the tip of her nose. "You forget, I'm good with kids. I can handle him if you can handle us leaving you alone for a short while. Of course, we'll wave at you when we have a break from our manly activities."

He wasn't surprised when she playfully punched him in the ribs. She was a toucher, and he felt the affection in her touch. "You'd better watch your attitude around my son. He's impressionable, and right now you're at the top of his list, bypassing Mr. Towers."

Nate stopped and tilted her chin up so he could look into her eyes. "I wonder where I am on your list," he mused. He wasn't disappointed or surprised when she lowered her eyes in embarrassment.

When she raised them, she thumped him on his chest. "You're going to have to keep wondering. I'm about to start believing that you're the baby in your family. Your sisters have spoiled you for all other women."

He laughed at her outrageous statement, and the pleasure of just having her in his life rippled through him. He ran ahead and scooped David up in his arms, lifting the boy high in the air. The child's peals of laughter were contagious, and soon both Nate and CeCe were laughing right along with him.

When Nate finally settled David securely on his shoulders, he scanned the bleachers for early arrivals. "Maybe you won't be alone after all. There are Anna Mae and Shay. Anna Mae's a regular, but it's been a while since Shay's joined us. I wonder if Marvin is here."

"I don't know, but I see Stuart."

He turned to her and frowned. "You would spot him first, now, wouldn't you?"

She batted her eyelashes in an exaggerated fashion. "You wouldn't by any chance be jealous, now, would you?"

"I'm not the jealous type," he said, giving her the once-over. "At least, I don't think I am, but we'd better not take any chances. Therefore, you should ignore Stuart today. Hey, you could pretend you've forgotten his name."

CeCe laughed. "Right. He's going to see right through that ploy, Nate. You have to come up with something better."

He patted the small sneaker-clad feet resting on his chest. "I could just punch his lights out and be done with it."

She laughed again. "You will do no such thing and you know it. I'm going to go right over there and thank Stuart for being so nice to me at the Gala."

She moved to cut across in front of Nate and make a beeline to Stuart, but Nate caught her arm. "I don't think so. We have to make sure Stuart has his own date before you make that move. 'Cause if he's here by himself, I could very well find myself going for pizza alone, while Stuart squires you and David around."

CeCe gave in with very little fuss and followed Nate to the section of the bleachers where Anna Mae and Shay were seated. Anna Mae had told her at this morning's workshop that she planned to attend the game, but Shay hadn't made an appearance, so CeCe was surprised—and happy—to see her. The bond of friendship between the three women had sprung up quickly but surely and was growing stronger every day. CeCe thanked God for bringing them into her life. She was especially glad to see their faces today. She needed the support of her friends. To tell the truth, she'd been a bit worried about her reception at the game. These people were Nate's friends, and she was an outsider. No doubt some might consider her not good enough for him.

Nate gave each woman a kiss on the cheek, then gave CeCe one too, before telling Shay and Anna Mae, "Watch this one for me. I don't want to lose her before the game is over." With that, he and an elevated and excited David headed for the ball field.

"Well, well, well," Anna Mae said, watching the man and boy walk toward the field. "He's sounding mighty proprietary, if you ask me. I think you've been holding out on me."

CeCe rolled her eyes at Anna Mae. "I'm not even going to respond to that," she said. Then she turned to Shay. "I'm glad you made it out today." CeCe took in her friend's bright yellow shorts and matching top. "I can see you're doing well. How's Marvin?"

Shay's smile lit up her whole face, and she pointed toward the ball field. "He's standing between Nate and Stuart. I'll introduce you before we leave. We want to have you and Nate over one day soon."

CeCe felt a bit awkward with the invitation. It was the first time she and Nate had been invited anywhere together, and she wasn't sure how to respond. "I'd like that, Shay, but I can't speak for Nate."

"Sure you can," Shay told her. "Anna Mae's already confirmed what I suspected."

CeCe turned to Anna Mae. "Exactly what have you been telling her, my friend?"

Anna Mae lifted her head in a haughty fashion. "Who, me? I'm insulted. You know that I never get in other folks' business. I haven't said a word."

Shay nodded in what CeCe thought was agreement with Anna Mae's outrageous statement. "She's right. She hasn't said a word—more like a dictionary of words. She already has you and Nate at the altar."

"Anna Mae!" CeCe reprimanded.

Anna Mae crossed her legs and developed a sudden interest in a splinter sticking up from the bench. "Don't 'Anna Mae' me. Everybody's talking about it. Everybody at our church at least. Nate taking a woman on a date is a big deal. I betcha we have more women from church at this game today than we've ever had at a game, because everybody wants to get a look at the woman who's struck Nate's fancy." Done with the splinter, she looked at CeCe. "I'm telling you, you probably were the cause of a lot of the crying that was done around the altar last Sunday. Every single woman in our church is wondering what you have that they don't."

CeCe shook her head in exasperation. "Stop exaggerating," she said. Though she knew Anna Mae was teasing, she also knew there was some truth to her friend's words. She had no doubt that a nice single guy like Nate had attracted the attention of more than one God-fearing woman looking for a God-fearing man. Unfortunately, she was as much at a loss as to why he was interested in her as the crying women were.

"You were there, Shay. You tell her," Anna Mae said. She turned to CeCe and said in all seriousness, "You're probably going to feel the stares boring into the back of your head all day."

At CeCe's dismayed look, Shay began to laugh. "Stop it, Anna Mae. You're embarrassing her. You're going to run her off before she and Nate get started good."

"I'm sure if she started running, he'd be running right behind her."

"Anna Mae!" CeCe and Shay said her name at the same time. They looked at each other and then at Anna Mae, who'd found renewed interest in her splinter, and the three of them gave a shout of laughter. CeCe felt as though she was among old friends.

When the game was over, Nate gave David the job of stacking the bats while he had a few moments with Marvin. "I'm glad you made it today, man."

"Shay made me come," Marvin answered honestly. "I definitely didn't want to be here." He swore. "Too many memories."

Nate glanced at David, wanting to make sure the child hadn't heard the word his friend had used. Nate was so glad that Marvin had come out that he didn't want to ruin it by chastising him about his language. He settled for, "There are still kids around here, Marvin. You've got to watch the language."

"I know, man; I'm sorry."

The men stood facing each other, but they didn't speak. Nate had never felt so far away from his friend. Marvin had been a major support for him since he'd known him. Until recent years, Marvin had been the counselor, the advisor of The Three Musketeers. Nate had been on the receiving end of Marvin's godly wisdom more than once. Now Nate felt inadequate to give his friend the help he needed.

"We're going out to get something to eat after we clean up here. Why don't you and Shay join us? She and CeCe seem to have hit it off well. What do you say?"

Marvin was shaking his head before Nate finished the invitation. "Thanks, man, but maybe another day. I know today has been hard for Shay, and I don't want to put too much on her." Marvin looked down at his feet. "I haven't been much support for her lately." He started to swear again but caught himself. "I haven't been *any* support. I probably need to take her home so she can relax. I know she looked like she was having a good time, but Shay's good at hiding her pain." He kicked up some dirt. "I wallow in mine and she hides hers. We're some pair, aren't we?"

Nate embraced his friend. "You're the best. Both of you. You're just going through a rough patch. If you can just reach out, the help you need is right at hand."

Marvin didn't meet Nate's eyes when he pulled away. "Thanks, man. I'll talk to Shay about going out with you and your girl. We'll let you know, OK?"

"OK."

Nate turned to David with a prayerful heart. He didn't want his friends' marriage to end as his had, and he was going to do everything in his power to make sure that it didn't. He'd lived through one failed marriage, and he wasn't sure he could make it through another.

After the ball game, a few games of pinball, and pizza, it was almost eight o'clock when Nate pulled into CeCe's driveway. By the time they got a tired and sleepy David settled in bed, shared a few minutes of chitchat with Miss Brinson, and settled themselves on the porch swing, it was nearing nine. CeCe sensed the tenseness in Nate and wondered at its cause. "Is something on your mind, Nate?"

"You," he said.

She smiled. "Cute, but not true. You've been somewhere else since we left the ball field. Did something happen?"

"Not really," he said. "I'm just a little worried about Shay and Marvin. How did Shay seem to you today?"

"Good," she said, remembering the teasing she'd been given by her new friends. "We had a lot of fun. In fact, she wants to invite us over for dinner one night. We didn't set a date or anything, but it's something both she and Marvin want to do. She introduced me to him when he came to get her. He seems like a nice man. A little sad, but nice."

Nate rubbed his hand down her bare arm. "This was the first game they've attended since their son's death about two years ago. It's been a long road back for them, CeCe, and they still aren't all the way back. Shay's only been to church a few times since the funeral, and Marvin hasn't been once. I wish there was something I could do for them."

"You pray for them, don't you?" she asked, touched by his concern for his friends.

"All the time."

"Well, you're doing the thing that needs to be done most. You'll know when there's something else you need to do."

He smiled at her, and she felt some of the tension in him abate. "I knew there was some reason I liked you. You're a smart cookie. Did you know that?"

She cocked her head to the side. "Why, sure I did. Tough woman, smart cookie—same thing."

He chuckled. "You're tough, all right. So tough that I hear you're making plans to go beyond your required one hundred and fifty hours of volunteer work at Genesis House. If we had more tough cookies like you, the world would be a better place."

CeCe plastered what she hoped was a stern expression on her face. "Hold on a minute. I'm not doing *that* much, and the little I am doing is not taking that much time. I just want to finish the job sessions and then work with Anna Mae on contacting some area employers about placing people. It's not that big a deal."

"If you say so."

"I say so."

Nate kissed her cheek and changed the subject. One day CeCe would learn to accept his praise, but he knew tonight wasn't the night. "We're having a gospel concert at church on Friday night. Would you like to go with me?"

CeCe had to think about that one. It was one thing to go to a ball game, but to go to his church was a totally different matter. That was second only to meeting his parents, and she wasn't sure she was ready for it yet. "Anna Mae said that the women at your church were wailing at the altar after they found out you'd taken me to the Gala. Now you've taken me and David to your ball game. Don't you think this gospel concert might be rushing things a bit?"

He glanced down at her. "Not really, but I guess you do. Does that mean you don't want to go with me?"

"It means we're moving pretty fast, Nate. That's all I'm saying."

"What would you suggest we do instead—sneak around?"

CeCe didn't know how the conversation had turned adversarial, but it had. "That's not what I'm saying at all. I just think we should be cautious. We don't want to give people the wrong impression."

"What impression would they get from your attending the concert with me?"

CeCe groaned. Nate was making this discussion much more difficult than it had to be. "Don't pretend you don't know, Nate. Everybody at your church is going to be speculating about us."

"Believe me, they'd speculate a whole lot more if we tried to act as though we weren't seeing each other."

"Is that what we're doing—seeing each other?"

"That's what I thought we were doing, but as you know, I've been wrong before." Nate's words were clipped. "Maybe you should tell me what we're doing."

"You're angry?"

He released a heartfelt sigh. "I'm not angry. I'm confused. I thought we had talked this through the other night, but now

I'm not sure we were having the same conversation. I need an answer, CeCe. What do you think we're doing?"

"OK, we're seeing each other."

"You don't sound too happy about it."

His words were still clipped, but now she saw the uncertainty in his eyes. Her heart went out to his vulnerability, and she decided to see if she could be as vulnerable with him. "I'm happy, but I'm also nervous. I told you, Nate, I'm not good at this relationship thing. I haven't had the best experiences with men, and I don't want to get hurt again. I really don't."

He looked into her eyes, as if willing her to read the sincerity in them. "I don't want to hurt you. I'd never deliberately hurt you, CeCe. You have my word on that."

Had she heard those words before? "I want to believe you, Nate—I do believe you, but I'm still afraid of getting hurt."

He traced a finger down her cheek. "It works both ways, CeCe. You can hurt me as easily as I can hurt you. While I understand your reasoning, it hurts that you don't trust me."

"But—" His finger against her lips stopped her words.

"I said I understood it, and I do, but it still hurts. I guess I'm just going to have to prove to you that I'm not like the other guys who've crossed your path."

She pulled his finger away from her mouth and folded her hand around his. "You don't have to do that."

"Yes I do, because I want you to trust me." He paused as if he were about to say something else but changed his mind. "Now, are you going to the concert with me?"

"Yes, I'd love to go to the concert with you."

She felt his smile. "That wasn't too hard, was it?" he asked, his voice full of the pride of victory.

"Yes, it was."

He grunted. "You're definitely a tough woman." They both chuckled at his statement.

A short while later, CeCe whispered, "Nate?"

"Yes?"

"I was a virgin before Eric—that was his name," she began.

"I've been celibate since then, and I don't plan to stop being celibate until, and unless, I get married. I've made a lot of mistakes in my life and have suffered the consequences of most of them, so I don't want to repeat them. I thought I was going to spend the rest of my life with Eric, but that didn't happen. I've decided that I'm going to do it God's way from now on. If you have a problem with that, or if you think you're going to get me to change my mind—"

He pressed a finger to her lips again. "I don't have a problem with it, and I'm not going to try to change your mind. You're singing to the choir. Why would you think I'd have a problem with your celibacy? I want to live my life for Christ, too."

"I know," she said, remembering the other men she'd known, "but some guys who call themselves Christians have different views. I considered myself a Christian and rationalized what Eric and I did as all right since we planned on getting married. I know now—and I knew it then too, if I'm honest—that I was deceiving myself. I had to accept responsibility for my actions and their consequences, and it was only by turning my face back to the Lord that I was able to do that."

"You've just been meeting the wrong guys," Nate explained. "I'm not like them, even if they do call themselves Christians. You should have hit them with a couple of Scriptures—maybe the whole Bible—and pointed them to the altar."

CeCe relaxed against him. They'd made it through the discussion. "I guess that would be one way to deal with the problem. Too bad I didn't think of it." Then she yawned. "Uh—excuse me."

"I guess that's my cue to hit the road. It's late, and we both have early days tomorrow. Would you like to pray together before I leave?"

CeCe felt her heart race. "Yes, I'd like that."

He took both her hands in his. "Any special requests?"

"Just Shay and Marvin."

Nate held her hands firmly as he petitioned the Father on their behalf. This was a brand-new experience for CeCe. She'd never gone out with anybody who wanted to pray with her. Maybe Nate was right. She'd definitely been meeting the wrong guys.

"Father, we ask that you bless our friendship. Show us how to support each other, care for each other, and build each other up. Direct our relationship in the way that you want it to go. We ask a special prayer for Shay and Marvin. We thank you for the healing work you've done in their hearts, Lord, and we pray that we don't get in the way of your continued work. Show us how we can love them and support them the way you want them to be loved and supported. We love you, Lord, and we thank you for loving us. In Jesus' name. Amen."

CeCe murmured an amen, then found herself being pulled up from the swing. Nate placed a soft kiss on her cheek as he'd done after the Gala and earlier today at the ballpark, and then he was gone. She entered the house wondering how it would feel to kiss him on his lips.

NINE

CeCe was both excited and anxious as Nate drove her and David to Shay and Marvin's for a Saturday afternoon cookout. Today marked six weeks since she and Nate had attended the Gala together. Since then he had become a vital part of her life. She was used to being with him, and his presence gave her a sense of security. She no longer worried about what people would say about them. Nate's friends and fellow church members had been nothing but gracious to her. Like Shay and Anna Mae, they cared about Nate and were happy to see him come out of his shell. Of course, she'd caught a couple of disappointed glares when they'd gone to the gospel concert some weeks back, but she understood how losing out on Nate could negatively impact any woman's disposition.

"What are you smiling about?" Nate asked.

CeCe hadn't realized she was smiling. "Just happy thoughts," she said evasively. "I'm excited about spending this time with Shay and Marvin. It's hard to believe I've known Shay for only a couple of months and already I consider her one of my closest friends. She's been a great help to me and Anna Mae with the workshops, and I really enjoy her company."

"You've been good for her, CeCe. You and Anna Mae both. You two were right there when Shay decided to reach out. I thank God for you both."

Though she should be used to it by now, Nate's praise still

caught her off guard. He valued her as a person and as a sister in Christ. She hadn't known how hungry she was for that kind of affirmation. "I think the three of us have helped each other. I thank God for bringing us together, too. I also thank him for allowing David and me to get to know you."

Nate didn't say anything, but CeCe knew him well enough now to know that the quiet smile on his face meant that her words had affected him deeply. "You don't think having David around is going to be too much for them, do you?" That question had been on her mind off and on since Shay had issued the invitation. She'd asked her friend straight-out if she would prefer they left David home, and Shay had assured her that she wanted the child to come. CeCe still wasn't sure.

"I think it'll be fine," Nate said, his eyes on the road. "If they can handle Little League games, they can handle an afternoon with David. I've been thinking that we've made it too easy for Marvin and Shay to shut themselves off. We shouldn't have allowed them to withdraw from us the way they have. I'll always regret that."

She smiled at him. If he could, Nate would take care of everybody he knew and probably quite a few people he didn't know. That's why the work at Genesis House was so good for him. Though he never talked about it, she knew he worked long hours. Not on the official Genesis House business of soliciting funds to carry out their programs, but with the personal caring for the people he served. "You can't control the world, Nate. You and everybody else did what you thought was best. Leave the rest to God."

"Are we there yet?" David called from the backseat.

"Sure are, sport," Nate said as he pulled into Shay and Marvin's driveway. As he opened his door, he said to CeCe, "I'll get David. You can head for the door."

Leaving Nate to unbuckle David's seat belt and assist him out of the car, CeCe headed for the door. Shay opened it before she had a chance to knock.

"It's about time you got here," Shay said, with a bit too much cheer. CeCe immediately suspected all was not well. "We've been looking out for you."

"Is everything all right, Shay?" CeCe asked, concerned about her friend. "If this isn't a good time—"

"Nonsense. Come on in." Shay took her hand and pulled her into the two-story foyer just as Nate and David came up behind her. Shay released CeCe and turned to Nate and David. "Hi, you," she said to Nate. To David she said, "I'm glad you could come, David. Why don't you get Nate to take you out back. There's a surprise out there for you."

"For me?" David asked, his eyes wide with childish wonder. He looked up at Nate.

"You don't even have to ask," Nate said to the boy. "I get the feeling they want to get rid of us anyway. Come on, sport." He picked David up, settled him on his shoulders, and headed toward the rear of the house.

"Tell me what's wrong, Shay," CeCe said as soon as Nate and David were out of hearing distance. She took her friend's hand. "I want to help if you'll let me."

Shay shook her head. "You can't help, CeCe. This is between Marvin and me. Things can't go on as they are. Something has to give."

"What happened? Did you two have a fight?"

Shay squeezed CeCe's fingers and led her to the white, over-stuffed sofa that dominated the living room. "I know you want to help and I love you for it, but believe me when I tell you there's nothing you can do. Right now, it's up to Marvin and me. We're either going to make it through this together, or I'm going to make it by myself."

All sorts of thoughts ran through CeCe's mind—none of them good. "Shay, you can't mean—"

Shay nodded her head in the affirmative. "I do so mean. I've loved Marvin since the day I met him. There was never a doubt in my mind that God had picked him especially for me. I still believe that, but right now we're not helping each other. We're bringing each other down. Something has to give." She took a deep breath and looked directly into CeCe's eyes. "Now I'm going to ask you to do something for me."

"Anything," CeCe said with all sincerity.

"OK, I want you to drop this subject and try to enjoy yourself today. I may look a little worse for the wear right now, but I promise you that I'm better than I've been in a long time. And I'm getting better every day. I can see God again, CeCe. There was a time when I didn't think I'd be able to see him." Shay stopped as her eyes filled with tears. "I can see him in you, in Nate, and I can even see him in me. That's the miracle. I can see him in me."

CeCe pulled her friend into her arms and hugged her close. "I've known you such a short time, Shay, but you've become very dear to me. I'm going to do what you want and enjoy myself today, but first you're going to have to give me a couple of minutes of crying time. Can you do that?" CeCe felt her friend's nod against her shoulder. "Good," she said, letting her tears fall.

Nate had picked up on Shay's discomfort as soon as he'd looked into her eyes. Now he didn't know what to expect when he saw Marvin. He hoped his friend was in good shape because he didn't want David exposed to anything negative. The boy had come to mean a lot to him, just as his mother had. Nate was protective of both of them. A part of him knew that Shay would never have allowed him to bring David out here if Marvin was in bad shape, but that didn't ease his anxiety.

"Hey, buddy," Nate called, grateful to see his friend standing at the grill. "You're looking good in that apron, my man."

"Just part of the job." Marvin waved his metal spatula. "Hiya, David. It's good to see you again. Did you enjoy the ball game last Saturday?" Nate had taken the child and his mother to several games since that first one, and last Saturday he and David had gone alone because CeCe had an appointment to show a house.

Nate set David down from his shoulders, and the tyke ran and stood next to Marvin. He began chattering about the game. "Where's my surprise?" he finally asked. Nate had begun to wonder if he'd forgotten.

"What surprise?" Marvin asked in mock ignorance.

"Miss Shay said you had a surprise for me."

Marvin rubbed his chin. "A surprise for you. Let me think. I wonder what she was talking about?" He looked over at Nate. "Do you know what she was talking about, Nate?"

Nate shook his head. "Not me. I want to see this surprise myself."

David looked from Marvin to Nate and back to Marvin again, his eyes showing his concern about the misplaced surprise. "Don't you know about the surprise, Mr. Marvin? Miss Shay said you did."

Marvin lowered his hand from his chin and snapped his fingers. "Oh, I think I know what she was talking about." He handed his spatula to Nate and winked. "Don't let the burgers burn. I've got to go show a surprise."

Nate chuckled as he took the spatula. "What if I want to see this surprise, too?" he called after the two of them, but neither turned around. Nate wondered what the surprise was as he watched Marvin lead David into the portable storage house he and Marvin had positioned in the backyard about three years ago. His mouth dropped open and tears welled up in his eyes when David zoomed out on a black-and-gold tricycle/go-cart. Marvin had done it. He'd finished the go-cart that he and Marvin Jr. had started building together. *Thank you, Lord,* Nate murmured to himself. *He's turning the corner.*

Nate continued watching as Marvin instructed David on the use of the go-cart. Once the little boy got a handle on it, he shot off again. "Look at me, Mr. Nate," he yelled across the yard. "I'm driving."

"I see you," Nate yelled back. Then he turned back to the grill and tried to get his emotions back in check.

"Hey," Marvin said, snatching the spatula back from him.

"I thought I told you not to let the burgers burn. You've been off your job. Look at that one there. I guess you'll have to eat it."

Nate looked down at the well-done burger and shook his head, almost back in control. "I'm sure I won't." He glanced back to make sure all was well with David, then turned to his friend. "Thank you for letting David play with the cart. I know how much it means to you."

"It's just a cart," Marvin said, his eyes focused on the meat on the grill.

Nate knew it was much more. That cart was a symbol of the relationship Marvin had shared with his son. His friend had been an excellent father. He'd had so much love for his boy, and that love had spilled over to every other boy he'd come across. That's the kind of man Marvin had been. The kind of man Nate hoped he'd become again.

"You're thinking too much, Richardson," Marvin said. "It's a bad trait."

Nate eased down into one of the patio chairs near the grill. "I know, but I can't help it."

"How are things with you and CeCe?" his friend asked.

That question caused Nate's face to split into a wide smile. "Good. Very good, in fact. How are things with you and Shay?"

Marvin took the burgers off the grill and added more. "They could be better. Then again, they've been worse. You know, sometimes I wake up in the middle of the night and just lie there looking at her. I love her so much that it scares me. How can I let myself love her that much? What if I lose her, too? I don't think I could live through it, Nate. I don't."

"Have you talked to Shay about this?"

He shook his head. "I can't. I can't talk to her about anything. I don't want to hurt her, but everything I do these days seems to hurt her. Sometimes I think she'd be better off without me."

"You don't mean that," Nate said. He didn't like the way his friend was talking.

Marvin gave Nate a look that let him know he did mean it.

"Don't you think I can see that she's getting better? I see the life in her. The life that drew me to her initially. But now it repels me. I can hardly stand it. I love her more than I love my own life, but I can't be in her presence for more than fifteen minutes before I start feeling as though I'm suffocating. What do you have to say to that?"

Fear snaked up Nate's spine as he considered the implications of his friend's words. "I say that you have a choice. You can tell Shay how you feel and share your pain, or you can continue to let thoughts like the ones you're having now rule your mind. But I'm telling you, Marvin, if you choose the latter, you're going to lose everything that's important to you."

David chose that moment to zoom by in the go-cart. "Look at me, Mama," he said as he breezed by.

Nate turned and saw CeCe and Shay coming their way. Shay looked a lot better now than she had when they'd arrived. CeCe, on the other hand, looked worse. Talk about a woman who wore her heart on her sleeve. That was his CeCe. And she thought she was tough. He laughed aloud.

"What's so funny, Nate?" Shay asked, taking the seat across from him. To his delight, CeCe took the patio chair next to him.

"Just thinking about my good fortune," he said, with a pointed look at CeCe. If her complexion had been lighter, he was sure he would have seen her blush.

"Will wonders never cease," Shay said in an exaggerated drawl. "A man who knows the value of what he has. I can't remember the last time I ran across one of you."

Nate's glance shot to Shay, who had directed her attention on Marvin. Was she deliberately baiting her husband? Nate wondered. If she was, the look on Marvin's face said he didn't appreciate it.

"David's enjoying his surprise," Nate said, hoping to lower the tension between his friends. It worked; Shay turned her attention back to him.

"Marvin did a great job with it, didn't he?" Shay watched her husband, her eyes full of love. "I'm always telling my husband that he can do anything he wants to do. He just has to want to do it."

Nate shot a second glance at Marvin, then one at CeCe. She took his hand and stood up. "Come on. I want to see this surprise up close," she said.

Nate didn't move immediately. He knew that CeCe was trying to give Marvin and Shay some time alone, but he wasn't sure that was a good idea. Shay seemed to be baiting Marvin, and given his friend's current state of mind, Nate thought she couldn't have picked a worse time.

"Come on," CeCe coaxed, tugging on his hand. "I have a feeling my son is going to be wanting a go-cart of his own. And guess who's going to have to build it?"

"You?" Nate asked, getting up. He'd decided to follow CeCe's lead and leave his friends alone.

"You've got it. And I'm sure I'm going to need some help."

"From me?"

"Give that man a cigar."

Nate chuckled as she led him away from the tempest brewing between his friends. They'd gone from silence to verbal banter. He prayed it signaled progress.

Later that night CeCe and Nate completed the ritual that had become theirs. They settled David into bed, spent some time with Miss Brinson, and then sat on the porch swing and enjoyed each other's company. "What's on your mind tonight?" Nate asked.

"Shay and Marvin. What's on your mind?"

"The same thing. They're not out of the woods yet, but they're getting there, I think. I pray."

CeCe remembered the way Nate had tried to referee the couple's budding argument, evidence of his concern for them. "Shay seems to think things may get worse before they get better. She's determined to move forward, preferably with Marvin."

"Preferably?" Nate repeated.

"Her words. Not mine."

"Do you think she's considering leaving him?"

CeCe sensed the change in Nate; she knew he was thinking about himself and Naomi. In a perfect world—in a world where God's creation was perfectly obedient to him—Nate and Naomi would be together. Sometimes she wondered about the hold that the past had on him. He didn't carry any banners to indicate his hurt, but CeCe felt it in his interaction with her. She knew his cautiousness and his care with her were a result of his past pain. "I don't think she's thinking about leaving him, but I do think she realizes that she has to be willing to give him up if they are to have any chance of coming out of this whole—and together."

Nate didn't say anything, and she wondered if he'd even heard her. As she looked at his profile, her heart hurt. *Lord, I said I wanted to be his friend, but I'm coming to care for him as more than a friend. How will I handle it if he can never feel more for me?*

"Did I ever tell you that I used to pray for a marriage as solid as Shay and Marvin's? I wanted a woman who'd suit me as well as Shay suits Marvin."

CeCe heard the fear and the pain in his voice, and wanted to comfort him. "They're going to be all right, Nate. We have to believe that."

"Sometimes things don't end up all right, CeCe. It takes two people to make a relationship work. Two people who want the same thing and who are pulling in the same direction. Sometimes one person has to carry the load for both of them, and the Lord will give that one the strength he or she needs to do it for as long as necessary. But when people leave and start lives separate from each other, the situation becomes more difficult. Not impossible, but much more difficult."

CeCe knew he was speaking from experience, and a part of her wanted to strangle the woman who'd caused him such pain. "Maybe it won't come to that."

He turned to her and took both her hands in his. "I want you to promise me something, CeCe. Promise me that you won't run away if things between *us* get difficult. Promise me that you'll talk to me, that you won't just leave."

"I promise, Nate." She squeezed his hand to reassure him. More than anything, she appreciated Nate's honesty. He didn't try to hide his feelings from her, and he didn't say things that he didn't mean. He never let her forget that she could hurt him just as easily as he could hurt her. In an odd way, that knowledge gave her confidence in their relationship. Though she wasn't sure he was falling in love with her, she knew that his heart had to be deeply involved in their relationship for him to ask for such a promise.

TEN

"Where is your other bag?" CeCe asked David. He stood near the door bouncing on his heels, hardly able to remain in the house long enough to gather the clothes he needed for the sleepover at Nate's. The boy looked around as if hoping the bag would magically appear at his feet. When it didn't, he raised questioning eyes to his mother. "Maybe you should try looking in the laundry room," she suggested.

At her words, her son scampered from the family room off in the direction of the laundry room. Nate and Miss Brinson both chuckled at David's quick movements, while CeCe just shook her head. "Are you sure you want to do this?" she asked Nate for the tenth time. He and Stuart were hosting this all-male event for their baseball team, and David had been invited to tag along. He'd become the team's unofficial—very unofficial—batboy, and he loved the job.

"I can handle it." Nate sat on the couch across from the two women who sat on the settee. "We've been doing this for three years now. David won't be a bother. The other guys love him, and I think they're a good influence on him, but if you're really worried, I won't take him."

CeCe shook her head, telling herself she was being the typical overprotective mother. "No, you have to take him. If you don't, he'll be crushed."

"And I won't get the peace and quiet I've been looking forward to," Miss Brinson said. "Of course, if you decide to leave David here, I can always go to the sleepover with you. It'll probably be quieter at your place, anyway."

"B.B.," CeCe began, "please stop teasing Nate. I do hate to see a grown man blush—especially when his complexion is as dark as mine."

David bounded back into the family room shouting, "I found it." He raised the bag in the air to get everyone's approval. "Can we go now, Mr. Nate? The guys are waiting for me."

The three adults shared a smile above David's head. "Seems like we're ready to hit the road," Nate said, taking David's hand. Miss Brinson and CeCe followed them through the family-room door and outside. CeCe reflected on the changes in her life since she'd met Nate. She felt very pleased with the way her life was working out. She was flourishing, her son was flourishing, and because she'd have the day free to meet with some prospective clients, her hopes rose that her real estate business would soon be flourishing as well.

"Are you going to meet us at church tomorrow, or should I plan on bringing David here afterward?" Nate asked, once they were all outside.

"Why don't you bring him here, Nate. I have a meeting at my church between Sunday school and morning service tomorrow, so I'll just stay there all morning."

Nate nodded his agreement, as she'd known he would. They'd decided to continue attending their respective churches and to visit each other's when possible. So far, the arrangement was working out well. On Labor Day they'd attended picnics at both churches, starting the day at hers and ending it at his.

Nate kissed both women on the cheek and headed toward his car. He turned around and faced them as he opened the rear door for David. "Oh, yeah," he called to CeCe, "my parents are coming to town next weekend, and they want to meet you and David and B.B. I told them that we'd make plans for the weekend. I was thinking the two of us could take them out Friday, then we'd have a cookout at my house on Saturday, and all of us go to my church on Sunday and back here on Sunday afternoon. We can talk more about it when I bring David back tomorrow."

CeCe's mouth fell open, but no words came out. Nate turned, arranged David in his booster seat in the back, waved again, then got in and drove away. CeCe's mouth was still open. Miss Brinson's laughter made her close it.

"He did that on purpose," she complained to Miss Brinson. "I know he did. I don't see why you're laughing. Nate's parents coming to visit is nothing to laugh about."

Miss Brinson shook her head. "I'm not laughing at Nate's parents. I'm laughing at you. You should see yourself. You look like you've just seen a ghost. Calm down, CeCe. They're just people."

Miss Brinson turned and went back into the house. CeCe followed her. "How can you say they're just people, B.B.? These are Nate's parents, and they want to see me. Why do they want to see me?"

"I'm not even going to try to answer that, CeCe." Miss Brinson went to the dishwasher and began unloading the dishes. "You know as well as I do why they want to meet you and David."

CeCe dropped down on the chair and covered her face with her hands. Miss Brinson was right. She did know why Nate's parents wanted to meet her and David. She knew, and it scared her to death. What if they didn't like her? What if they didn't think she was good enough for their son?

"Stop it, CeCe," Miss Brinson said. "I know what you're doing. You're going to make yourself sick with worry over nothing. They're going to love you because Nate loves you."

CeCe nodded. She could do nothing else. *They're going to love you because Nate loves you,* B.B. had said. Except Nate had never said that he loved her. She and Nate needed to talk. It was unfair of him to drop this on her and then leave the way he had. She had half a mind to drive over to his house and confront him. If he wasn't having the sleepover, she'd do just that.

She didn't know if she was ready to meet his parents. Everything was moving so fast. It had been only three months since they'd gone to the Gala together. Her life was changing so much. All good, but still very fast. She knew that she'd grown as a person and as a Christian since she'd started working at Genesis House and met Nate, Anna Mae, and Shay, but the relationships were still very new to her.

How she wished she could talk to Nate. He had become her best friend, and she wanted to talk this out with him. She raised her eyes to the clock on the wall above the television. It was just five o'clock. It would be ten or later before Nate called her tonight, if he called at all. She was going to kill him, she decided. She was definitely going to kill him.

The first time Nate called, CeCe was in the bathtub and missed his call. When she tried to call him back, his line was busy. Finally, after a terribly long half hour, he called her again.

"Are you still upset?" he immediately asked.

She was wise enough to know his question was a tactic designed to disarm her, and she wasn't going to fall for it. Besides, the laughter in his voice was barely disguised. "What you did was cruel, Nate."

The man had the nerve to laugh outright. "It wasn't cruel, CeCe. You're just so predictable. Have you pulled out all of your hair yet?"

OK, she got his point. Maybe she had overreacted. "Last time I looked, I was as bald as you."

He laughed again. "Oh, CeCe, I do love you."

CeCe thought her heart stopped beating. Did he know what he had said? Why was he saying this now?

"Are you there, CeCe?" Nate asked. He was no longer laughing.

"I'm here," she said in a small voice. Did he really love her? Oh, how she wanted him to love her!

"What are you thinking?"

What does he mean, What am I thinking? When she didn't answer, he said, "I know what I said. I didn't plan to say it now, but it's true. I love you, CeCe, and I want to spend the rest of my life with you."

Her heart was too full for her to even speak. He loved her and wanted to spend the rest of his life with her. Was she dreaming?

"Well, aren't you going to say something?" he asked. His impatience warmed her heart, because she knew it was an indication of how vulnerable he was with her.

"I'm here." This time her voice was weepy.

"Look, the boys are in bed. Stuart is here. I can be there in about thirty minutes. Meet me on the porch so we don't wake B.B."

CeCe nodded. Of course, he couldn't see her assent.

"Say something, sweetheart," he said.

"I'll meet you on the porch." Her mind focused on the fact that this was the first time he'd used an endearment when he spoke to her.

"I didn't mean to make you cry, sweetheart. I'll be there as soon as I can. OK?"

"OK." The tenderness in his voice did nothing to quell her tears.

Nate hung up the phone and quickly changed out of his pajamas and into a pair of jeans and a shirt appropriate for visiting. He hadn't planned to tell CeCe that he loved her this soon or in this way, but it had happened. Now he needed to see her and tell her to her face before he lost his courage. This verbal confirmation of what he was feeling was a major step for him, and he didn't want to think too closely about it. No, he didn't want to analyze it and judge it; he just wanted to enjoy it. He loved CeCe, and he was pretty sure she felt the same way about him. He just didn't know if she was ready to say the words yet. That was all right, though. He was willing to wait. CeCe was worth waiting for.

Fully dressed, Nate padded down the stairs to the family room, where Stuart and he were bunking on the floor with the boys. He put his finger to his lips and shook his friend awake. They tiptoed out of the family room and went to the foyer.

"Where are you going?" Stuart asked, fighting back a yawn.

"To see CeCe," Nate said. He was sure his grin covered his entire face.

"This late?" Stuart was immediately fully awake. "Is something wrong? What can I do?"

Nate put his hand on his friend's shoulder to calm him. "Nothing's wrong. In fact, everything's right."

"You're not making sense, Nate. What's going on?"

He put his other hand on Stuart's other shoulder. "I just spoke to CeCe on the phone, and I told her that I love her."

Stuart yawned and Nate dropped his hands. "It's about time," he said simply. "If you had waited any longer, I think I might have told her for you."

Nate chuckled. He wasn't surprised that Stuart knew his feelings. He certainly hadn't been trying to hide them. "Hold down the fort. I should be back in a couple of hours."

"Don't rush. All we're doing here is sleeping. Or trying to sleep."

Nate didn't bother responding to his friend's last words. All he wanted was to see CeCe. He loved her. And he'd told her. He felt so good that his heart played a song all the way to her house. He saw her in the shadows of the porch as soon as he pulled into her driveway. He was out of the truck as soon as he cut off the ignition. He bounded up the three steps and lifted a teary CeCe in his arms. "I love you, CeCe Williams. I love you. I love you. I love you." Nate began swinging CeCe around the porch, and soon her tears of joy turned to giggles and then to full-fledged laughter. By the time he put her back down, he was laughing himself. He took her hand and pulled her to their place on the swing. Tonight, though, he pulled her close in his arms. "Do you have any idea how good it feels to tell you what's in my heart? Oh, sweetheart, it feels so wonderful. How does it make you feel?"

She looked up at him, and he could read the love in her eyes.

Yes, he could wait for the words. He knew they were there. "Oh, Nate," she said. "I can't believe it. You love me. You actually love me."

He chuckled. "Silly woman. You sound as though you're surprised. Surely you must have guessed my feelings by now. I would hope that I've shown them to you enough."

"You have. You have," she assured him. "And in so many ways that I can't even count, but it feels so good to hear the words."

He pulled her close and savored the moment. This was the woman he loved. The woman God had given him when he'd doubted there was a woman for him. Oh, but he'd been given a gem. A precious gift directly from the Father. *Thank you so much for sending her to me, Lord. Teach me to love her as you want her to be loved. More than anything, I want her to be confident in my love for you and my love for her and David.*

"Nate." CeCe's voice was quiet.

"What, sweetheart?"

She pulled back just far enough to look into his eyes. "I love you too."

Pleasure flowed from the top of Nate's head to the bottom of his feet. He wanted to shout his joy to the entire neighborhood, but he settled for pulling her close again and thanking God for his love and for CeCe's. His heart shouted his joy to the angels in heaven. That was enough for tonight. When tears filled his eyes, he didn't try to stop them.

"Nate?" CeCe queried again. When he didn't answer, she pulled back and looked at him. Seeing his tears, she pressed her fingertips to his face. "Oh, Nate," she said, "isn't it wonderful?"

Nate looked through his tears at this woman he loved. "It's more than wonderful. It's a miracle. A miracle straight from heaven."

And for the first time since Nate had known CeCe, he did something he'd wanted to do for a very long time: He pressed his lips against hers for a brief kiss before pulling her back into his arms and repeating his vow of love.

The ringing of the telephone shattered CeCe's most wonderful dream. She and Nate were sitting in rockers on their front porch, watching their great-grandchildren play in their yard. She fought against waking as long as she could, but the phone continued to ring. She sat up and reached for the phone, casting a glance at the clock and wondering who could be calling this early in the morning

"Hello?"

"CeCe, it's me, Nate."

CeCe slid down in the bed. A stupid grin, she knew, spread across her face. Nate was going to tell her he loved her again. It wasn't a dream. "I love you, Nate," she said, wanting to say it first.

She felt his smile and his love through the telephone lines. "I love you, too, sweetheart, but we have a little problem this morning."

CeCe sat straight up in bed. "What's wrong? Is it David? Is something wrong with my baby?"

"No, sweetheart," Nate said. His calm voice relaxed her. "David's fine. He and the other boys are still asleep. Our problem is with Shay and Marvin."

"Oh no, Nate. What's happened?"

Nate expelled a weary sigh. "Marvin just showed up here about thirty minutes ago with his suitcase. He says he's moved out of the house."

CeCe slumped down in the bed. *Poor Shay,* she thought. "What about Shay, Nate?"

"That's why I'm calling you, sweetheart. I've called the house a couple of times, but her line's busy. I don't want to panic, but I think somebody should go and make sure she's all right."

CeCe was getting out of bed. "I'm about to get dressed now," she said. "I'll call you as soon as I see her. Don't worry."

"I won't," he said.

CeCe heard the pain in his voice. "You shouldn't, Nate, but you will. Are you still planning to take the boys to church?"

"I think so. Marvin seems to be all right." He gave a dry chuckle. "In fact, he seems to be handling the entire situation a lot better than I am. He was asleep as soon as his head hit the pillow."

"He has to be hurting, Nate, but you do what you think is best. Whatever you decide, don't worry about bringing David back here. I'll stop by there and get him."

"Thanks, sweetheart."

"Well, I need to hang up so I can get dressed. I want to be with Shay. I know she can use a friend right now. I'll talk to you later, OK?"

"OK." CeCe was about to hang up when Nate said, "CeCe?"

"I'm still here."

"I do love you with all my heart. I just wanted to tell you that this morning."

"I know you do, Nate. I love you too. Now take care of yourself and try to get some sleep if you can."

CeCe didn't wait for Nate's agreement because she didn't expect to get it. She hung up the phone, rushed to the bathroom to wash up, and then threw on some clean clothes. She knocked on Miss Brinson's bedroom door on her way out and told her what was going on.

Since nobody was on the street but her, it took her only fifteen minutes to reach Shay's house in southwest Atlanta. *Please, God, show me how to help her through this. She loves Marvin so much. I just know she's going to be crushed.*

CeCe rang the bell and then rocked back and forth on her heels while she waited for Shay to answer. She was about to ring it again when Shay opened the door. "CeCe, what are you doing here? Is something wrong?"

CeCe took in her friend's nightgown, bare feet, and barely opened eyes and realized that she'd been in bed—asleep. A close inspection of Shay's eyes revealed no trace of tears. *Maybe she doesn't know that Marvin is gone,* CeCe thought. "I have something to tell you, Shay. I think we'd better sit down."

Shay stepped back and let CeCe in the house. "Let's go to the kitchen. We're probably going to need some coffee," Shay said.

CeCe followed her friend, praying for the wisdom to break the news in the best way. Once Shay had put on the coffee and they were both seated at the Formica-topped kitchen table, CeCe took her friend's hand. "Marvin arrived at Nate's this morning with his suitcase."

Shay looked down at her nails. "You know," she said when she looked back up at CeCe, "I really should get my nails done. I've let them go in the last year or so. Just as I've let a lot of things go."

CeCe wondered if her friend was in shock. "Did you hear what I said, Shay? Marvin has moved into Nate's."

"I heard you, CeCe. I knew Marvin was gone. I just couldn't decide if he went to Nate's or to Stuart's. I should have guessed Nate's since you're here." She turned to the coffee. "I think it's ready. Do you want cream, sugar, or both?"

CeCe reached across the table and placed her hand on her friend's arm to keep her seated. "Shay, you're scaring me. Don't you care that Marvin's gone?"

Shay pulled her arm away. She got up and took cups from the cabinet. Then she turned back to CeCe. "Of course I care," she said, her voice wavering. "I care more than you'll ever know, but leaving was Marvin's decision. I can't live his life for him, and I can't live my life through him." She turned back to the coffee. "I'll have this ready in a minute."

CeCe wanted to weep for her friend, but she couldn't because Shay wouldn't allow herself to weep. She watched as Shay poured the coffee as if this were an ordinary day. When she gave CeCe her cup, she said, "I bet Nate was pretty surprised to see Marvin on his doorstep, wasn't he? I imagine that was a funny scene."

CeCe didn't know what to say. She didn't find any humor in this situation, and she didn't see how Shay could, either.

"I've shocked you, haven't I, CeCe?"

She nodded. What else could she do?

Shay idly stirred her coffee. "You're not alone. I shocked myself. Marvin and I argued last night, and he said he was leaving. And you know what? I didn't cry. Not even when he packed his bags and went downstairs. He's been gone since around eleven. After he left, I checked the locks, set the security system, and went to bed. And I slept through until you got here."

CeCe didn't understand Shay's pride in herself. She was still a bit unsure about her friend's mental state. "Nate said he tried calling you but the phone's been busy."

Shay gave a sheepish half smile. "Oh, yeah, I forgot. I took it off the hook. If Marvin wants to talk to me, he has to come home." She reached for CeCe's hand. "I wish I could stop you and Nate from worrying about us, but I know I can't. The least you can do is not let what's happening with us cast a dark cloud over your own happiness. I believe with all my heart that Marvin and I are going to be all right, and I need you to believe it, too."

CeCe squeezed the hand holding hers. "I'll believe with you."

Shay smiled. "Good. Now tell me some good news about you and Nate. We can't go through the day with just the news of Marvin and me." CeCe didn't say anything, but apparently she didn't have to. "Come on," Shay said, "I can tell by your eyes that something's happened. You'd better tell me before I start guessing."

When CeCe still didn't answer, Shay explained, "I won't be any more unhappy because of your happiness, CeCe. In fact, I want to share in your happiness, so just tell me."

"Last night Nate told me that he loved me," she blurted out.

Shay snorted. "Well, it's about time. A blind man could see that you two are meant for each other."

"Is it that obvious?" CeCe asked, not bothering to hide the wonder in her voice.

Shay laughed. "A blind man wearing a mask could see it."

CeCe opened her mouth, then closed it. By the time she called Nate to let him know all was well at Shay's house, she was laughing herself.

ELEVEN

"Nate," CeCe whispered against his mouth, "we have to stop."

"I know." Nate pressed his mouth against hers again.

CeCe felt herself melt against him. Kissing him this way felt so right, but she knew they had to stop. Though she knew that the love she and Nate shared was different from what she had shared with Eric, she knew that both emotions could lead to disaster. She pulled herself out of Nate's arms and settled back against the swing, her eyes closed.

"I'm sorry," Nate said, his voice warm and comforting. "I mean, I'm sorry for making you uncomfortable but not sorry for kissing you." He chuckled softly. "I've wanted to do it for a very long time, but I promise you, CeCe, it won't go any further. I don't expect it to go any further."

CeCe nodded, but she didn't open her eyes. "I know, Nate. I trust you." But she wondered if she could trust herself. Nate had proven he could control his passions, for he'd lived a celibate lifestyle for four years. She knew she could control hers as well, but the intensity of her feelings for this man she had come to love surprised her. *Well, CeCe,* she said to herself, *you wondered how it would feel to kiss Nate's lips, and now you know. Maybe you would have been better off not knowing.*

"Come on," Nate teased. "Tell me what's going on behind those eyelids. I don't like it when you think so much. It usually means you're worrying unnecessarily."

She opened her eyes, but she still didn't look at him. "You have nothing to be sorry about, Nate. I was as willing as you were. I should apologize to you. I didn't mean to lead you on."

Nate placed his index finger on her chin and turned her face to him. "What are you talking about? You didn't lead me on. Now tell me what's on your mind."

CeCe turned her face away from the tenderness and acceptance in his eyes. What did he really know about her, anyway? How could he love her when he didn't know her? He didn't know the awful things she'd done and the price she still had to pay because of them. Would he still love her if he knew?

"I'm not him," he said, when she didn't speak.

CeCe's head jerked back in his direction.

"I'm not Eric," he repeated. "I want to marry you, CeCe, and spend the rest of my life with you. And I want everything to be right between us. That means waiting until we've said our vows before sharing any intimacies beyond the kisses we've shared. I don't want us to start our lives together with guilt or shame over sex. Our marriage is going to be a celebration of the love God has given us. We're not going to tarnish it. Neither one of us wants that." He grinned. "Even if it means we never sit on this porch alone again."

CeCe smiled, feeling relaxed because of his obvious desire to comfort her. Nate's sensitivity to her needs and emotions made her feel cherished. She wanted him to feel the same way. "I don't think it'll come to that. I'd hate to have to give up our special place."

He pulled her close to him and pressed a kiss on the top of her head. "Neither would I. Besides, I'm still not sure B.B. doesn't have a double-barreled shotgun aimed at me even as we speak."

"You're so bad," CeCe said with a giggle. "You know she doesn't have a gun."

She felt his smile against her head. "If you say so."

They were quiet for a few moments, then CeCe said, "Your parents will be here tomorrow."

"They sure will."

She waited for him to say more. When he didn't, she gave voice to the fear she'd harbored since he'd told her about the visit. "What if they don't like me?"

"They'll like you," he said in a voice that brooked no disagreement. "In fact, I think they'll love you."

CeCe wasn't so sure. Parents had high standards for only sons, and she was sure Nate's parents were no different. After his disaster with Naomi, they were probably even more concerned about the woman in their son's life. It didn't take a genius to figure out that most parents would not consider a single mother with a four-year-old son as prize daughter-in-law material. And if they knew the details of her past. . . . She shook off the thought. "Aren't they going to think this is awfully soon?"

"This what?" he asked, and again she heard the smile in his voice.

She punched him playfully in his side. "You know what I'm talking about. What if they think our relationship is moving too fast?" In truth, CeCe had wondered that herself.

"They won't."

"They might."

"They won't."

CeCe gave a loud sigh. "How can you be so sure? I think we should talk about this."

"We only need to talk about it if *we* think we're moving too quickly. We don't." He pulled back and looked down at her. "At least, I know I don't. Do you think we are?"

CeCe didn't answer immediately, and when she spoke, her voice was soft. "It's only been about three and a half months." She felt him tense at her side, then quickly relax again.

"If you want to be technical, I probably could have told you I loved you a month ago. Maybe even six weeks."

"You're kidding."

He tilted her face up to his. "Do I look like I'm kidding?"

The love and honesty in his eyes told her he wasn't. He'd known he loved her all that time. "But how . . . ?" she asked.

He shrugged as if the how didn't matter. "I don't know. When

God puts two people together it doesn't have to take long for them to realize it. Besides, we're not getting married tomorrow. We have a lot to do before we get formally engaged and set a date. You have to meet my parents. I have to meet yours. We have to talk to our pastors. We're going to do this right, every step of the way."

He wants to meet my parents, CeCe thought. She didn't know why she was surprised. She should have known he'd want to meet them, that he'd have to meet them if their relationship continued to progress. So here they were. Her parents. She wondered if she could get them to make the trip up here, or if she and Nate would have to go to Alabama. She only went once or twice a year—for no more than two or three days at a time— and she dreaded every trip. She didn't want to even think about taking Nate into that environment.

She relaxed against Nate's side without commenting on his words. She'd think about all of that later. They were in no hurry to get married or formally engaged, for that matter, which meant there was no rush for him to meet her parents. Besides, she wanted to enjoy his loving her for as long as she could. *Who knows what the future holds, anyway?* she asked herself; but even as she asked, she prayed silently, *Lord, please don't let me lose the only person I'll ever love this way. Let everything work out so that Nate and I can get married and build a life together.*

CeCe shouldn't have been surprised at how nice the Richardsons were—given they had a son like Nate—but she was. She and Nate had met the older couple at the airport and taken them out to dinner the night before. She'd fallen in love with them over the Chinese food and laughter they'd shared. She smiled as she remembered how Mrs. Richardson had fussed over Nate and how embarrassed it seemed to make him. Mr. Richardson had been cute with the bear hug and slap on the back he'd given his only son.

David and Miss Brinson had won the couple over and been won over by them as well. CeCe had held her breath when she'd introduced them to David, knowing she wouldn't be able to tolerate in-laws who didn't accept her son. Now as she watched David, Nate, and Mr. Richardson assemble the go-cart the three had gone out and bought earlier in the day, her heart filled up, as did her eyes.

"What's the matter?" Mrs. Richardson asked, coming up behind her. The older woman had been out back chatting with Miss Brinson when CeCe had excused herself to check on the homemade ice cream that was cooling in Nate's freezer.

CeCe tried to suck in her emotions. "Nothing, really," she said to Nate's mother. "I'm just happy, I guess."

Mrs. Richardson put her arm around CeCe's shoulder. "You should be," she said. "I don't think I've seen my son this happy in a long time, CeCe. I love you for the role you played in giving him that happiness."

CeCe turned to look back out the window at the man they were discussing. Today he and David wore matching khaki shorts and tan polo shirts. They had been dressing alike fairly often since the sleepover. She knew her son was as much in love with Nate as she was. "Well, your son is very much responsible for my happiness, and for David's. Nate is a very good man, and very, very rare."

Mrs. Richardson's eyes crinkled at the corners as her lips curved in a proud smile. "I'm biased, I know, but I agree with you. I'm glad the woman he's chosen appreciates and loves the man he is, for Nate can be nothing other than what he is." She paused. "He's not perfect, not by a long shot, but he has a loving heart, and he can ask for forgiveness when he's wrong, and he can forgive when he's been wronged. I have no complaints with the man he's become or with the woman he's chosen."

CeCe lowered her eyes. This woman's total acceptance of her still surprised her. She wondered if Mrs. Richardson would still think so highly of her if she knew everything about her past.

"I don't know who's having more fun," Mrs. Richardson said, "grandpa, daddy, or son."

CeCe's eyes filled up this time, and she couldn't stop the tears from falling. She turned to the woman she hoped would one day be her mother-in-law. Mrs. Richardson must have read the uncertainty only slightly masked by the tears in CeCe's eyes, because she added, "Nate told us that you two aren't officially engaged yet, but he also told us that he loves you and wants to marry you. And that you feel the same way."

CeCe nodded through her tears. "I want to be his wife," she said.

Mrs. Richardson placed her hands on CeCe's shoulders. "Then don't worry about David, CeCe. We already think of him as our grandson, and we'll love him just as we love our other grandchildren. You're both going to be part of our family, and we consider ourselves blessed to have you."

"But—," CeCe began, wanting to say something but not sure what. How could this woman accept David so lovingly into her family, when his biological father and paternal grandparents had rejected him? It seemed too good to be true.

"As I've already told Nate and Gert," Nate's mother was saying, "you all have to come to Chicago for a visit. We would all come to visit you, but Nate's oldest sister is expecting again, and she's not traveling. Nate has told them all about you, and they can hardly wait to meet you." Mrs. Richardson took a deep breath. "Now, do you need any help in here?" she asked, as if knowing CeCe was too overcome with emotion to continue their previous line of conversation. CeCe shook her head. "OK, then, I'll go back out and sit with Gert. You come back out when you're ready." CeCe nodded again.

Mrs. Richardson turned back to her before she went out the door. "I'll be calling you to arrange the trip."

CeCe watched the door long after Mrs. Richardson had gone through it. When Nate's family liked you, they really liked you, she guessed. They didn't seem to have any reservations about her relationship with Nate, which was just too good to be true. Though a part of her questioned her good fortune, CeCe decided to accept the Richardsons at their word. She wasn't going to go looking for trouble today, because she knew for a certainty that trouble knew all too well how to find her.

"Why are you hiding out in here?" came the voice of the man she loved, the man who loved her. "We need your help with the go-cart."

She shook off her thoughts and greeted Nate with a grin. "Sure you do. What do you want me to do? Pass the hammer?"

Nate chuckled, then pulled her into his arms and hugged her briefly. Setting her away from him, he said, "You can pass the nails, too."

CeCe laughed. "So, are your parents enjoying themselves?"

Nate hopped up on the counter and sat. "Can't you tell? If they enjoy themselves any more, I may have to pry them out of my house." He frowned at the idea, or seemed to. "Right after I pry Marvin out, that is."

Nate had been complaining about Marvin since he'd shown up the other week. His friend had settled in for the long haul, it seemed, though he had made himself scarce since Nate's parents arrived. CeCe assumed he was at Stuart's. "I thought you said nothing could make your parents leave their grandkids in Chicago."

"Grandkids in Atlanta might," he said, all trace of humor gone. They hadn't talked about children, and CeCe warmed to the thought of sharing a pregnancy with this man. She hadn't had a husband by her side when she was pregnant with David, and the thought of sharing that experience with her baby's father filled her heart to overflowing.

"They'll have to wait a while on that, won't they?" she said.

He inclined his head toward the window where they could see David with Mr. Richardson. "Seems to me they already think they have one here," he said. "But I'm sure that the more there are, the greater the chance of my parents being willing to move here. Between my three sisters, they have six—seven if you count the one on the way—in Chicago. I'd be up for trying to break that record, but I guess it would ultimately be up to you. And the Lord."

CeCe sucked in her breath. This conversation was getting out of hand. No way could Nate be serious about the two of them having seven children. He couldn't be.

Nate hopped down off the counter and kissed her cheek. "Don't look so worried," he said. "Seven children could take us at least seven years." At her shocked expression, he turned and, whistling, left the house.

David wasn't the only one sleepy when Nate took him, CeCe, and Miss Brinson home later that night. The boy and Miss Brinson immediately went off to bed, giving a tired Nate and CeCe a few quiet moments together. When CeCe yawned, Nate said, "I guess this means no sitting in the swing tonight. The honeymoon is over before it even starts."

CeCe gave him a sassy smile and reached for the mail scattered on the kitchen counter. Nate had brought it in while she and Miss Brinson made their way into the house.

"And now, even the mail is more important than a few quiet minutes with me," he teased. "By the time we're married, I fear you'll have forgotten I'm alive. You'll start treating me like the furniture."

"Stop," she said, slapping his wrist with one of her letters. "We'll have to go through the mail when we're married, so we should start practicing now."

"All right," Nate said. "I think you have a point." He walked behind her and hugged her.

When he massaged her shoulder, she smiled and said, "That's not exactly—"

CeCe stopped in midsentence. Nate felt her tense against him. "What is it?" he asked, looking over her shoulder at the letter she held in her hand. "Is it bad news?" He didn't see how she could know something was wrong, because she hadn't opened the envelope, but it was clear something was dreadfully wrong.

CeCe seemed to make an effort to relax. "It's nothing."

"Oh no you don't," he said, turning her around. "We need to start being completely open with each other now—even before we get married. Now tell me what's wrong. Was it that letter?"

He watched her look at the letter, and the shutter in her eyes let him know that the letter was indeed the problem. "What is it?" he asked.

With a sigh, CeCe handed him the letter. He noticed she did it with reluctance, and he almost refused to take it. Almost. "It's from Alabama. Is that your hometown?"

She nodded.

There was no name on the return address, just a street and city. "So who's it from?"

She turned away from him. "Eric's parents."

"Oh," he said. It was all he could think to say. He'd expected the pain to be caused by *her* parents, not Eric's. He handed the letter back to her and watched as she tore it up without opening it.

"Why did you do that?"

"Because I know what they want."

He waited for her to tell him more, and when she didn't, he asked, "What do they want?"

She sighed as if she'd told him this story a million times before and resented having to tell it again. "They want to be part of David's life. Can you believe that?"

He certainly could believe it, but CeCe's tone told him she probably wouldn't appreciate his sharing that opinion.

"Where were they when David was born?" she asked. He knew she didn't expect an answer. No, she was getting rid of the pain. It was so intense he could feel it. Any other time he would have reached out to comfort her, but tonight his arms stayed at his side. "*Your* parents were more accepting of David than *they've* ever been. Can you believe that?"

Obviously, she couldn't believe it. She turned back to him. "You aren't saying anything," she observed. "What are you thinking?"

Her question sounded like an accusation, and Nate wasn't sure how to respond. "Why don't you want them to see David?" he asked.

Her eyes widened as if she thought the answer should be obvious to him. "Because it's too late. Because David wouldn't understand."

Her argument was weak, and Nate knew she knew it was weak, but her tone dared him to challenge her. Since he loved her, he had no choice. "Are you sure this isn't more about you than it's about David?"

"What do you mean by that?" she asked, her tone again daring him to disagree with her.

He didn't want to hurt her, but he wanted to understand and he wanted to help. "I can see how upset you are, CeCe, but to be honest, I can understand their wanting to see their grandson."

"He's not their grandson," she said, her voice tight with anger and pain. "They didn't want him when he was born. How dare they think they can be part of his life now! How would I explain to David that he has grandparents but he doesn't have a father?"

Nate didn't know what to say. CeCe was clearly distraught, and he didn't think she was ready to listen to reason right now. "Look, we don't have to solve this tonight," he said. "You're tired. I'm tired. The problem will still be here tomorrow. Let's talk about it then."

"I don't know what else we have to talk about." She lifted her chin in defiance and finality. "I've said all I have to say."

"I know," he said, pulling her into his arms. "Now walk me to the door. Tomorrow is going to be a long day. You're still going to church with us, aren't you?"

CeCe raised surprised eyes to his. "Of course. Why would you think I wasn't?"

Nate didn't answer her. He kissed her briefly, and then he was gone. As he walked to his car, he prayed, *Lord, Lord, please help her to forgive them. And help me to help her.*

When he got into his car, he wasn't smiling. The joy of the day had been tarnished. If there was one thing he knew two people absolutely must possess in order to build a life together, it was the ability to forgive. He knew CeCe had the capacity in her to do it. He just prayed that she knew it too.

TWELVE

"Don't look so sad, CeCe," Mr. Richardson whispered in her ear as he hugged her good-bye. She and Nate had driven them to the airport and waited with them for their plane to board. Now that their seats had been called, it was time for them to part. CeCe felt both sad and relieved. Sad, because she'd enjoyed the older couple so very much. And relieved, because the happy façade she'd been wearing since her discussion with Nate last night had not been very effective.

"All couples disagree," Mr. Richardson was saying. "Like I told Nate, it's good the two of you have to work through this problem now. In working it through, you'll find out whether you're willing to do what it takes to make a marriage work." He pulled back from her and chucked her under her chin with a loose fist. "Now give me a smile. I don't want tears to be the thing I remember about you when I get home. It'll be all right, I promise you. You love Nate, and he loves you. Most important, I think you're a fighter. To be married, you have to be a fighter, because you have to fight for your love against the obstacles that will surely come against you."

"Dad, it's time," Nate called from near the boarding gate, where he stood with his mother.

"That's my girl," Mr. Richardson said when CeCe smiled. "Fighters do what has to be done. They don't give up, even when the going gets tough. That's the kind of woman my boy needs,

CeCe, and the kind of man you need, too. Now enough of that. I'm tired of hearing myself talk, so I know you're tired of it, but thanks for listening to an old man."

CeCe leaned over and kissed his cheek. "Thank you," she said, taking his arm and following him to Nate and Mrs. Richardson.

"What are you trying to do, Dad?" Nate asked, moving from his mother's side to CeCe's. "Take my girl?"

The older man laughed and shook his head. "She's mighty tempting, Son, but I think your mother is about all the woman I can handle."

Nate and CeCe grinned at the glare Mrs. Richardson gave her husband. "Just come on," she said. "We're going to be the last ones on the plane as it is."

He winked at Nate and CeCe. "She nags me to death, but I still love her."

Mrs. Richardson took her husband's arm and began to lead him to the jet way. "He doesn't know what he'd do without me," she said. She, too, winked, then added, "I hope he never has to find out. You children take care. CeCe, I'll be calling you about your visit to Chicago." When she and her husband reached the boarding gate, she turned back to them. "You two need to hurry up and make up. You both look terrible." With that and a smile, she turned, and she and her husband made their way down the jet way.

CeCe felt Nate looking at her, so she wasn't surprised when he spoke. "They're right," he said. "You look about as bad as I do." He gave a weak smile. "I'm going to take that as a good sign. I hope it means that you don't like the tension between us any more than I do. Am I right?"

She nodded her head twice in answer. "I couldn't sleep after you left last night. I wanted to call you, but I didn't know what to say. I wasn't sure what you'd say."

"I love you," Nate said in a strong, clear voice. He took her hand in his. "Let's get out of here and find a better place to talk."

CeCe leaned close to him as they walked down the crowded concourse to the escalators. During the brief train ride to the ground transportation area where they had parked, she took strength from the love that flowed between them. They would work out their differences. She'd make him understand about Eric's parents. She had to.

Nate drove with one hand because he didn't want to lose contact with CeCe. Last night had been awful for him. He'd been scared, so very scared. Last night had been the first time since he'd started seeing CeCe that he wondered if they might not end up together. He'd tried to shake the thought, but he hadn't been successful. Instead, he'd tossed and turned all night long. Even while they'd been in church this morning, his thoughts had been on CeCe and Eric's parents. After the service, he'd been more convinced than ever that the real issue here was whether CeCe would forgive Eric's parents. After she did that, she'd know how to deal with their request to be part of David's life.

He drove her to his favorite spot at Stone Mountain Park, a shaded spot with a clear view of the huge granite rock, but off the beaten path so they'd have some privacy. He sat and pulled her down next to him.

She spread out the skirt of her denim jumper to cover her legs. "I'm glad you thought to come here, but what made you think of this place?" she asked, as if needing to say something.

"I used to come out here sometimes when I needed some peace and quiet to think, to pray." He'd found the spot quite by accident during one of the early morning runs he'd taken around the mountain when he lived in an apartment complex nearby.

"I'm glad you're sharing it with me."

He turned to her, the seriousness of the moment weighing heavily on him. He knew, he just knew, that what they said here now would greatly affect the course of their relationship. "This isn't all I want to share with you, CeCe. I want to share your life. I want to build a life with you. That means that your burdens become my burdens. That's the love I feel for you."

CeCe launched herself against him, wrapping her arms around his neck and holding on as if their life together depended on it. He knew then that she felt the gravity of the moment just as he did. "That's what I want, too, Nate. Really I do. I love you so much it hurts. Sometimes I think something will happen and you'll realize that I'm not good enough for you."

He pulled her away from him so he could look into the eyes that so enchanted him. "You—not good enough for me?" He gave a dry, empty laugh. "If anybody's not good enough, it's me." He paused and cleared his throat. "You have no idea how special you are to me. I thought you did, but you don't. Don't you know that you are God's gift to me? To *me*." He thumped his chest. "I love everything you are and everything the Lord is making you to be. I want to be there during your times of trials and failures as well as during your successes. There is no part of you that I don't love—and that includes the parts that I don't know."

"How can you say that, Nate?" CeCe asked, her eyes shadowed with pain. "I still remember the way you looked at me last night when we were talking about the letter from Eric's parents. I felt your disappointment with me and your withdrawal. I thought I was losing your love."

"Never that," he said, and he meant it. He knew he'd always love her. If he didn't spend the rest of his life with CeCe, he knew he would spend it alone, for he didn't believe there could be anyone else for him. "What you saw last night was concern, very deep concern."

"You think I should let Eric's parents back into our lives, don't you?"

"No—"

"Don't lie to me, Nate."

He caught her by the shoulders. "I would never lie to you. Never. You should know that. What I was going to say was that it's your decision what you do about Eric's parents. My only concern was the anger you displayed. That anger comes from hurt, CeCe."

CeCe looked away from him and toward the mountain. "Of

course I'm hurt. They hurt me. They rejected me. They left me to go through all that by myself. While they planned one of the biggest weddings people in our town had ever seen, I was suffering through a pregnancy all by myself. Where were they then?"

Nate felt her anger and her hurt, and he hurt for her, but he knew she had to let it go. "They were wrong, CeCe. But the letters seem to indicate that they want to right their wrong. Have you ever opened one of them?"

She nodded slowly—begrudgingly, he thought. "When they first started coming almost a year ago, I opened them. I wrote back and told them I didn't think the time was right, but they keep writing as though I'd never answered the first letter. You'd think they'd get it by now. I wonder why this sudden interest in David, anyway. What have they been doing for the past four years?"

Nate took a deep breath. *Lord, please give me the right words to comfort the woman I love.* "I don't know. What were you doing for those years?"

She jerked her head in his direction. "What kind of question is that? I was raising David. Alone."

He shook his head. "I don't mean that. I mean what were you doing here." He placed his hand across her heart. "What was going on here during those years?"

"I told you," she said, a bit more relaxed now. "I rededicated my life to Christ and began living my life to please him."

"So you think your response to Eric's parents is pleasing to God?"

She didn't speak immediately, and he thought that was a good sign. When she did speak, she said, "They—Eric and his parents—hurt me so much. I'd known them all my life, Nate, but after they found out I was pregnant, it was as though I was a monster from an alien planet. They acted as though I'd seduced their son, or worse yet, that I was making the whole thing up."

"Is it possible that Eric told them that you did?" he asked, trying to reach beyond her emotions to someplace where she could reason.

"It doesn't matter what Eric told his parents," she answered. "They knew me. They should have known I wouldn't lie about a baby. They should have known."

Nate clasped her hand in his. "Eric is their son, and they wanted to believe him, to believe in him. How do you think they'd have felt if Eric had told them the truth?"

Nate wasn't surprised when she didn't answer. She was so wrapped up in her own pain that she couldn't see—didn't want to see—the pain of others. He bowed his head and began to pray. "Lord, we need your strength today. You told us to forgive, and you showed us how. You continue to show us. Help us to show your love the same way. Help us to forgive the people who hurt us. I love CeCe so much that the people who hurt her also hurt me, so help me to forgive Eric and his parents for their mistreatment of her. Help me to pray earnestly for their souls. I thank you again for bringing CeCe into my life. Build us together as one in you. Teach us to serve you and to serve each other. Let us spur each other to growth in you. Let us be better servants together than we would have been apart. We love you, and we thank you for loving us. In Jesus' name. Amen."

Nate wasn't surprised to see Stuart's Expedition and Marvin's Altima parked in his driveway when he arrived home later that evening, but he couldn't decide whether or not he was glad they were here. Of course, Marvin was here because it seemed that he now lived here, but Nate's instincts told him that Stuart was here to find out how CeCe had gotten along with his parents. He suspected Marvin had mentioned something to their mutual friend about his demeanor last night. Nate hadn't been able to hide his feelings from Marvin, though he hadn't discussed them with his friend, either.

Nate took a deep breath before entering his home, or maybe he should call it a shelter, since Marvin had sought and found refuge here. He heard sounds from the family room and considered bypassing his friends for some quiet time in his bedroom, but he knew he'd only be putting off the inevitable. He decided to brave the tigers head-on.

He entered the room and found his two friends, each stretched out on one of the matching leather sofas, engrossed in some interview on ESPN. "What's up?" he called to them as he came forward. Stuart sat up and made room for him, while Marvin merely threw up a hand in greeting.

"We should be asking you that, my man," Stuart said. Nate sat down on the couch with him and helped himself to a handful of what he suspected were his own peanuts. "Your family loved CeCe, right?" Stuart asked without preamble.

Nate threw back a few of the nuts. "Of course they did. Why wouldn't they?"

Nate didn't miss the glance Stuart sent Marvin. "Is something wrong between you and CeCe, Nate?"

Nate shook his head. "Nothing we can't handle." He wasn't being flippant, he told himself. He was being confident.

"You're sure?"

"I'm sure."

Marvin leaned over and reached his hand into the bowl of peanuts. He popped a few into his mouth. "Spoken like a true optimist, if you ask me."

"I guess it's good we didn't ask you then, huh, Marvin?" Nate said, letting loose on his friend. He'd been waiting for an opportunity to discuss how Marvin was handling his situation with Shay, and tonight, with Stuart present, seemed the right time. "Besides, you don't seem to be doing so well with your own woman. When are you going home?"

"Tired of me already?" Marvin quipped.

"As a matter of fact, I am," Nate said.

Stuart lifted his right hand like a child wanting to ask a question in a classroom. "I'd like to jump in and say that I'm tired of you, too, Marvin, and you aren't even living with me."

Marvin and Nate looked at Stuart and then at each other before breaking up into laughter. Stuart could always be counted on to use his dry wit to lower the temperature on any situation. When their laughter subsided, the men were quiet, each lost in his own thoughts. Nate thought how fortunate he was to be able to count Marvin and Stuart as his friends and brothers. Time had proven that theirs was a relationship that would endure— through law school, marriage, death, divorce, joy, and sorrow. Yes, he was blessed to have these two men in his life.

"I'm serious though, Marvin," Nate spoke up after a few moments. "I still don't see how your being here is helping you to work out anything with Shay. In fact, it seems the distance you've put between the two of you is making things worse, not better."

Marvin tossed a few more peanuts into his mouth. "You don't understand, man. Things couldn't get any worse between Shay and me. We don't even share the same bed anymore."

Stuart and Nate shared a disconcerted glance. "Are you saying Shay put you out of your bed?" Nate asked slowly. "Somehow I can't believe that, Marvin, unless you did—"

Marvin shook his head, his eyes directed on the television. "Shay didn't put me out," he clarified. "I moved out on my own accord."

Stuart jumped up, surprising both Marvin and Nate. "How could you be so cruel, Marvin? Shay loves you, always has, though God knows, I'm beginning to wonder at her wisdom in doing so. Just how much do you think she can take? She lost a son, too, remember, and now she's losing her husband."

The tension in the room became so thick that you could have cut it with a knife. Stuart had broken the two unspoken rules that had reigned between them since Marvin Jr.'s death: Don't question Marvin's grieving process, and don't bring up Marvin Jr. Well, Stuart had broken the rules, and Nate was glad he had. They had been too easy on Marvin. They'd tried patient love; now they were going to try tough love.

"Don't talk about my boy," Marvin said, his mouth tight, his words clipped. "You just don't talk about my boy. When you lose a son, you can talk about it, but right now, you don't talk about my boy."

Nate sighed. *Lord, help us.* "Marvin, somebody has to talk about him. Look at what's happening to you and Shay. Is this what you want? Are you intentionally hurting her? Do you want to lose her?" When he didn't respond, Nate added, "Say something, man."

"You know I love her," Marvin said, his words broken. "You know I do, but like I told you before, it's just too hard being with her. She'll be better off without me. I'm no more than a millstone around her neck. I'll suck all the joy out of her life." He sat up then, placing his feet on the floor. "Do you know how many times a day I drive by my house, hoping to get a glimpse of her? Do you know whose face I see before I go to sleep every night? Shay and Marvin Jr. were the first family I'd ever had. I swore before God to love and protect them." He snorted his disgust. "I did a good job of that, didn't I?"

"Don't do this to yourself, Marvin," Nate pleaded, feeling his friend's pain. He didn't want to think how he'd feel if something happened to CeCe or David or one of the other children he prayed they would have. But he hoped that if he lost one of them, he'd find a way to go on—if only for love of the ones left. "All this self-pity is only making your situation worse. You're in a hole, and you need to reach for help. You haven't forgotten how to do that, have you?"

Marvin didn't answer. He stood up instead. "Look, if you want me out of here, I'll leave, but I'm not going back home."

Nate waved him back to his seat. "Nobody's putting you out. Yet. But the time is going to come when you're going to have to deal with Shay. You don't want to go where I've been, Marvin. If you love Shay, if you want to keep the vows you made to her before God, you're going to have to face her and deal with this."

Marvin sat down again. "Is that what you're doing with CeCe?" he challenged.

Again Nate sighed. "I'm trying, man. CeCe and I made a promise early on that we wouldn't run away from each other. I think we can face anything together. We're going to have our problems—like the one we're facing now—but together we can work through them. I'm not so sure what would happen, though, if one of us walked away. The only experience I've had with that is Naomi, and you both know how that turned out."

After those words, Nate got up from the couch and headed for his room. He'd said what he had to say, and he was glad he had. In supporting Marvin, he had found encouragement for himself and the situation he faced. He did believe he and CeCe could weather this storm they were facing. He loved her too much to believe anything else.

When he reached his bedroom, he went directly to the cedar chest and opened the top drawer. The small box he sought was easy to find. He flipped open its top and stared at the diamond engagement ring he'd bought for CeCe soon after pledging his love to her. When he'd bought it, he'd thought the only thing keeping him from giving it to her was the formalities of talking to her parents and their pastors. As he closed the box and the drawer, he prayed he'd been right.

CeCe knew she was going to spend another restless night in bed. What should have been the happiest time in her life had now been marred. Eric and his family had somehow reached into her life to bestow even more pain on her. Why couldn't they leave her alone? She and David had done all right without them. More than all right, even if she had to say so herself.

But Eric was always there in the back of her mind, CeCe admitted. That day on the back porch when she'd threatened to tell his precious Yolanda their little secret always hovered over her, poised to destroy any chance she had for happiness. If she could take that day back, she would gladly do it. She'd hurt so much then that all she'd wanted to do was hurt back.

She'd told herself that her reasons were practical. After all, she was going to be a single mother and she'd had needs. But she knew now—had known a long time—that had been only part of it. No, her primary goal at the time had been to inflict pain on Eric, with no consideration of the price she'd have to pay for her actions down the road.

She'd asked the Lord to forgive her for what she'd done, and sometimes she was able to go for days—weeks even—without thinking about it. Then the letters had started coming. And with the letters, the reminder of what she'd done. Now those reminders were infringing on the future she wanted with Nate, the man she loved and who loved her in return.

How could this be possible? she asked herself. She didn't want much out of life. Why did it sometimes seem that she was destined not even to have that? She turned over, and her eyes found the Bible on her nightstand. *Open it and take comfort in the words*, she told herself. She kept staring at the Bible, then flipped over on her other side. She wasn't ready to be comforted, at least not in that way, not tonight.

THIRTEEN

Nate stared at his bedroom ceiling. It was only four o'clock in the morning, but he was wide awake. This was becoming a regular occurrence. He found himself waking up in the middle of the night thinking about his relationship with CeCe. He usually prayed during those times and was able to fall back to sleep. Tonight was different. He couldn't get back to sleep.

Since that day at Stone Mountain a little over three weeks ago, he and CeCe had reached a kind of truce concerning Eric's parents. Nevertheless, the question of how she was going to deal with them hung over their relationship like a dark shadow. He loved her, but he knew it took more than love to make a marriage work. He considered CeCe his and he still wanted her, but how could they begin a life together when she still carried so much hurt from the past? If only she could let it go and forgive Eric and his parents, Nate and she could move forward. As it was, they hung in limbo, and he wasn't sure how long they'd be able to continue that way.

Nate thought too much time had passed already, but what was he to do? He had promised himself and God that he would follow CeCe's lead and not pressure her to move faster than she was ready to move. Well, CeCe seemed to be dragging her feet big-time on this one. He wasn't quite sure what to make of it. She loved him and wanted a life with him, didn't she? He had to face the facts. CeCe hadn't made any moves to get them closer to a formal engagement. He'd told her that he wanted to meet her parents first, and she'd made no move in that direction at all. He didn't feel it was his place to push the issue, though he was sorely tempted to do so. He didn't like dragging things out like this.

Was he going too fast for her? he wondered. Maybe he'd had her meet his parents too soon. Maybe he should have waited until after he'd met her parents and they'd gotten formally engaged. Nate didn't know anymore. He knew the engagement ring he'd bought for her was still in his cedar chest. He knew he wanted to move forward with CeCe, but he was no longer sure that was what she wanted. *Lord*, he prayed silently, *show me what to do.*

The ringing telephone interrupted his thoughts and caused his pulse to race. Who could be calling at this hour? He turned and picked up the handset from the nightstand. "Hello," he said.

"It's me," came CeCe's voice, soft and tense.

He sat up in the bed and began praying for her. *Please let everything be all right, Lord.* "What's the matter?"

"It's my grandfather. He's sick. Really sick."

This was the first Nate had heard about a grandfather. CeCe didn't talk about her family, which, if he allowed himself to think about it, was yet another concern he had about their relationship these days. "Are you going to see him?" he asked.

"I think I should, don't you? They think he's dying, Nate," she said, the weariness in her voice obvious.

He nodded, wishing he was there to offer her physical comfort. "Of course you should go, sweetheart. You need to say your good-byes."

"That's what I was thinking, too," she said, as if in a trance. "OK, well, I'll go to Alabama today. Do you think I should take David? I'm not sure if I should take him."

Nate responded to her controlled panic. She needed him to make the decisions for her. He was the man in her life, and he welcomed the challenge. "Yes, you should take him. Look, CeCe, I can take off a couple of days and go with you if you think that'll help. I can take care of David while you do what you need to do. How does that sound?"

"Could you, Nate?" she asked. The anxiety in her voice let him know that she wanted him—needed him—to go with her. When all this was over, he'd have to tell her how much her needing him meant to him. He'd started to doubt that she did.

"CeCe, I love you, and I want to go with you. Now when do you want to leave?"

She gave what sounded like a relieved sigh. "I think we should leave soon, but I don't want to wake David."

Nate considered their options. "How long a drive is it?" he asked.

"About two hours."

"OK, why don't we do this? You get up, get dressed, and throw some things in a bag. Then wake B.B. and tell her what's happening. I'll call Shay and tell her you're going to be gone and ask her to stand in for you on Saturday with Anna Mae. I'll ask Marvin to step in for me. It just might do him good. Then when I get to your house, we'll wake David and get him in the car. He can sleep all the way there. Do you think you can do that?"

"I'll do it. How long before you get here?"

He glanced at his clock and considered everything he needed to do. "Give me about forty-five minutes, OK?"

"OK."

"I'm hanging up," he said.

"Nate?"

"Yes?"

"I love you, and thanks. I really needed you this morning. You were the first person I thought of when my mother called. I just wanted you to know that."

Nate's heart soared. He'd needed the confirmation of her love. "Thanks for telling me, sweetheart. I'm glad that you thought of me first. I'll see you in about forty-five minutes."

Nate hung up the phone with a smile on his face. This was not a happy occasion, but he felt renewed. He dressed, threw a couple of days' worth of clothes in a bag, and then trotted down to Marvin's room. He quickly told his friend the situation and asked him to step in for him at Genesis House.

"I don't know" was Marvin's first response.

"Look, man," Nate said, not bothering to keep the irritation out of his voice, "I wouldn't ask you if there was anybody else, but CeCe needs to get on the road *now*, and there's nobody else I can call at this hour or on such short notice."

"How about Stuart?" he asked.

Nate shook his head. "You know he has court. You're my only option. If you don't agree, I'll have to try to get in touch with somebody after I get to Alabama, and I have no idea how we're going to find things when we get there."

Marvin looked at his friend, then allowed his gaze to skitter away. "I'll do it."

Nate sighed with relief and prayed that something good would come out of Marvin's return to Genesis House. His friend had done little of anything in the last eighteen months. Maybe this return to Genesis House would have a positive impact on him. Returning his thoughts to CeCe, Nate left Marvin's room, grabbed his bags, and headed for the door. He was downstairs before he remembered he needed to call Shay. Using the phone in the family room, he called to tell her the situation. He woke her up, of course, but she readily agreed to step in for CeCe. "Be sure to tell CeCe my prayers are with her," Shay said.

"I'll do it," he said.

"Nate," Shay added, "I'm glad CeCe has you. I'm glad you have each other."

Nate considered telling Shay that Marvin would be stepping in for him at Genesis House, but he decided to let her find out when she saw him there. He didn't want to give her false hope. He said his good-byes and was out of the house and on his way to CeCe's in the next instant.

CeCe sat on the porch and waited for Nate. She needed to see him, needed him to tell her that everything was going to be all right. She accepted that she'd come to rely on him, and while that might have caused her concern under other circumstances, right now she was just glad that he was in her life. That he loved her.

The pain in her stomach that always appeared when she was preparing to go back home was there this morning, more intense than usual. Maybe it was because she knew she'd see Eric's parents, and she knew the stakes were higher this time than they'd been in the past. Nate hadn't said anything about them or the letters since their talk in the park, but she knew he hadn't changed his position. She could feel him waiting for her to make a move. She knew what he wanted her to do—or she thought she did. She just wasn't sure she could do it.

Her thoughts skittered to her parents and her grandfather. She'd disappointed them so much, and every time she saw them, she could see the disappointment in their eyes. They'd loved her and raised her to live a Christian life, and she'd strayed from them and from God. But CeCe was also disappointed in them. If they had—

Nate's headlights brought her thoughts back to the present, and she got up from the swing and went to meet him. When she saw him step out of the car, it was as if her legs took on a life of their own, and she found herself running toward him, tears streaming down her face. He caught her to him and held her close, whispering words of comfort she didn't really understand. She did understand and feel his love and concern, and that was enough. After a few minutes—too few for her—she pulled away. "I'm glad you're here."

"Me too," he said. He put his arm around her shoulders and led her back to the house. "Are you about ready?"

She nodded. "We just have to get David up. The bags are packed."

"Let me put them in the car, and then we'll go get David. Is B.B. up?"

CeCe gave him a wobbly smile. "She's in the kitchen. There's coffee, and she's making us breakfast for the road."

"She's a sweetheart," he said. They entered the house. Nate

gave B.B. a good-morning kiss on the cheek before taking the bags CeCe had packed and putting them in his car. When he returned, B.B. made him drink a cup of coffee.

While he and B.B. were alone, B.B. said, "I think I should go with you. CeCe is going to need you with her, and you won't be able to take David everywhere you go. I haven't mentioned this to CeCe because I know she'll refuse. But I've already lined up someone to take care of the day-care kids. Maybe the two of us can convince CeCe."

Nate nodded, deferring to B.B.'s wisdom. He knew she loved CeCe, too. B.B. went to pack while he went looking for CeCe. He found her in David's room and moved to help her put clothes on the sleeping child.

"B.B. wants to go with us, and I think we should let her," he whispered. "She can stay with David while we're at the hospital. Is that OK with you?"

"B.B.'s done so much for me, Nate. I'd hate to inconvenience her about the kids."

He placed his hand over hers, which was lacing David's sneakers. "She's got somebody to take care of the kids, and she wants to do it, so let her."

Reluctantly she nodded her assent, and in short order the four of them were off to Alabama—CeCe and Nate up front, B.B. and David in the back. The backseaters were asleep shortly after they hit the road.

CeCe sat close to Nate as he drove. He held her hand, periodically squeezing it to give her strength and to remind her that he was with her all the way. Once they were on Interstate 85 South, which would take them all the way to her home, she pulled their joined hands to her lips, kissed his softly, and then lowered them back to the car seat.

"I only see them about once or twice a year," she began, when she mustered up enough courage to tell him about her family and the estrangement they suffered. "It's just too hard for me to go home. Too many memories. Too many things said, too many things left unsaid. It's easier to stay away. Since my folks don't like to travel, they rarely, if ever, come to Atlanta." She looked out the passenger window, the landscape marred by her thoughts of the past. "I don't know if that's a good thing or a bad thing. A part of me wishes they'd sought me out. I know I disappointed them. We live in a small town, and everybody knows everybody else's business, so they had a lot to live down when I got pregnant and everybody learned Eric was going to marry somebody else. Rumors started. Some said that the reason he wasn't marrying me was that the child wasn't his. Others said that I'd gotten pregnant to trap him. It was awful. I think my parents wanted to support me, but they didn't know how. To be honest, I didn't give them much time. I left town before I started to show and moved to Atlanta."

"Thank you," Nate said, giving her hand another squeeze.

"For what?" she asked.

"For sharing that part of your life with me. I know it was hard for you, and I'm just happy that you trust me and love me enough to share yourself with me this way."

CeCe looked at his profile as he watched the road unfold ahead of them, but she didn't speak.

"You know," he continued, "intimacy comes in a lot of different ways, and while I eagerly await the time we'll share physical intimacy, I'm glad we don't have to wait to be intimate in the other parts of our lives."

CeCe continued to stare in amazement at this man who wanted to share her life. How could she—CeCe Williams—have been so blessed to meet him and to have him love her, of all people?

"I know this isn't the best of situations, and I wish the circumstances were different," he was saying, "but I'm glad I'll meet your parents and your grandfather, and visit the place where you grew up. I think it'll help me understand you better, and in understanding you better, I'll be better able to love you."

CeCe knew tears were again forming in her eyes, but she didn't bother trying to stop them. She moved closer to Nate, placing her head on his shoulder, as he placed his arm around her. They didn't talk much during the long drive, but she didn't think words were necessary. Their hearts were being bonded more tightly together by the invisible and loving hand of God. She knew it, and she knew Nate did, too.

Nate decided that they should check into a hotel before they went to the hospital. CeCe agreed because she didn't think the sleeping David and B.B. were up to sitting around a hospital all morning. They reserved two rooms—one for the men, and one for the women—which they knew would please David. Once B.B. and David were settled in the women's room for the time being, Nate and CeCe headed for the hospital. Nate drove, following CeCe's directions, and soon they were pulling into the hospital parking lot.

Nate took CeCe's hand and helped her out of the car, and she left it there as they walked into the hospital and then to the Intensive Care Unit, where her grandfather was. Nate guessed she took strength from his touch, and that pleased him very much. When they stepped off the elevator on her grandfather's floor, her grasp tightened. Wondering what was wrong, he turned his head to see what had attracted her attention. Hands together, he allowed her to lead him along the corridor toward an older couple who stood a little away from the nurses' station. He could see only their profiles because they were turned sideways from him and CeCe. He assumed she knew these people, and he wondered if they were her parents.

When they were within ten feet of the couple, CeCe slowed and said, "Mama, Daddy." The man and woman turned around so fast it seemed to Nate as if they'd been wired to CeCe's voice. The joy and relief and love in both their eyes surprised him. The two people before him now did not appear to be disappointed in their daughter.

Both of them stepped forward together and pulled CeCe into a three-way embrace. Nate didn't realize CeCe still held his hand until she let it go and wrapped her arms around her parents. They held each other as though they'd been separated a very long time and were happy to see each other again.

When they pulled apart, he noticed that all three pairs of eyes were damp. CeCe reached for Nate's hand again, and he moved closer to her. "How's Big Daddy?" she asked.

"Not too good, baby," her mother answered. Nate could see CeCe in the older woman's face and knew that CeCe, too, would age with grace. "The doctors don't think it's going to be more than a day or so now. They're putting him in a room so that we can sit with him until the end."

Nate squeezed her hand to give her his strength. "Does he know you're here?" she asked. "Will he know I'm here?"

Her father patted her shoulders in a clumsy manner that made Nate doubt the man was naturally affectionate. "He'll know, baby, and he'll be glad you're here."

CeCe turned to Nate and placed her head on his shoulder while she cried. He felt a bit awkward with her parents watching, but he didn't see what else he could do. In an effort to make them all a bit more comfortable, he extended a hand to CeCe's father and nodded to her mother. "I'm Nathaniel Richardson." Because he could think of no other way to describe his relationship to CeCe, he added, "I'm in love with your daughter."

Surprised didn't adequately describe the look that crossed the couple's faces. *Shocked*, maybe. *Pained*, even. Obviously, CeCe hadn't told them anything about him, and Nate wasn't sure how that made him feel.

When she'd gathered herself together, CeCe pulled away from him, "I'm sorry. Mama, Daddy, I love him too."

That seemed to break the ice. Mr. and Mrs. Williams smiled at him, though Mr. Williams's smile was a bit wary. Nate wouldn't be surprised if the older man requested a private moment with him at some point. In fact, he'd welcome it. He wanted to make his intentions known and formally ask for CeCe's hand in marriage.

"Why don't we sit for a spell?" Mrs. Williams said. "The nurses said they would tell us when your grandfather was settled and we could go in." She led them to a small waiting area with six blue vinyl chairs surrounding a glass-topped table littered with magazines. "How's David?" Mrs. Williams asked as soon as they were all seated. "I bet he's grown a lot since we last saw him. Thank you for the pictures. They're almost as good as being there, but not quite."

Her voice sounded wistful as she asked about David, and that surprised Nate. She sounded exactly like his mother when she talked about her grandchildren. The picture he was getting of CeCe's family did not match the picture she had painted for him with her words.

"David's at the hotel with B.B.," CeCe answered. "He was asleep when we left Atlanta, and we weren't sure what the day was going to be like, so we left them at the hotel."

"Why are you staying at a hotel?" her father asked in the gruff tone that Nate suspected was his trademark. "We have plenty of room at the house. No cause for you to waste your money."

Nate felt CeCe stiffen next to him, and he wondered why. Her father's words had been cordial and welcoming, despite the gruff tone of voice. "It was just easier, Daddy," CeCe explained. Her voice held a note of defensiveness.

"Well, you'll just have to move out," the older man said, folding his arms across his chest as if daring CeCe to defy him. "We have enough room for you, David, B.B., and your friend, Nate."

"That's right, CeCe," her mother added. "Besides, it's not every day our grandson comes to visit."

When CeCe didn't say anything, Nate squeezed her fingers. "Thanks for the hospitality, ma'am, sir," he said to her parents.

The man waved away Nate's comments. "Ain't no hospitality. It's CeCe's home, even if she acts like she don't know it."

"Now's not the time for that," CeCe's mother said, placing a calming hand on her husband's arm and giving him a pleading glance. "CeCe's here now, and that's all that matters. We'll work out the rest later." When she turned those pleading eyes to her daughter, Nate knew the peacemaker role was one she regularly played. "Won't we, CeCe?"

CeCe nodded, but Nate couldn't tell what the nod meant. He didn't know if CeCe planned for them to remain at the hotel or if she wanted to move into her parents' home. All he knew was that somehow the signals between these parents and their daughter had gotten crossed. For it was obvious to him after being in their presence only a short while that CeCe's parents loved her dearly. It was just as obvious to him that CeCe didn't see it.

Lord, Lord, what's going on here, and what does it all mean?

FOURTEEN

Nate took CeCe down to the hospital cafeteria for breakfast after her grandfather had been situated in his room and she'd had a chance to sit with him. They didn't linger over their food and were soon back upstairs again. Nate sat with her parents while CeCe called to check on B.B. and David.

"B.B. says David's a little anxious I wasn't there when he woke up," she told them after her call, "so I think I need to go and get him settled."

Nate stood at those words, prepared to go with her. Her mother's words stopped him. "Why don't I go with you, CeCe? I want to see my grandson." She turned to her husband. "You'll be all right, won't you, Kurt?"

Seated comfortably with his legs crossed at the knees, Mr. Williams waved off his wife's concern. "I'll be fine. Don't worry about me." To his daughter, he added, "Why don't you leave the young fellow here with me? There are some things we need to discuss."

"Daddy—"

"Kurt—"

Both women spoke at the same time. Their chastising tone almost made Nate laugh. It was apparent they were worried about what Mr. Williams would say to him.

Nate placed a hand on CeCe's shoulder. "I'll be fine," he said. "Unless you need me, I'll stay here with your father. Will you be OK driving to the hotel?"

CeCe nodded, but he could tell she was still uneasy leaving him with her father.

"He doesn't look like he'll bite," Nate whispered in a blatant effort to tease her out of her concern.

"Looks can be deceiving," she whispered back. She glanced at her father and then at her mother and Nate. She sighed. "All right," she said in a voice loud enough for them all to hear. "But you—," she said, pointing a finger at Nate—"have to escort us to the car."

"Yes, ma'am," Nate said, causing her parents to chuckle and CeCe to groan.

After he'd seen the two women safely to the car, Nate headed back upstairs to CeCe's father. The older man was still seated in the waiting room.

As soon as Nate sat down, Mr. Williams asked, "How long have you known my girl?"

Here it comes, Nate thought. *Give me wisdom, Lord. I don't know exactly what CeCe's relationship is with her parents, but this man is her father and I want his respect and his blessing.* "Almost five months."

Mr. Williams nodded, as if considering that length of time. "Not very long, yet you say you love her."

"With all my heart. I want to marry her, and I'd like your blessing."

"What about the boy?" The question was asked casually enough, but the tight expression on Mr. Williams's face made clear its importance.

Nate cleared his throat and prepared to show Mr. Williams his heart. He didn't want CeCe's parents to have any doubts about his feelings for her and David. "I love David, too. I haven't talked to CeCe about it yet, but I hope she'll grant me the privilege of adopting him. I hope that God blesses us with more children, and I want them all to carry my name. I won't have David feeling as though he's different."

Mr. Williams nodded but gave no clue to what he was thinking. "What about the boy's father?"

"You mean his biological father?" The older man's brows rose at the question, and Nate knew his point had been made. "Eric will always be David's biological father. I want to be a real father to the boy."

Nate felt as though he'd passed some test when Mr. Williams uncrossed his legs and relaxed back in his chair. "CeCe's a good girl," he said, "but she's too hard on herself. She always has been. Even when she was a little bitty thing." He smiled as if he was remembering one of CeCe's childhood antics. "There was never any need to punish her, because most times she punished herself."

Nate knew CeCe's father was telling the truth. CeCe *was* hard on herself.

"I'm glad she's found somebody to love," the older man said, his voice gruff but affectionate. "Me and her mama worried that, after Eric, she never would. That boy broke my girl's heart." The old man stopped for a moment, and Nate knew then that he'd shared his daughter's pain. "'Course he wasn't nothing but a kid himself. Both of them were. They both sinned, but CeCe had to bear the consequences alone. Or so it seemed to her."

Nate was gaining some insight into CeCe's relationship with her parents. It seemed to him that her parents had never cast Eric in the role of the evil seducer, but rather they considered him a kid, like their daughter, who'd gotten in over his head and fallen into a trap of the enemy. He could see how CeCe would interpret this attitude as not supportive of her. She had cast Eric in the role of the villain, and her parents refused to go along with it. Consequently, she felt betrayed by the people who were supposed to love her.

Nate was also beginning to see that CeCe's parents were special people. More than a few parents would have placed Eric in the role of the devil just to make their daughter look better, but the Williamses had been stronger people. Of course, they'd been hurt because of the role Eric had played in their daughter's unhappiness, but they'd been compassionate toward the man-child he'd been at the time.

"Are you a good man, Nathaniel Richardson?" Mr. Williams's question interrupted his thoughts. "I don't want my little girl hurt again."

The question surprised Nate, though he supposed it really shouldn't have. It was probably the question all fathers most wanted answered. "I try to follow Christ in my life, Mr. Williams, if that's what you mean by good."

Mr. Williams nodded, seemingly satisfied with the answer. "Now then, tell me about this man who wants to marry my daughter."

Nate did as instructed. He told Mr. Williams about his family, his marriage and divorce, his work, and the joy of having David and CeCe in his life. "I know CeCe could do a lot better than me, but I love her, and I promise to do my best to keep her safe and to make her happy."

Mr. Williams nodded again. "Well, I don't guess a father can find fault with that." He extended his hand. "As long as you two don't rush into marriage, but get to know each other and make sure you're listening to God's voice, you have my blessing. Welcome to the family, Son."

CeCe returned to the hospital alone. Nate stood when he saw her get off the elevator. Mr. Williams was in the room with his father. "How is he?" CeCe asked, referring to her grandfather.

Nate kissed her cheek and then led her to the chair next to his. "No change," he said, squeezing her hand. She looked like she could use some sleep. "Where's your mother?"

CeCe leaned back in her chair, keeping her hand in Nate's. "She decided she wanted to spend some time with her grandson." Nate wondered at the skepticism in her voice, but before he could ask her about it, she added, "Mama decided we'd be better off staying at the house, so we are now checked out of the hotel and officially checked in at the place where I grew up."

Nate smiled. Though he could tell CeCe wasn't too optimistic about the change of venue, he was. "I like the idea of staying in the house where you grew up. I just may learn some of your secrets." He was teasing, but the shadow that crossed CeCe's face made him doubt she realized it. "Hey, I'm teasing."

"Oh," she said.

"Tell me what you're thinking," he encouraged. He didn't like her to keep her thoughts bottled up inside. He was beginning to think she'd done that too often in her life. He was still amazed that she didn't realize how much her parents, her father in particular, adored her.

"I'm worried about my grandfather and feeling a little guilty that I haven't spent as much time with him as I should have." She became quiet.

"Why haven't you?" he asked.

She squeezed his fingers. "It's a long story. Let's not talk about it now. Mama is fixing lunch for you and Daddy. I'll stay here while you two take a break."

He shook his head. "I'll stay here with you. I can get something from the cafeteria."

She leaned over and kissed him softly. "I love you for the offer, but I want you to get some rest. I woke you up early this morning—"

"You were up too."

"But you drove all the way." When he was about to offer another objection, she said, "You have no idea how much you helped me this morning, Nate. I was a basket case, and you just stepped in and helped me through it. If I hadn't loved you before, I would love you now. But now it's my turn to take care of you, and I want you to go home and get some rest. I'm going to need your strength later."

Nate felt as though he'd grown ten feet at her appreciation of him. "Well, when you put it that way, I don't guess I have a choice."

Her lips curved in the sweet smile he'd come to cherish. "You're right, you don't. Let me go get Daddy so you two can get out of here."

He watched her make her way to her grandfather's room. *Lord, you've given me a complex woman in CeCe Williams, and I need you to show me how to best love her. She doesn't know how loved she is by her parents, and I wonder if she understands how much I love her. Open her eyes so she can see and her heart so she can feel.*

Mr. Williams came out of the room just as an older couple rushed down the hallway toward them. A short, stout woman and a tall, thin man approached him, and the woman threw her arms around his waist. Holding the woman, Mr. Williams extended his hand and affectionately clasped it with the man's. Then he introduced his sister and brother-in-law, the Howards, to Nate. CeCe must have heard the commotion because she came out into the hallway and was given a big hug by her aunt and uncle. The couple had just arrived from their home five hours away. They suggested that CeCe go home with her father and Nate, while they sat with the patient. After a short debate, CeCe agreed to leave with the men.

Nate was glad CeCe's relatives had arrived. While she was worried about his getting enough rest, he was more worried about her getting enough. He knew she was physically tired and emotionally drained, and he suspected that every trip she made home was exhausting for her.

Mr. Williams acted as tour guide on the short drive to the Williamses' home. He pointed out several landmarks of significance to their family—their church, CeCe's high school, the police department. Of course, Nate didn't actually see the buildings. Rather, Mr. Williams pointed out the streets they were on and coerced CeCe into promising to take him for a closer inspection before they left town.

Nate was surprised when he saw CeCe's home. He'd expected a place much smaller than the sprawling ranch before him. The house was surrounded by an immaculate, still-green lawn covered by a kaleidoscope of leaves from the row of trees running along the far side. A big oak tree overhung the porch, which sported a wooden swing.

Nate leaned over and whispered to CeCe, "At least we still have our swing." He was pleased when she lowered her eyes, because he knew she was thinking of the quiet times they'd shared on the swing in Atlanta. He squeezed her fingers as he followed her and her father into the house. Nate almost bumped into her when she stopped suddenly just inside the room. Her father had already scooped David into his arms and, with a gleam in his eyes, listened to his grandson describe the toy truck he held in his hands.

"What—," CeCe began, but her mother cut her off.

"They dropped by to ask about Grandpa," Mrs. Williams said quickly. Nate noted the way she was twirling the ties of her red-and-white checkered apron. Something was not right with the scene before him.

CeCe glanced at the distinguished-looking man and woman seated in the living room with Mrs. Williams and B.B. She didn't smile and she didn't speak. When she turned back to her mother, she frowned. "They came to ask about Big Daddy?" CeCe asked with obvious skepticism. Nate wondered what was going on. It was pretty obvious CeCe was surprised and upset to find the other couple here.

"Look, Mr. Nate," David said to him. The child was oblivious to the undercurrents in the room. *Who is this couple?* Nate wondered again.

Nate nodded a greeting to the unknown couple and moved to Mr. Williams's side so he could see David's truck better. He tried to listen to the boy and to CeCe at the same time.

The guest couple stood abruptly. "I guess we should go," the woman said, looking at CeCe with pleading eyes. *Pleading for what?* Nate wondered.

"Thank you for coming by, Von, Harold." Mr. Williams spoke as if he were as unaware of the tension in the room as David was.

"What do you have to say, David?" The question came from B.B.

The boy turned his attention from Nate to the departing couple. "Thank you for the truck."

CeCe gasped, and the room became so quiet that you could have heard a pin drop on the soft carpet. "You're welcome," the woman mumbled, and then she and her husband rushed out the door.

CeCe shot her mother an angry glare. B.B., always the diplomat, took David from his grandfather's arms. "Why don't we go outside and play with your truck?" she suggested.

David was all for it. "You go too, Grandpa, Mr. Nate."

Mr. Williams shook his head, and Nate looked to CeCe for direction. She didn't notice him. B.B. didn't wait. She took David and went out the front door.

As soon as they were out of the room, CeCe asked in a tight voice, "How could you do this, Mama? How could you do this to me? I knew I shouldn't have left David alone with you."

"I didn't do anything to you, CeCe," the older woman said. "They came by. What was I supposed to do? Not let them in the house?"

CeCe looked as if she thought that would have been a very reasonable action. "You're my mother," CeCe answered, and Nate heard the tears in her voice. "You could have stood up for me and my wishes this one time. David is *my* son."

Mr. Williams stepped in. "Don't talk to your mother in that tone of voice, Cecelia Williams. We're still your parents."

"Well, you should act like it," CeCe murmured.

"Just what are you saying, young lady?" Mr. Williams asked as if he were talking to an out-of-sorts teenager. Nate half expected him to pull off his belt.

"Just forget it, Daddy. If you haven't seen it in all these years, you won't see it—"

"CeCe—," Mrs. Williams began, but the ringing telephone startled them all into silence. Nate knew everybody was wondering if it was bad news. Mrs. Williams answered the phone. When she hung up, she said, "We'd better get to the hospital."

CeCe's grandfather died less than an hour after they returned to the hospital. He was surrounded by people who loved him, including his pastor, who'd arrived while CeCe and her parents were away. Nate stayed close to CeCe, lending his strength. The rest of the afternoon and evening passed in a blur of planning and supportive calls and visits. By the time David was in bed, they all felt they wanted to follow his lead. B.B. did. Mr. and Mrs. Williams stayed up talking in the kitchen with the Howards, who were staying at the Shoney's Inn that CeCe and company had recently vacated. Nate and CeCe sat quietly in the living room.

Wanting some private time with her, Nate took her hand and led her to the front-porch swing. After they were seated, CeCe said, "There's one on the back porch, too."

Nate was pleased by her teasing, even though her eyes were cloudy with sadness. It had been a tough day for her. He knew the argument with her parents still weighed heavily on her mind, and now she had to deal with the death of her grandfather, too. He pulled her close and kissed the top of her head. "I guess we'll have to try that one out tomorrow. I'm sorry about your grandfather, CeCe."

She took a deep breath. "I'm sorry too," she said. "Sorry I didn't spend more time with him. But I'm also happy that he had made his peace with Jesus."

Nate nodded. That had to be a big comfort for her. Had her grandfather died without knowing the Lord, his soul would have been lost and CeCe's heart would have been broken.

"I really didn't have much choice—about spending so much time away," she explained. "I had to protect David."

Her words confirmed what Nate had already begun to suspect: That couple was Eric's parents.

"I don't know why I'm surprised that my mother let them see David behind my back. They've always taken his side," she said absently. Nate wondered if she realized she was talking aloud. "I just don't understand. I'm their daughter, but they take his side."

Nate squeezed her shoulders in a show of support and comfort. "What don't you understand?" he asked.

She sighed and pressed closer to his side. "They were never angry with Eric. After all he put me through, they were never angry with him. They even tried to defend him to me, if you can believe that."

Nate wondered if she thought the only way for her parents to support her was to blame Eric. Faulty reasoning, he knew, especially for a Christian. In his opinion, CeCe would have been better off if she'd adopted her parents' attitude.

"Instead they looked at me with disappointment in their eyes and made me feel as though I was the worst person in the world," CeCe was saying. "Why were they angry with me, but not with him?"

"Have you ever asked them?"

She didn't speak immediately. When she did, her voice was soft, unsure. "No, but I came close a couple of times. Sometimes I think I don't want to hear their answer."

"Why is that? What they say can't be any worse than what you think they'll say. Your imagination could have you suffering a lot of unnecessary pain."

CeCe intertwined her fingers with his. Nate knew she was absorbed in thoughts and regrets from the past. "How did your parents react when your marriage was falling apart?" she asked.

Nate recognized the change in topic for what it was and went along with it. He tried to recall that time in his life, which now seemed so long ago. All he remembered was his parents telling him to do what he thought was best and agreeing to pray for him. He also remembered the sadness in their eyes when he'd told them Naomi was gone. "They hurt *for* both me and Naomi. I could see my pain reflected in their eyes, and oddly, I found that reassuring."

She lifted her eyes, sharp with awareness, to his. "That's all I wanted from my parents. I never felt that they hurt *for* me.

I always felt that they hurt because I had hurt them, because I had disappointed them so badly."

Nate wasn't sure CeCe was interpreting her parents' actions correctly. From what he'd seen of Mr. and Mrs. Williams, he couldn't imagine them not sharing their daughter's pain. Mr. Williams had practically told him so. But CeCe's parents had also suffered Eric's pain. Nate prayed that given the same circumstances, God forbid, he would be as generous and forgiving as they had been. Especially since Eric had been able to walk away from the situation while CeCe had to endure pregnancy and then raise a child alone. "I think you need to talk this out with your parents, CeCe. It happened too long ago for it to still cause this rift between you."

She shook her head. "It's not in the past, Nate. It's in the present. Today my mother deliberately went against my wishes and allowed Eric's parents to spend time with David. It's obvious my parents think I'm handling the situation the wrong way."

Though it was hard for him to accept, Nate realized that CeCe really didn't see the connection between the past and the present. *Oh, Father, what am I to do?* "It may be happening in the present, CeCe, but it's rooted in the past. You can't keep running away from your past and your parents. You've got to deal with them both." *And soon,* he added silently.

CeCe rested her head on his shoulder, quiet, but Nate didn't mind. He just hoped she'd open her heart to his suggestion. He prayed that all the work God wanted to do in her she would allow to be done. For her sake—and theirs.

"Nate," CeCe said sometime later. They were still seated on the swing, her head resting on his shoulder, his arms draped loosely around her waist. "They're going to wait three or four days before the funeral to give the out-of-town relatives time to get here. You don't have to wait around. You should go back to Atlanta."

He stiffened at her words. He didn't want to leave her to face her demons alone. "What if I want to stay?"

She pulled away and looked up at his face. "As much as I want you here, I need more for you to go."

"But why? I want to be with you." *And you need me to be with you,* he added to himself.

She lowered her head back to his shoulder. "Because I'm no good here. I don't want you to see me like this. Something inside me changes when I come here, and I'm not myself. I can't explain it. Everything good in me now seems to get overshadowed by everything bad from my past." She paused. "When we were at Shay and Marvin's for the cookout, Shay said that she could see God in herself now, when for a long time she couldn't. Well, when I'm in Atlanta I can see God in me, but when I'm here, it's as though the old person comes back. I don't want you to see me like this. I regret that I got so angry with my mother today, and I regret that you had to see me that angry."

Nate knew she had no idea how much her words pained him. She was suffering too deeply in her own pain to be aware of his. He wanted to tell her that the old person was dead, not to be resurrected again, but he held his tongue. She knew the Scriptures as well as he did, and he suspected she wouldn't appreciate a sermon. "I'll go," he said, though he desperately wanted to stay. "But I'll be back for the funeral."

"Thank you" was her only response.

FIFTEEN

Nate's thoughts had been with CeCe the entire time he was away from her. He knew now that what he'd initially thought was a serious miscommunication problem between her and her parents was much more than that. CeCe still carried burdens from her past, and the weight of those burdens was becoming more and more difficult for her to bear. As he pulled his car into her family's driveway, he asked the Lord to show him how to best support her and give her strength until she realized this truth for herself.

David ran out of the house, CeCe right behind, just as Nate was getting his overnight bag from the backseat.

"Mr. Nate, Mr. Nate!" David called, bouncing on his heels. Nate couldn't help but smile at the two of them. Mother and son both wore bright smiles, acknowledging their pleasure at seeing him. It warmed his heart to know that his love for both of them was returned.

"Hey, sport," he said, walking to them. He leaned down and kissed the top of David's head, then pulled the boy to his side for a hug. One hand still pressing David against his side and the other holding a garment bag, he leaned forward and pressed his lips against CeCe's. "How are you?" he asked, though he'd spoken with her on the phone last night and again this morning before he'd left Atlanta.

She smiled, taking his bag and leaning against his side. "Fine, now. I've missed you."

Nate draped his free arm around her shoulders and hugged her closer to him. "Good," he said. "I like the sound of that." He kissed her again briefly.

The day went by in a flurry of activity. There were last-minute details to take care of for tomorrow's funeral and housing arrangements to make for the late out-of-town arrivals.

"I can go to the hotel, CeCe," Nate offered later that day when he was able to get a private moment with her outside in the backyard. Leaning against the chain-link fence that separated the Williamses' yard from that of their neighbors to the back, Nate rested his arm on CeCe's waist as they watched David play with some neighborhood kids. "It won't be a problem."

She was shaking her head before he finished. "You're staying here. Mama and Daddy wouldn't have it any other way." She turned to him with a big smile on her face. "You've won them over. What exactly did you and Daddy talk about when Mama and I left you alone at the hospital?"

He tapped his finger against the tip of her nose. "Man things," he said, teasing her. "You wouldn't understand." Since he now had her father's blessing, Nate had considered bringing the engagement ring with him and giving it to her, but he'd decided against it. He wanted everything to be perfect when he put his ring on her finger.

"Chauvinist."

"Honest."

"Oh, you." She punched him playfully in the ribs as she so often did. He'd come to look forward to those touches.

He chuckled. "Do you still want to leave tomorrow night, or do you want to stay longer? I have the time, so it's up to you."

She shook her head. "I think we should leave as planned. I need to get back to work."

Nate suspected it was more than work that made her ready to leave. "I'd like to come back here again," he said, not sure what her response would be. "Soon."

She turned back to David and the other children. "I'm not sure that's a good idea, Nate. You saw what happened the day we came home for lunch and found Eric's parents here. My parents disagree with the way I'm handling this situation. It's painful for me to watch them take Eric's side—or the side of his parents—against mine."

He rubbed his hand down her back, then squeezed her shoulders. "I don't think that's what they're doing, CeCe. Your parents love you, don't you know that?"

She shrugged. "I know they love me."

"But . . . ?"

She sighed deeply. "I can't explain it. David is my son, and they should respect my feelings about how to deal with Eric and his parents. I've apologized to my mother for the way I reacted, but I still think she was wrong. They've made me feel like a failure as a daughter, but I won't let them make me feel like a failure as a mother."

Nate sensed finality in her words, but he pursued the topic because he also heard pain. "You can't keep running from your family, CeCe." *Or is it Eric she's running from?* a small voice inquired.

CeCe moved away from him. "So you're on their side, too? You think I should let Eric's parents see David. Is that what you're saying?"

He pulled her back against him and pressed his lips against the top of her head. "That's not what I'm saying at all. Right now, I'm talking about you and your parents. You're giving Eric too much power in your life. He's controlling your relationship with your parents by keeping you from your home. He kept you from spending time with your grandfather during his last years, and now you're letting him keep David from his grandparents the same way."

CeCe didn't say anything, and Nate knew they had reached an impasse. She wasn't ready to give in on this issue now, and he knew they'd have to revisit it. As he kissed the top of her head, he prayed, *Lord, give me the words when the time is right to bring it up again.*

Though CeCe had been pretty quiet with him since their discussion in the backyard yesterday afternoon, Nate stayed close by her and David during the day of the funeral, ready to give her support when and if she needed it. He knew her grief was magnified by the guilt she felt at not having been more a part of her grandfather's life. She should have been able to celebrate his salvation and rejoice that he was now in a better place. Instead, she regretted that she hadn't spent much time with him during his last days. Even though Nate knew God could use her pain to increase her faith, he would have gladly taken her pain to spare her.

As the day wore on, Nate watched CeCe withdraw from him and from those around her. She was still present physically but absent emotionally. It was as if she'd detached herself from everybody. Everybody but David. But even that connection was distorted. She didn't let the child out of her sight. Most of the time she held him on her lap. Nate grew more and more uneasy at the change in her. By the time they were ready to leave for Atlanta, her withdrawal from him had progressed to the point that he couldn't get her to say more than a few disjointed words to him, though she continued to fake engagement with others.

Nate took their luggage to the car while CeCe and David said their final good-byes to her parents. Nate held Eric responsible for the change in CeCe, and he felt a deep anger toward the man for the pain he had inflicted on her. If Eric were here now, Nate knew it would be a struggle not to punch his lights out. By the time he'd finished loading their luggage and the food Mrs. Williams had prepared for them, his anger toward Eric had dissipated, and he began to feel a tinge of pique toward CeCe. Her withdrawal from her parents he could understand, even if he didn't agree with it, but why would she withdraw from him? All he'd done was love her—or try to. Had she expected him to agree with everything she said or did? Was that what she wanted from him?

He wanted to build a life with CeCe, but he wanted that life to be based on the principles of God. He wanted God to use him to build her up and use her to build him up. "As iron sharpens iron," he muttered. He knew that meant there would be times when they wouldn't agree, but he believed they'd be able to work through those differences if they were committed to work together and to stay together.

But now CeCe was going against that. He'd asked her early in their relationship not to walk away from him, but rather to talk to him, and she'd agreed. Yet here she was, walking away from him. OK, she hadn't physically walked away, but the way he looked at it, her emotional detachment was the same as walking away, if not worse. At that moment Nate experienced déjà vu. He'd been here before. Naomi had pulled away from him physically, just as CeCe was now pulling away from him emotionally. He was sure the latter hurt much worse than the former had. He and CeCe had the benefit of their past experiences, so they shouldn't repeat the mistakes of the past. At least that's what he had hoped.

When the three of them were settled in the car, Nate didn't try to engage CeCe in conversation. Had it not been for David's chatter, the two-hour drive home would have taken place in total silence. The child forced both adults to come out of their thoughts.

Cece stood against the porch railing, looking out into the night, her back to Nate. They had completed their evening ritual of putting David to bed and spending some moments with B.B.

Nate was seated on the porch swing. "So, are you going to cut me off the way you cut off your parents?" he asked.

Surprised, Cece turned to face him. "What's that supposed to mean?" she demanded.

"Come on, CeCe. You've been giving me the silent treatment ever since we left Alabama. I just want to know what's coming next."

"I wasn't giving you the silent treatment. I just didn't have anything to say."

He stood up, lifted her chin, and peered into her eyes. "Let's be truthful with each other. You're angry with me for the things I said about your relationship with your parents and with Eric's parents."

"You don't understand, Nate," she said, neither agreeing nor disagreeing with him. "Everything is black and white to you; you don't understand."

He opened his arms wide. "I'm here. Help me to understand," he pleaded. "I want to understand. I love you, CeCe. Don't shut me out."

She walked into his arms, and they closed tightly around her. "I'm not shutting you out," she said, but even as she said it, she knew she was. The secret she held inside forced her to shut people out. She couldn't risk their finding out the truth. Would Nate love her if he knew? What would her parents think if they knew? Sometimes she suspected they did, but they'd never said anything to her about it. No, it was the way they looked at her sometimes that made her wonder if they knew, the disappointment in their eyes that became impossible to endure. If Nate knew the truth—the whole truth—would he look at her the same way? Would disappointment replace the love and concern she saw in his eyes now?

She hadn't really believed she'd find anyone to love. Not after Eric. But miracle of miracles, God had sent Nate her way. And he loved her. *But would he still love me if he knew everything, Lord?*

A small voice said, *Trust me. And trust him.*

CeCe ignored the voice, blocked it out as if she hadn't even heard it. She'd lose Nate if he learned the truth, and she couldn't bear to lose him. "Things will be back to normal tomorrow, Nate," she told him, the fear evident in her voice. "I told you that going to Alabama did something to me. Now you see what I mean. I didn't want it to touch us, but it has."

He pulled back and looked closely at her. "Nothing can touch us unless we allow it to, CeCe," he said simply. "Places and people don't just do things to us. We have to give them permission first."

"So you're blaming me?" she asked in a soft voice.

He shook his head. "It's not about blame. It's about dealing with the issues in our lives so we can move on. God's not going to let us move forward until we learn what he wants us to learn. We can run away from one situation, but the issue will only surface in another. I think that's what's happening with us."

"You mean with me?" she asked. She was beginning to feel a tinge of anger.

Nate tightened his hold on her. "No, I mean us. We're in this together, CeCe. What you do affects me, and what I do affects you."

"But you think it's my problem to fix? Don't deny it, Nate. I know you do."

He nodded solemnly. "You brought Eric into our relationship, and you have to ask him to leave. He's only here because you brought him here."

CeCe gave an unladylike snort. "You make this sound like a party and Eric is a guest."

"I hadn't thought of it that way, but maybe you're right. Do you want him here, CeCe? I asked you before if there was somebody else, and you said no, but maybe you do have some feelings for Eric. Maybe the reason for all of your anger is that you still care for him."

CeCe pulled out of his embrace and glared at him. "How can you say that after everything that man did to me?" she asked, her voice tight. She was making a conscious effort to keep her emotions in check and her voice low, but she found it difficult to do so. "How could you think I'd feel anything but hatred toward him?"

CeCe folded her arms around her waist, her back ramrod straight. Nate just stared silently at her. "*Hate* is a very strong word," he said slowly. "How can you hate him and love me? You know as well as I do that hate and love can't occupy the same vessel."

She didn't move, and she didn't answer.

He sighed deeply. Then he tilted her face up and placed a soft kiss on her forehead, taking care not to touch her anyplace else. "I do love you," he said. Then he walked down the steps and to his car. He didn't turn around, so he didn't see the tears that fell from her eyes as he backed out of her driveway.

CeCe would have been happy to cry herself to sleep, but she was not that blessed. After her tears subsided, she was wide awake and more heartsick than she'd ever been before. Her life seemed to be falling apart around her, and she knew it was her own fault. The past was catching up with her. The past she'd tried so hard to escape.

Nate was right. She hadn't been able to admit it to him, but he had been absolutely right. She *was* giving Eric too much power in her life, and she knew the time had come for it to stop, just as she knew what she had to do in order to make it stop.

She also knew she owed Nate an explanation—and an apology. She loved this man, but she didn't deserve him. He'd been nothing but open with her, and what had she given him in return? Half-truths. She should have told him the full story about Eric—she knew that now—but she'd been so ashamed. And, she admitted, she'd been afraid of Nate's reaction when he heard her shameful story. Would his eyes still look at her with love, or would they mirror the disappointment she saw in her parents' eyes?

CeCe wasn't sure, but she needed to find out. She couldn't torture herself with what-ifs, and she couldn't continue to hide herself from Nate. She might have been able to continue her charade if he hadn't gone to Alabama with her and seen the ugliest part of her. She might have been able to hide if she hadn't seen the vulnerability in his eyes when he'd kissed her goodnight and sadly told her that he loved her. She might have been able to continue along the path of least resistance if she hadn't known that Nate was questioning her love for him.

She glanced at the clock on her nightstand, the fluorescent numbers screaming the early morning time to her. It was too early to call Nate, she knew, but she had to make the call while she still had the courage. She picked up the handset and dialed.

"Hello," he answered in a wide-awake voice. Her heart ached because she knew she was the reason he couldn't sleep.

"I know it's early, Nate." She pushed the words out quickly, still not sure if her courage would abandon her. "But we need to talk."

"OK, let's talk."

"Not on the phone. Can you meet me for lunch around noon at Woodruff Park?"

"Sure I can meet you."

CeCe expelled the breath she hadn't realized she'd been holding. She'd deliberately chosen the place they'd eaten their first lunch together because she wanted to go back to the familiar. She'd known during that lunch that Nate could touch her heart in a way that no man had ever touched it before, or would again. It was fitting that Woodruff Park also be the place where she confirmed for him that her heart belonged to him as well.

"I'll see you then," she said. "And Nate, I do love you."

SIXTEEN

CeCe arrived at Woodruff Park about fifteen minutes early. She'd gone in to work early and was prepared to stay late in order to take whatever time was necessary to work out her problems with Nate. Their relationship was too important to let a ghost from her past tear them apart.

It was a warm, cloudless day, and the park was crowded with downtown workers taking advantage of the extended warm weather of late fall. As she sat down on a vacant bench in the midst of the horde, she wished she had chosen a place that would have provided them more privacy. She should have gone for practicality instead of sentimentality.

"Hi."

CeCe looked up, surprised to see Nate standing before her but happy he'd decided to arrive early, too. That was a good sign, wasn't it? She smiled at him, his probing eyes reminding her of their first visit here. Then his look had made her cautious. Now it made her feel safe. And loved. "Hi," she said.

His lips curved in a slight smile. "Do you want to get something to eat and bring it back here?"

Standing, she nodded, though she hadn't given a thought to food. Then she almost burst into tears when he enclosed her hand in his and gave it a little squeeze. *Lord, why did you send this man to me? Never in my wildest dreams could I have imagined him.*

Beyond what you can ask or think, a soft voice said. *Those are the plans I have for you.*

CeCe looked up at Nate and smiled again, knowing he could see the tears in her eyes. "I do love you, Nate, even if sometimes it doesn't seem that way." She pressed her free hand to his clean-shaven face. "I don't know how or why God saw fit to send you to me, but I'm so very glad he did."

Nate covered the hand on his face with his free one. "We're already becoming one," he said softly, his loving emotions clear in his eyes. "You're stealing my lines." He smiled and then pressed a kiss against her forehead. He pulled back and looked down into her eyes. "I think I'd rather talk than eat. How about you?"

She nodded. "I'd rather talk too, but I don't think I picked the best place for serious conversation." They both looked around, taking in their busy surroundings.

"What time do you have to get back to work?" he asked.

"I'm pretty flexible. I went in early, and I'm prepared to stay late."

"Good." He squeezed her hand again. "I know the perfect place, but we'll have to drive."

She followed him without question. They went back to Genesis House, where they got Nate's car. They didn't talk much during the drive, but CeCe didn't mind. Nate still held her hand and periodically gave it an affectionate squeeze. He was encouraging her, she knew, and that consideration strengthened her belief that all would be well between them.

CeCe wasn't sure of their destination until they reached Highway 78. She knew then they were going back to Stone Mountain Park, to Nate's spot there. She couldn't think of a more appropriate place. He'd brought her here the first time they'd been at odds.

He led her to the same area, his spot littered now with the brown and gold leaves of autumn, slipped off his light denim jacket, sat, and pulled her to sit down next to him on the jacket. "I love you," he whispered. "More than you know."

She believed him because she loved him the same way. "Nate, I don't have any unresolved feelings for Eric. You have to believe me."

He squeezed her shoulders. "How can you be sure?"

"Oh, I'm sure all right. All my feelings for Eric are definitely resolved." She was positive her disdain for the man was clear in her voice.

"You know, people say love and hate are two sides of the same coin," Nate said, gently massaging her shoulder. "I think that connection is especially true for us as Christians. I know you well enough to know that you don't hate Eric, not in the sense of wanting him to die or anything like that."

At those words, she shot him a glare that suggested maybe he didn't know her as well as he thought, but even as she glared at him, she recognized the truth in his words. She didn't want anything to happen to Eric. The thought brought rumblings of sadness in her—which surprised her.

Nate ignored her glare and continued talking. "So I have to conclude that your hate, or your so-called hate, must have its roots somewhere else. I know you loved him at one time, CeCe, or you thought you did. Maybe a part of you still does."

She shook her head. "Maybe I don't want anything to happen to him, but I can assure you that I don't have any loving feelings for him." When Nate would have contradicted her, she stopped him by pressing her hand against his chest. "I need to tell you the truth about Eric and me. I think that once you hear the whole story, you'll see why Eric is still so much a part of my life, and you'll know that it has nothing to do with any loving feelings I still harbor for him."

"OK," he said. "I'm listening."

She sighed deeply and felt fear build within her. *Lord*, she prayed, *give me the courage to tell this story. Help me to get past the shame.* "Eric and I practically grew up together," she began, looking away from Nate and off toward the mountain. "I think I developed a crush on him in first grade, if you can believe that." She gave a self-deprecating laugh, to which Nate responded with a soft squeeze of her shoulder. "Well, my crush didn't go away as most crushes did. Instead, it grew and grew and grew. By the time I was in high school, I was practicing writing my name as Cecelia Bradshaw. Mrs. Eric Bradshaw. Eric and Cecelia Bradshaw. I was undaunted by the fact that Eric never looked at me as anything more than a friend. I think he told me that he was falling in love with Yolanda—that's the woman he married—even before he told her." She still remembered the pain she'd felt the day he'd shared his joy with her and thought she'd done an admirable job of hiding her feelings.

"Yolanda was a big deal because she wasn't part of our group. Eric and I were both active in the InterVarsity Christian Fellowship group when we first went off to college, but Eric stopped coming after he started seeing Yolanda. Of course, we were all worried about him. Anyway, Yolanda broke his heart, as we knew she would. When Eric told me about it, I encouraged him to come back to the group, but he said he was too ashamed. So we started having Bible study together."

She shook her head at the memory of how naïve she'd been and the easy prey she'd made for the enemy. "This is when I went crazy. I just knew that everything that was happening between Eric and me was a sign from God that we were meant to be together. I don't know how it happened, but before long I was avoiding the other members of our group just as Eric was. Now that I look back, I can see why. You see, deep down inside I knew that Eric was lonely for Yolanda, not lonely for God. But all I wanted to see was that he was with me. I had wanted him with me for so long."

She paused. Reliving this part of her past was harder than she'd imagined it would be. Nate must have understood, because he didn't say anything. He just waited patiently for her to start again. If he had spoken, she wasn't sure she would have been able to continue.

"Anyway, one thing led to another, and one night after our one-on-one Bible study, Eric told me he thought I was pretty." She turned her lips downward in regret. "You would have thought he told me I was Miss America or something. It was as though he was finally seeing me as a woman. I was ecstatic. Then he started telling me how different I was from Yolanda and how he'd been crazy not to see that before. I was eating this up, of course, because I knew he was right."

She stopped again and took some time to pluck a blade of grass. This was the hard part. "Then one night I told him. I don't know how I told him or why I told him, but I told him that I loved him. He was surprised, I could tell, but he kissed me and told me that he loved me, too." Her happiness at that moment had been unlimited but, unfortunately, short-lived.

"After that, our Bible study sessions turned into kissing sessions. When our feelings began to get physically intense, we started talking about marriage. Once we started talking about marriage, it became easy to go beyond the kissing. He was going to be my husband, after all, I told myself. We were already married in our hearts." She laughed at herself again, laughter that substituted for the tears she refused to shed. Oh, how she'd deceived herself back then! "We were together during the summer after Eric graduated, but like summers have to, ours ended and Eric went off to med school. We planned for me to visit him for the Howard-Morehouse football game and for him to visit me at Thanksgiving, and then we'd both go home for Christmas. We had it all planned. But when I went to visit him for the Howard-Morehouse game, I could tell things had changed. I didn't want to see it, but I did. And for the first time I was the initiator in our physical relationship. I don't know, I just felt that I had to be close to him." She'd been a very foolish girl, she knew now.

"Anyway, I went back home telling myself everything was OK. I learned I was pregnant about a week before Thanksgiving. I should have been devastated, but all I could think was that now Eric and I would get married sooner. It had been Eric's idea to wait until I graduated to get married. That should have told me something." As she looked back, she realized she'd had more than one signal, or sign, that she should end the relationship, including the conscience she had often battled. Unfortunately, she'd ignored them all.

"Eric came home for Thanksgiving as planned. Before I could tell him I was pregnant, he told me that he and Yolanda had reconciled. Apparently, she'd had second thoughts, and to prove herself to him, she'd taken a job in D.C. so they could work out their problems."

Nate pressed his lips against her hair, and she accepted the comfort he offered. "Now I was devastated. Talk about your world crashing down around you. Mine did. I couldn't say anything, and when I finally did, it wasn't what Eric wanted to hear. He didn't come right out and say it, but he hinted that our only alternative was abortion. That was when I hit rock bottom. It was as though my whole life flashed in front of me, at least the last couple of years. I felt ashamed and worthless and stupid. Eric left, upset. I concentrated on making it until the next time I saw him. Of course, I convinced myself all the while we were apart that Eric would come to his senses and realize that he loved me and not Yolanda. But it was not to be." CeCe took comfort in the soft brush of Nate's fingers on her neck.

"Eric didn't have to tell me he didn't love me the next time he saw me, because I could read it in his eyes. He told me anyway, of course, and then he told me that he and Yolanda were getting married in the summer. They were going to announce it at Christmas. I knew then that I'd just been a substitute for Yolanda. That hurt. Really hurt. Eric had been my friend for a long time, and then he'd used me that way. I was hurt and I was angry. And since I was hurt, I wanted to hurt him back."

She paused again. Everything she had admitted up to this point was bad enough, but what was yet to come was even worse. She breathed deeply, then continued, "So I told Eric that I would tell Yolanda I was pregnant." Nate's fingers stopped briefly, then started again. CeCe waited for him to ask the question she knew was on his mind, and when he didn't, she answered him anyway. "That got to him, of course. He had to hide the truth from Yolanda. One thing led to another and—"

CeCe stopped. She couldn't say it. She covered her face with her hands. If only she had walked away as soon as she'd seen that Eric didn't love her. If only she'd acknowledged the signs she'd seen while she was in D.C. If only, if only, if only. She shook her head sadly. But she hadn't, and things had spiraled way out of control.

"CeCe?" Nate's question was soft, nonthreatening, and most important, noncondemning. "CeCe," he said her name again. "It's all right. You've told me, and we'll work though it."

CeCe managed a nod. After a few more seconds she lifted her head. She knew Nate thought he knew the rest of the story, but he didn't. She had to tell him. He had to know. She took another deep breath and told herself life would not end if he walked away. She'd never really thought she'd get married and live happily ever after. She'd been content to live a single life, and she could become content again. She had a wonderful son, and that was enough.

"You haven't heard all of it yet." At the question in his eyes, she nodded. *Lord, please help me to make it through this part.* "I had planned to tell Yolanda I was pregnant, expecting that she'd refuse to marry Eric and then he'd do the right thing and marry me. Except it didn't quite work out that way." CeCe remembered it as if it had happened yesterday.

"Why do you want me, CeCe?" Eric had asked her, oh so calmly. *"I don't want you and I don't love you. I've never loved you. You were just there. I'm sorry, but that's the truth."*

How could he have stood there and said those words to her so carelessly when she'd been carrying his child? What kind of monster had he been to treat her with such cruelty?

"CeCe?" Nate's tender voice brought her out of her thoughts.

"Well," she continued, willing herself to tell him all of it, "Eric told me that he didn't want me and he didn't love me, had never loved me."

Nate reached for her to pull her close, she knew, but she couldn't accept his comfort right now. She used her hands to ward him off, and thank God, he followed her lead. Just thinking about the way Eric had used her made her feel dirty. Five years later, she still felt dirty. She couldn't bear to have Nate touch her when she felt this way.

After a long while, it seemed to her, the pain of the past went back to that place where it lived, and she was able to speak again. She turned pleading eyes to Nate, willing him to understand what she was about to tell him. "I was so hurt, Nate. I had loved Eric so much, and now I was so hurt. All I wanted to do was hurt him back. So I said the first thing that came to my mind. I told him that if he didn't give me twenty thousand dollars, I was going to tell Yolanda everything."

She lost her courage and had to lower her eyes. She didn't want to see the disdain she was sure Nate now felt for her. Why shouldn't he feel disdain? It was no less than what she felt for herself. She stared at the blades of grass before her and thought how simple life could be if a person just followed the Lord's direction. So very simple. "Of course, Eric didn't have that kind of money," she continued. "I didn't let his money situation bother me, though. I told him it wasn't my problem. Before he left to go back to school, he told me he'd get the money. Over Christmas, his parents announced his upcoming marriage, and he gave me a check for twenty thousand dollars."

She raised her eyes to Nate's again. "And that really is the end of the story," she said, repeating the phrase she'd used when they'd talked after the Gala. "I used the money for the down payment on the house B.B. and I now share, and for my living expenses until I had the baby, finished school, and found a job."

Nate didn't know what to say or where to start. Cece had sinned, and she'd suffered because of it. But all that was in the past. She'd repented and was already forgiven by God. She just had to accept it. But Nate knew she couldn't accept it until she forgave Eric.

He admitted surprise at CeCe's story. It wasn't what he'd

expected, but then he didn't know what he'd expected. He'd heard a lot of things in her story, things he wasn't even sure she heard. He knew Eric had broken her heart, but he also knew CeCe hadn't been as much a victim as she tried to convince herself she was. She and Eric had been coconspirators. A part of him wondered if CeCe, consciously or unconsciously, had wanted to get pregnant as a way of forcing Eric to marry her. He knew pain had caused her to blackmail Eric. Pain resulting from unrequited love. And that bothered him. He was now even less convinced that CeCe no longer had feelings for Eric. She had to. And if she still had feelings for Eric, where did that leave him?

"So what happens now?" he asked.

CeCe turned to him. "I want to pay Eric back his money," she said, with such confidence that Nate knew she'd thought long about her course of action. "I feel so guilty for taking it. If I paid him back, then I wouldn't have that guilt."

Nate nodded. He agreed that restitution was needed, and he was glad CeCe had decided to do it, but he didn't think it was enough. CeCe was looking for the restitution to change her heart, when in fact, it should have been a changed heart that prompted the desire to make restitution.

"My debt to Eric is the major debt standing between me and the day-care center that B.B. and I have talked about. You know, the day-care center was something I wanted to do for B.B. She was keeping kids in the house, and it seemed that if I could give her this day-care center, I could show her how much I appreciated everything she had done for me, been to me." She shook her head back and forth sadly, defeated. "But I couldn't even give her that because Eric and the money he'd given me stood in the way. I knew I couldn't start anything new until I dealt with that debt. But the whole situation with Eric was just so hard to deal with that I kept putting off repaying the money, and thus the day-care center started to seem farther and farther away. But now I have to deal with it. It'll take a while," she continued her explanation, "but I should have the money saved in two, three years at the most. Then I can repay him, and he'll be out of our lives."

"You're going to wait two or three years to deal with this?" Nate said, his voice louder than he would have liked, but he couldn't believe what he'd just heard. What were they supposed to do with their relationship for two or three years?

CeCe turned to him. "It'll take me that long to get all the money," she said in such a matter-of-fact tone that Nate knew she didn't see any problem with her plan.

He wanted to yell at her that money wasn't the issue. Didn't she see that? He opened his mouth to tell her, but he closed it without uttering a word. He knew this was not something he could tell CeCe. He couldn't make her see; she had to see for herself. Besides, he had his own problems to deal with. He didn't want to make a life with a woman who didn't know how to forgive or one who still harbored feelings for another man. He'd been down that road once, and once was one time too many.

CeCe was true to her word. She wanted to pay Eric back and, over the next couple of weeks, she threw herself into her real estate business with a vengeance. Nate had sensed that before now she'd been hesitant to follow up on the contacts she'd made the night of the Gala, but she dropped those hesitations with seeming ease. One of her first calls had been to Mr. Cronin, who'd been out of town for a couple of weeks. His office staff scheduled her to meet with him as soon as he returned. The timing of the appointment seemed providential. Cronin put her in touch with a broker who was serving as the sole representative for a new development he was soon to begin construction on in southwest Atlanta. He'd suggested CeCe talk to the broker because he knew she was looking for another assistant, someone part-time. He thought it would be the perfect opportunity for CeCe to get her foot in the door and begin to build a solid foundation for her own business.

When CeCe had met with the woman, Margaret Thomas, they'd immediately hit it off, and Margaret had offered CeCe the job right on the spot. Margaret had been especially willing to work with CeCe's schedule since she herself had started in the business when she was a single mother with a full-time job. They agreed that Margaret would leave CeCe's assignments in the office each afternoon, and CeCe would have the tasks completed by the next day, or whatever due date Margaret set. The work would primarily consist of research CeCe could conduct on the computer, lead follow-ups, document filings and tracking, and as many showings as CeCe wanted to conduct. The arrangement gave CeCe the freedom to do the work on her own schedule and also gave her the opportunity to establish her own base of clients while working with one of the top producers in the city. She was giddy with excitement when she told Nate about it later that night.

"I can't believe the timing," she told him. "Mr. Cronin spoke with Margaret just yesterday, and then my appointment with him was today. I'd say God was opening doors for me."

Nate wasn't sure he agreed. "How are you going to do your regular job, put in time at Genesis House, and work with Cronin's sole representative? What about David?" *And me?* he added silently. "You're only one person, CeCe."

She smiled as if she found his concern amusingly endearing. "It'll take some managing, I know, but I can do it. I *want* to do it. I want to repay Eric this money so that we can put the past behind us where it belongs. That's my incentive. It'll work, you'll see. I'll make it work. Besides, working as Margaret's assistant will be more manageable—and probably as lucrative, if not more so—than freelancing and having to handle multiple clients for multiple properties. I'll be able to do the work at night after David is in bed, and on Saturday and Sunday afternoons. It's the perfect setup."

Nate wasn't so sure, but he didn't want to squelch her happiness. If she wanted this new job to work, then he wanted it to work for her. He'd said he would follow her lead, and he was going to do that, but he was beginning to wonder if her future included any place for him.

She yawned, then apologized.

"I can take a hint," he said. "Let's pray so I can hit the road."

Nate watched David scamper back over to the older boys huddled around the new science exhibit at the Fernbank Museum. He'd come to love the child as if he were his own. *Funny how that happened,* he thought with a wistful smile. He and David had been hanging out without CeCe a lot since she had started her new job. He didn't think he was seeing the child that much more than he had in the past; it was just that he wasn't seeing CeCe much at all. While he enjoyed the time with David, he missed CeCe, and he regretted that the three of them weren't sharing moments that would become tomorrow's shared memories.

He knew CeCe tried to make sure that David wasn't short-changed as a result of her new work schedule. She came home every evening after her day job and didn't go to the Cronin job, as he referred to it, until after David was in bed. Despite her efforts, he still thought she was shortchanging the boy. And him. Besides, things were bound to get worse. She could do most of her work at night now because they were in the preconstruction phase of the development. He wasn't so sure that would continue after they moved to the construction phase.

"You're crazy about that kid, aren't you?" Stuart asked. He'd returned from verifying the rest of today's schedule with the museum's tour group assistant.

Nate nodded. "I guess it's pretty obvious, huh?"

"Sure is. Just like it's obvious that you're preoccupied. What's up with you and CeCe?"

Nate shot his friend a questioning glance. "What makes you—"

"Don't even try it, Richardson. I know you, remember? So don't tell me it's nothing. Either tell me what it is, or tell me it's none of my business."

Nate laughed. Stuart, his feet-on-the-floor friend, was always true to form. "I miss her," he told his friend simply. "I just miss her." He'd already told Stuart about the job Cronin had hooked up for CeCe. His friend had laughed when he remembered the older man's attentiveness to her at the Gala.

"Have you talked to her about it?" Stuart asked.

Nate shook his head. "I'm being understanding."

"You don't look like it. Your expression says you're angry with her."

Nate didn't respond immediately, but his friend was right. If CeCe had been working out of necessity, he didn't think the hours would bother him as much. Since he knew why she was working, he was more than bothered. Every time she couldn't do something with him and David because of work, like attend the museum with them today or spend Thanksgiving with his family in Chicago next week, or when she cut their private times on the swing short with a yawn, he was reminded that what she was doing was not necessary.

Why didn't she just call Eric, tell him how she felt about what she'd done, ask him to forgive her, and then arrange a repayment schedule with him? Why did she have to get all the money together and give it back to him in a lump sum? He'd been asking himself those questions for a while, but he'd yet to pose them to CeCe. Maybe it was time he did. He might even offer to give her the money. He'd made a profit when he'd sold his home in Chicago, so he had a little put away that he didn't need right now. What was the point of having money if you didn't spend it when you needed it? Besides, this wouldn't be the first time he'd dipped into the pot to help out a friend in need.

"Whatever it is," Stuart continued, "don't let it fester. You and CeCe have something special. You've had pretty smooth sailing until now, but your relationship is going to be tested. You know that. You've got to be ready for the test, and you've got to go through it the right way."

Nate accepted his friend's counsel. He hadn't expected his relationship with CeCe to be without bumps. It was just that this bump was not the bump he had expected. Not her past.

Not her relationship with another man. "You're right, Stuart," Nate said to his friend. "What do you say about letting me buy your dinner tonight to show my gratitude?"

Stuart laughed. "I'll take dinner as partial payment. I think my advice is worth a lot more than the price of a single meal."

SEVENTEEN

CeCe was late getting home. Since today was the day before Thanksgiving, she'd shuffled her schedule a bit, going to work for Margaret directly after leaving her day job instead of coming home first. She'd hoped that would give her some time with Nate before he left for his family's for the holiday weekend. She couldn't go with him, since she had to finish up her contribution to a major presentation Margaret was making to Cronin the following Monday. She had also hoped to get home before David went to bed, but she knew she was cutting it close.

Nate's car was in the driveway when she pulled in, and she had no doubt he and Miss Brinson had tucked her son safely into bed. While that gave her a measure of comfort, she still preferred that hers be the last face David saw each night.

She met Nate as he was coming down the stairs. "Hi, stranger," he said to her. Though he was smiling, she heard a tinge of censure in his voice.

"Hi, yourself," she said, greeting him with a light kiss. "David in bed?"

"Just put him down." He smiled again. "After I read him three stories."

CeCe laughed. "Three? Nate, you're a real pushover."

His smiled faded, and she wondered what he was thinking. "Maybe I am," he said. "I hadn't thought of myself that way before, though."

CeCe had the feeling Nate was no longer talking about David, and though she wanted to know what he meant, her first priority was getting to David. "I'll go say good night. Will you be here when I come back down?"

He brushed his finger down her cheek, a message in his eyes she couldn't quite decipher. "I'll be waiting for you," he said. "It's something I'm getting pretty good at doing." He dropped his finger from her face and put his hands in the pockets of his slacks. Then he moved around her so she could go up the stairs.

After spending a few minutes with her son, CeCe went to her room, put down her belongings, and slipped off her shoes. "Ohh," she said, wiggling her hose-encased toes, "that feels so good." She sat down on the side of the bed and rubbed her feet with her hands. It had been a long day and a long three-day workweek. Balancing three jobs was becoming more and more difficult. This was her first job as an assistant and she was learning a lot, but she hadn't realized how much time and effort would be involved in working with a top producer like Margaret. The woman was a dynamo, and she kept CeCe extremely busy.

If she didn't need any sleep, CeCe knew she could handle all three jobs without a problem, but as it was, she found herself getting more and more tired. She knew she couldn't keep up this pace forever, but she hoped she could hang on just a little longer. She had only a few more hours to put in at Genesis House, and when that duty was done she should have more time. She sighed. "I'll probably just spend that time sleeping," she murmured. When she reminded herself of the reason she'd taken on the additional work, she guessed her sacrifices were worth it.

She breathed deeply, then stood up and slipped off her jacket and skirt. She pulled on a multicolored jumper over a long-sleeved shirt, put her feet in a pair of comfortable flats, and made her way down to Nate. She'd been happy to see him, and her happiness had been dimmed only slightly by his peculiar behavior. She'd have to find out what was wrong and make it right. After working through the Eric problem together, she was confident she and Nate could work through any problem they faced.

When she got downstairs, she checked to see if Nate was in the kitchen with B.B. Once there, she found B.B. on the phone, but no sign of Nate. She waved at B.B., mouthed a greeting, and then went to the front porch, where she was certain she'd find Nate. She smothered a yawn as she reached the door. She was tired. Very tired.

"Hi, again," she said, coming to sit next to him on the swing. She pressed a kiss against his cheek. "Miss me?"

"Always."

"Me too." She placed her hand in his. "Things will get better."

He arched a brow. "When? You've been saying that for a month now."

CeCe pulled away from him so she could see his face. "Are you upset with me, Nate?" His clipped words suggested he was.

Nate shrugged, and she almost laughed. Was Nate pouting? She couldn't believe it. Her manly man was acting like a spoiled child. "You are upset. I know you are. You could be honest about it, you know."

He gave her a sheepish grin. "OK, I'm a little upset, but I'm trying to be understanding about your work."

"But . . . ?" she coaxed. "Come on now, I know there's a *but* in there somewhere." CeCe was still in a teasing mood. She was a bit flattered that Nate missed her so much. So much so that she thought she could put up with his pouting every now and then, as long as it didn't become a habit.

"But I'm having a hard time understanding."

"Well, you know what I'm trying to do and why I'm trying to do it," she said calmly, thinking he needed to be reminded of the reasons and reassured of her love. "I miss you as much as you miss me, but we agreed this was what I needed to do."

Nate shook his head. "We didn't agree."

CeCe's teasing mood vanished immediately. "Yes, we did. The day in the park, remember?" Of course he remembered. He'd just momentarily forgotten, she told herself.

He shook his head again. "We didn't agree. You told me what you were going to do, but I didn't agree."

Now CeCe was getting angry. "As I recall, you didn't disagree," she challenged.

He expelled a sigh. "I didn't agree or disagree. You didn't ask my opinion. You told me what you were going to do."

"I guess you're telling me now that you don't agree? You don't think I need to pay Eric back? I don't understand."

Nate rubbed his hands down the front of his pants. "It's not that I don't think you should pay Eric back," he began. "It's just that I don't think you need to kill yourself in order to return all of the money in one swoop."

CeCe leaned back in the swing. She could see that Nate had been doing some serious thinking. Why was he just now telling her? she wondered. What did he expect her to do now that he was? "Do you have some other suggestion for how I can pay him back?" she asked, choosing to go with her second question first.

"I can give you the money," he offered with a careless shrug. "Or loan it to you, if that makes you feel better."

"No, you can't," she said with a strong shake of her head. What made him think she'd take twenty thousand dollars from him? "You know that wouldn't be right."

"Why wouldn't it?" His probing eyes challenged her. "We're going to be married, aren't we? Your debts are my debts."

She shook her head again. "No way, Nate. This is my problem, my debt, and I'm going to repay it myself. I have to."

"No, you don't *have* to. You *want* to." CeCe could tell by the tightening of Nate's jaw that he was angry. "Besides, you don't have to give it to him all at once. You can pay it back in installments."

Since he was angry, she tried to keep a rein on her emotions. "No," she said calmly, "I want to give it back in one lump sum. That way, I just have one call to make to Eric."

"Yeah," he said, the word full of sarcasm. "Three years from now. Why don't you just call the guy up, tell him you're sorry for what you did, ask his forgiveness, and work out some repayment plan?"

Nate's sarcasm freed CeCe from her need to be calm. "You

can't be serious! You don't really expect me to just up and call him, do you?" She began shaking her head again. "No way. I don't talk to Eric until I can hand over all the money."

He sighed again, and his anger seemed to dissipate. "What's this all about, CeCe? Are you afraid to talk to him again?"

She turned her gaze away from him and studied the darkness that now surrounded them. "I don't know where you're coming from, Nate. I thought I explained all of this to you when we went out to Stone Mountain. I thought you understood." Her voice grew soft, and she willed him to know how much his words hurt her. "I guess I was wrong. You didn't understand. You don't understand."

"I think I understand a great deal, CeCe," he retorted, either uncaring or unaware of her feelings. That added to her pain. "You're holding on to Eric. You're not ready to let him go."

Anger suddenly allowed her to see beyond her own pain, and she turned her attention back to him. "What? What are you talking about? You know Eric means nothing to me. How can you even suggest that after everything I've told you?"

His eyes never left hers. "Actions speak louder than words," he accused. "Your actions say that you aren't ready to get Eric out of your life, not yet."

CeCe couldn't respond. She didn't know how to respond. At a loss, she asked, "Are you jealous of Eric, Nate? Is that what all this is about?"

His flinch told her she'd hit the bull's-eye. He was actually jealous of Eric, a man he hadn't met? A man who meant nothing to her? She couldn't believe it. "Come on, Nate, you can't be serious."

Nate didn't answer. He sat there with his arms folded across his chest like a small child. She would have laughed if she wasn't so angry. "I don't know what else I can tell you, Nate. Either you trust my feelings for you or you don't. I don't know what else I can do."

"You can let him go, CeCe. Call him and let him go."

She shook her head. "I'm beginning to think this isn't about

Eric and me," she said, enlightenment dawning. "Maybe you're the one who can't let go of the past. Maybe you can't let Naomi go."

He flinched again. "Don't be ridiculous."

She began to feel the evening's chill and rubbed her hand down her arm. "I'm not being ridiculous. I'm right and you know it." She sighed. "You know, Nate, I've always resented Naomi's place in your life. She hurt you, and I knew you'd carry the remnants of that hurt around a long time, but I accepted it because I knew I had my own baggage. When you asked me not to walk away if we had problems, that was more about Naomi than it was about me or about us. Our whole relationship has been built on the foundation of your not repeating the mistakes you made with Naomi. Well, in case you haven't noticed, I'm not Naomi. Eric is not some long-lost love that I'm going to go rushing back to as soon as I get over being angry with him. You've gotten your women mixed up."

Nate opened his mouth to speak, but CeCe raised her hand. "Not tonight, Nate. We've both said a lot, maybe too much. Let's not say anything more. Right now, I don't trust myself to listen so I know I don't trust myself to speak. Maybe we should just pray and call it a night."

After eating an early breakfast with David the following Saturday morning and hearing about the plans he and Miss Brinson had for the day, CeCe dressed and made it over to Genesis House to meet with Shay and Anna Mae. With her new work schedule, they had agreed to meet an hour before the workshop to go over their plans, so CeCe didn't have to meet with them during the week. The Saturday morning meetings with her friends had turned out to be one of the best things to result from her added responsibilities. Though they met to discuss the workshop, which was now in its third session, they used the time to share about their week and to pray for each other. After her argument with Nate this past Wednesday night, she needed the support of her friends.

Shay and Anna Mae were at the Center when CeCe arrived. They pulled three chairs together in a small circle near the front of the room, and Anna Mae started the week's session. "I need you two to join me in prayer about Danita. Something's going on, but I don't know what. She broke up with her boyfriend all of a sudden, and she won't talk about it. You both know I thought they were getting too serious too fast, so this breakup could be a good thing for the both of them. But Danita looks so sad that it breaks my heart. Every time I ask her what's wrong, she says 'nothing.' I don't want to push, but I don't know what else to do."

Shay and CeCe nodded their understanding. "You've raised a good girl in Danita," CeCe offered. "The best thing you can do right now is to let her know you're there for her. Don't assume she's done anything wrong. You don't want to send those signals. Tell her that you love her and that you're there to help her. Leave the rest to God."

"CeCe's right, Anna Mae," Shay added. "Being a teenager is hard enough without parents who are always assuming the worst."

"I'm trying to do that," Anna Mae acknowledged with a dramatic wave of her arm, "but it's hard."

"We know," Shay said. "Sometimes it's very hard to do the right thing."

CeCe pressed her hand against Shay's knee. "What's up with you this week, Shay?" she asked, sensing her friend was struggling to do the right thing in her life as well.

"Same old, same old." Shay lifted her shoulders in a light shrug. "I miss Marvin so much that it's become a physical ache. Things were much better when we were physically in the same house, even though we weren't communicating that much. But I'm believing that God is going to take this separation and work it for our good. I believe that with all my heart. I have to because I'm not ready to give up my husband or my marriage. Not now. Not ever."

CeCe was inspired by the fervor of Shay's words. "I'm so glad you said that, Shay," she said. "You both know that Nate and I have been having our share of issues. I thought things were getting better, but now I'm not so sure."

"What happened?" Shay asked.

CeCe looked from one friend to the other and took comfort in the concern and support that she felt transmitted from their hearts to hers. "We had an argument Wednesday night, before he left to spend the holidays with his family in Chicago. A serious one, I think. The conversation started with Nate telling me how he felt about my long work hours. It ended with him accusing me of still having feelings for Eric, and me telling him that he's gotten me confused with Naomi."

"Whew," Anna Mae pushed the word out. "You didn't pull any punches, did you? Do you really believe Nate's confused you with Naomi?"

CeCe shook her head. "I know he knows I'm not her. He knows I'm CeCe, but I think that when he sees similarities in us, he begins to extrapolate those similarities to the point of absurdity."

"Look," Shay said. "I know I can be slow, but I'm not getting your point, CeCe."

CeCe was still learning how far to go in sharing her and Nate's problems, but she trusted Shay and Anna Mae completely. "The man Naomi married, the one she left Nate for, was an old boyfriend. So in the back of Nate's mind is the possibility that I'll realize some hidden feelings I have for Eric and go back to him."

"Nate actually said that?" Anna Mae asked.

"Not exactly. I said it, and then I didn't allow him to respond."

"Well, that was one way of doing it," Shay put in.

"I know, but we had said so many things already. I thought we needed to stop before one or both of us said something that we regretted. I'm not sure we didn't." CeCe saw the look that passed between her two friends. "What?" she asked.

The women exchanged another look. "We've just been a little

concerned about you and Nate," Shay said. "It's hard not to notice that he's not as happy as he was."

CeCe stood up and began pacing around the circle of chairs. Was her life falling apart, or did it just feel that way? And why did everything have to fall apart now, just when she'd started to think all was well? "I didn't know Nate was so unhappy," she said.

"We aren't saying he's unhappy," Anna Mae explained. "It's just that he's not as happy as he has been. It's obvious to those of us who know him well that something is on his mind. We just guessed the something was you and him. We could be all wrong."

CeCe stopped behind her empty chair. "You're not wrong. I thought Nate and I had passed the hurdle, but Wednesday night and today I'm seeing that we haven't."

"You will," Shay reassured her. "Just keep talking and keep praying. And keep taking those cooling-off periods. What you did Wednesday night was probably the right thing to do. It gave both of you a chance to take a breath."

"Shay's right," Anna Mae agreed.

CeCe accepted her friends' encouragement and support. She counted on it, in fact. She was missing something, she knew she was, but she didn't know what. "Look," Shay said, "I think we'd better pray. All this talk is making us think too much about problems and not enough about solutions."

Nate and Stuart took David and his friend Timmy, along with their boys groups, to Seabrook Village, a re-created slave community just south of Savannah, the following Saturday. Though the two boys were too young to understand slavery and its effects, he thought the trip was a good introduction to discussions they would have as they got older. After taking David home that night, he walked through his front door just as Marvin was walking out of the kitchen, sandwich in hand.

"Hey, man," Marvin said. "I didn't expect you home this early. You and CeCe have a fight?" Nate supposed his expression alerted his friend to his mood, for Marvin quickly added, "I was just joking with you. What's up with you and CeCe?"

Nate followed his friend into the den. Tonight he could use Marvin's company. Though he had called CeCe on Sunday to let her know he'd gotten back from Chicago and to pass along greetings from his family, he hadn't had a serious discussion with her since their argument the Wednesday before Thanksgiving. Tonight he had deliberately left her house before she got in from a late night at work because he still wasn't ready to talk to her. The things she had said to him last week had thrown him for a loop. Of course, he hadn't confused her with Naomi—that was ridiculous—but CeCe may have had a point about his being jealous of Eric. He wasn't jealous, not really, but he did feel a bit of insecurity that he knew was rooted in his experience with Naomi, just as CeCe had accused.

The fact that Naomi had left him and rushed quickly into the arms of an old boyfriend had been hard for him to swallow. That was a part of their breakup that he didn't dwell on. Not dwelling on it didn't change the facts: Naomi had left him for another man. Not just any other man, but a man from her past. Dwelling too much on such thoughts always led him to the inevitable question: Had she ever cared for him, Nate, or had she always been in love with the other man, the man she was now married to? That was a painful question. Only less painful than its answer. He didn't want to believe that he had been happily married to a woman who had never loved him. Though still difficult, it was much more palatable to think that she'd fallen out of love with him, or that she'd grown bored with the marriage, or that he'd lost her because he hadn't paid her enough attention.

"I'm probably not a good person to discuss relationship problems with," Marvin was saying. "But if you need to talk, I can listen."

Nate appreciated his friend's support, but he wasn't yet able to discuss what was going on with him and CeCe. "Thanks, man, but not tonight. If I talk to anybody, I need to talk to CeCe, and I guess I'll do that tomorrow."

Marvin took a sip from the soda can on the cocktail table in front of him. "After church?"

Nate nodded. "I think I'll go to her church in the morning. Maybe I'll get an invitation to dinner. Or I'll offer to take them out."

Marvin nodded also, but he didn't say anything.

"What's going on with you and Shay?" Nate asked his friend. Neither Marvin nor Shay had said anything about seeing each other when they'd stepped in for him and CeCe at Genesis House when CeCe's grandfather was ill.

"Same old, same old."

Nate didn't like that answer. He'd thought that by allowing Marvin to live with him, he'd be giving his friend the space and time he needed to come to his senses. Unfortunately, events weren't unfolding according to plan. "Are you going home anytime soon?" Nate asked.

Marvin stopped and looked at Nate, his can midway to his lips. "Are you kicking me out?"

Nate stood up, ready to head for his bedroom. He didn't have the energy to argue with Marvin tonight. He had too much on his mind. "Not yet, Marvin," he answered, "but the day is coming. You can't stay here forever. Shay's not going to wait that long."

EIGHTEEN

"Mr. Nate, Mr. Nate!" David called when he spied Nate entering the church. The boy ran across the vestibule to greet him.

Nate scooped the child into his arms. "Hi, sport. Does your mother know you're out here running around?" Nate had planned to get to church in time for Sunday school, but after a restless night, he'd slept late and arrived during the break between Sunday school and the start of the eleven o'clock service.

David lowered his lashes, giving Nate a chance to smile at the child's antics. "Mama's inside." Nate didn't say anything, just stared at the top of the boy's head until David looked up at him. "I'm not supposed to run in church."

"I didn't think so," Nate said, settling the boy back on the floor. "What do you think we should do about this?"

David stared at his feet. "Tell Mama."

Nate nodded. "That's right. Where is she?"

David put his hand in Nate's and led him through the swinging double doors into the sanctuary. CeCe was down front talking to the Sunday school superintendent. Nate couldn't remember the woman's name. When David would have pulled him down to join the women, Nate held back and directed the child to a pew about a third of the way back from the front of the church. CeCe would see them as soon as she turned around.

Nate nodded a greeting to the faces that were familiar to him because of his visits to the church with CeCe. He knew quite a few names, though he rarely saw the people outside of church. He and CeCe had formed a core group of shared friends in Shay and Marvin, Anna Mae, Stuart, and Miss Brinson, and they spent most of their time with them. That most of their circle had been his friends before he'd met CeCe he attributed to CeCe's work at Genesis House. Her close friendships with Shay and Anna Mae had developed there. The only one of CeCe's friends Nate had gotten to know was B.B., and he supposed that was because she was CeCe's best friend. She'd probably been the only person that CeCe considered a close friend until Shay and Anna Mae joined her circle. Nate knew she now considered him a friend as well. He wanted to be her friend and her husband, if the Lord allowed it, and he hoped she still wanted that kind of intimacy with him. Recent events were making him wonder more and more where they were headed as a couple.

He felt David fidgeting next to him and glanced down to see what the child was doing. He'd somehow knotted the laces in his shoes and was trying unsuccessfully to unknot them without taking off his shoes. Nate reached down, picked up a foot, unknotted the lace, and relaced the shoe in short order. He quickly did the same for the other foot. David smiled his appreciation, and Nate leaned down and pressed a kiss against his adorable head, knowing that the place the child had secured in his heart would remain forever. Regardless of what happened between CeCe and him romantically, he hoped their friendship would always give him a place in David's life.

Just as Nate raised his head, CeCe turned from her conversation with the superintendent. Their eyes met, and she gave him a wobbly smile. He gave her a stronger one in return. At least, he hoped his was stronger. He knew his insides were as wobbly as the smile she'd given him.

"Good morning," he said when she reached the pew.

"Good morning." She settled in next to David. "I didn't expect to see you here today. You didn't tell me you were coming."

"Is that good or bad?" he asked, teasing her but wanting to hear her answer.

She gave the barest hint of a smile. "I think it's good."

Nate nodded. "I thought we could have dinner together after service."

Her eyes brightened, and he took encouragement from the change it brought in her. "Of course. You can come over to the house. B.B. cooked something before we left this morning."

"Do you think she made enough for me?" Nate knew Miss Brinson always cooked more than enough, but he wanted to keep the light in CeCe's eyes.

"There's always enough for you, Nate," CeCe said in all seriousness, her eyes locked with his. "You shouldn't even have to ask."

"Just checking," he said, but he smiled as he did so, and so did she.

Their conversation was cut short by the start of the devotional. As usual, the deacons led the combination prayer-praise service, which set the tone for the morning worship. Their first song, "How Great Thou Art," was one of Nate's favorite hymns. He closed his eyes and joined in the deacons' chanting rhythm. His soul was comforted by the greatness of the God he served. The spirit of worship encompassed Nate, and his heart overflowed with love and gratitude for his Father, his Savior, and his Comforter. Before he knew it, David was telling him "See ya" and scrambling over his mother's legs to join the other children for children's church. Nate slid closer to CeCe, taking the space David had just vacated so there was no room between them.

CeCe was very conscious of Nate's presence. She'd been surprised but very happy to see him when she'd turned from her conversation with Alma Thompson. Though he'd called when he'd gotten back to town last Sunday, she missed seeing him, being with him, talking to him, despite the fact that their last conversation had been an argument. Now he would be spending the rest of the day with her. Well, not exactly the whole day, because she had to go to work. She could arrive as late as three, but she had to go. She sneaked a glance at Nate. She was sure he was aware of her schedule. She just hoped her leaving wouldn't become awkward.

She turned her attention back to the pastor when he began reading the Scripture lesson for the day. He'd chosen the story of Mary and Martha from the Gospels. She opened her Bible so she could follow along with him. As she read along, she looked and listened for some word or advice that applied directly to her situation with Nate. Was there something in the story of Mary and Martha? Was she Martha, so busy with the unimportant work that she was leaving the important work undone? CeCe didn't think so. Yes, she was working a great deal, but there was a purpose to her work. She wasn't busy merely for the sake of being busy. When the service ended, she was disappointed that she hadn't gotten any guidance on her relationship with Nate.

"Great service," Nate said to her after the benediction.

CeCe guessed he'd gotten whatever it was he wanted out of the service because his eyes were bright and content. Maybe she would have gotten more if her attention hadn't kept straying from the pastor's lesson to her relationship with Nate.

"Pastor Reeves always preaches a good message," she said before turning to greet her fellow church members. She and Nate made their way to the doors, stopping here and there to give a greeting and share a hug or a kiss. David was waiting for them in the vestibule. Not waiting exactly, more like playing around with his friends.

"Are you coming to our house, Mr. Nate?" he asked when he saw them.

"Sure am, sport," Nate told him.

David turned to his mother. "Can I ride with Mr. Nate, Mama?"

CeCe shook her head. "Not today, David. Nate would have to take the booster out of our car, and that's too much trouble."

David shook his head. "No, he won't. I have a booster in his car. Tell her, Mr. Nate. Tell her about the booster."

CeCe looked up at Nate, a question in her eyes. "I picked it up a couple of weeks ago." He palmed David's head. "My buddy here and I were spending too much time moving the seat from one car to the other."

"Yeah, Mama, now I have three boosters. One in your car, one in B.B.'s car, and one in Mr. Nate's car. So I can ride with Mr. Nate, can't I, Mama?"

CeCe nodded her head. "I guess you can, David."

"Yeah," David shouted. "Let me go tell Rodney." David scampered back off to his little friend. CeCe called after him, "David—"

"Let him go, CeCe," Nate said. "He's having a good time."

CeCe looked at her son with love in her eyes. "I know he is, but we have to get home so we can eat. I have to go to work this afternoon."

"That's right," Nate said. "Why don't you go on ahead? We'll follow right behind you. We'll be ready to eat as soon as we walk in the house. You won't be late for work."

CeCe sensed rather than heard Nate's displeasure. "Don't do this, Nate," she said quietly.

"Go on," Nate said, not responding to her plea. "I promise David and I will be only a few minutes behind you."

CeCe wanted to make Nate understand, but she couldn't find the words. She just stood and watched as he walked over to David and his friend. She was losing him. She knew she was.

Sunday dinner would have been very awkward had it not been for David and B.B. CeCe wasn't sure if it was she or Nate who was causing the tension at the table, but she was sure that he and B.B. felt it, just as sure as she was that David didn't.

"Can I go now, Mama?" David asked CeCe. "Mr. Nate wants to see my game. I have to go set it up."

She glanced at Nate and accepted his nodded agreement before answering her son. "Sure," she said with a smile. "But you have to set it up in your room. Mr. Nate can see it up there."

"OK, Mama." He hustled out of his chair. "I'll go set it up now."

"Change your clothes first," she called after him, hoping he'd heard her in all his excitement.

After David left the room, B.B. made a production of clearing his plate and hers from the table. Then she remembered some task she needed to do in her room, leaving CeCe and Nate alone, not just in the dining room but on the first floor of the house.

"Thank you for being so good with David," CeCe said, though she knew they had other issues to discuss. She also knew those other issues would take more time than she had right now. She didn't want to be late for work.

The corners of Nate's mouth turned downward in a frown. "You don't have to thank me, CeCe. I love David. I thought you knew that by now."

Why was he turning her words around? she wondered. "I know you love him, Nate, but that doesn't mean I can't thank you for the way you are with him. Not many real fathers are as good, as patient, as loving with their children as you are with David."

Nate leaned back in his chair and tossed his white cloth napkin on the table in front of him. "I want to be a real father to him, CeCe, just as I want to be a husband to you. I thought that was what you wanted too, but now I'm not so sure."

CeCe didn't have the time for this conversation now, and Nate had to know it. So why was he bringing it up? "You know it's what I want. How can you say you're not sure?"

His eyes widened in surprise or anger, she wasn't sure which. "How can I *not* say it? The last time I talked to you, you were on the fast track to paying Eric back his money. A fast track that's going to take two or three years. That must mean you're thinking it'll be two, three, four years before we get married."

CeCe shook her head. She wasn't going to get angry with him.

"We haven't talked about a date, Nate. We aren't even officially engaged yet, but—"

Nate lifted his arms in the air. "Whose fault is that?" he asked, his voice clipped and louder than usual. "You've been dragging your feet about the entire matter. I told you that I wanted to talk to your parents first, and I didn't see you making any move to get us together. Had your grandfather not gotten ill, I'm not sure you would have ever gotten around to getting me together with your parents."

"That's not—"

Nate shook his head and laughed a dry chuckle. "Do you know that I have a diamond engagement ring in my chest at home that I've been wanting to give to you?"

He'd already bought the ring. She didn't know. Why hadn't he told her? "Nate—"

He lowered his voice to its normal decibel level. "Don't 'Nate' me, and don't look so surprised. Why wouldn't I have a ring? I want to marry you, CeCe. This isn't a game for me."

She bowed her head. "It's not a game for me either."

He took her hand in his. "Then tell me what we're doing, where we're going, because for the life of me, I don't know anymore."

She raised clear eyes to him. "I want to marry you, Nate, and I also want to pay back Eric's money. There's nothing that says we can't get married before I pay the money back."

Nate shook his head, his eyes sad. "You don't get it, do you?"

"Get what?" CeCe asked, anger running up her spine trailed closely by fear.

"There is no *us* until you deal with Eric." He spoke slowly, deliberately, each word clearly enunciated. "How can we even think about getting married with him consuming all of your thoughts and energy?"

She jerked her hand away from his, her anger and fear equally matched now. "We aren't back on that, are we? Eric is nothing to me, Nate. I'll tell you again. Maybe it's your own heart that you need to consider." Before he could respond, she pushed back from the table and stood. "We need to talk this through without interruption, and we can't do it now because I have to go to work. I'll be back around six. If you're here, we can talk after David goes to bed."

"I'll be here," he answered with a barely perceptible bow of his head.

"Good. I have to go change. I'll talk to you tonight." As she turned and left the room, the fear of what was coming consumed all of her anger.

CeCe arrived back that night a little earlier than she'd expected. She and Nate had some time together with David, which she really enjoyed, and then she listened as Nate read David a story before they left him to sleep for the night. Her heart lightened a bit when Nate took her hand in his as they walked down the stairs and out to the porch.

He continued holding her hand when he spoke. "I'm sorry for my attitude today, CeCe. I've been upset about things, and I let my feelings show in the wrong way. I hope you can forgive me."

"There's nothing to forgive, Nate," she said. Then she added, "Nothing much, at least."

He gave a grim smile and squeezed her fingers. "I don't know where we're going, CeCe, and that concerns me. I thought we wanted the same things—"

"We do." She placed a hand against his cheek. "You know we do. I love you, and I can think of nothing better than spending the rest of my life with you."

"Even though you think I'm treating you as though you're Naomi?" he asked, his eyes probing hers. "Is that what you really think, CeCe?"

It was her turn to squeeze his fingers. His voice betrayed his vulnerability. "I think you're comparing Eric and me to Naomi and the ex-beau she ended up marrying."

He dropped her hands and leaned back on the swing. "Maybe

I am guilty of making those comparisons, but I don't think I've been unreasonable. I never want to end up in another relationship like that one, which is why I asked you that first night if there was anybody else."

"I told you there wasn't, and there isn't."

He leaned forward. "But there is."

She sighed deeply. "We seem to be at a stalemate, Nate. I don't know what else I can do to make you believe what I tell you. Tell me what I have to do to prove to you that Eric means nothing to me."

He took her hands in his again. "Call him. Ask him to forgive you for the blackmail, and make reasonable arrangements to repay the money." This time CeCe pulled her hands away from his. He sighed. "Why is that so hard for you to do?" he asked.

She rubbed her hands down her arms. Though she wore long sleeves, the late-November air felt chilly. Or was the chill she felt from Nate? "I'm not sure. I just don't think I can do it now. How can I talk to him after everything that has gone on in the past? I need to be able to give him the money, and then I can talk to him. Not before."

"Why is having the money so important, CeCe? The money isn't the issue. The issue is your letting go of the past so we can move on to the future."

"I just need more time, Nate." Why couldn't he understand?

"How much time?" he asked, his voice soft. "It's been five years now. How much more time do you need?"

CeCe stood up, still rubbing her hands down her arms. "Just let me get the money. Then I'll be able to face him. I can't face him now. I'd be too ashamed. I can't do it. After everything he's done to me, I can't go crawling to him for forgiveness. I can't. Not now. Not yet."

Nate inhaled a deep breath and then let it out. "That's my problem."

CeCe dropped her hands from her arms and turned to face him. "What's your problem?"

"You," he said, inclining his head toward her. "If you can't let him go, there's no room for me. If you can't forgive him, CeCe, I have to wonder if there'll come a time that you can't—or won't—forgive me."

She raised her arms in exasperation. "That's ridiculous, Nate. You'd never—"

He cut her off. "Never say 'never.' Besides, true forgiveness has very little to do with the actual wrong that was done. True forgiveness comes from a loving heart, CeCe. True forgiveness is a decision, much like love, not just a feeling."

CeCe felt as though a dull knife stabbed at her heart with each of Nate's words. "But once I get the money—"

"OK, CeCe," Nate said calmly, too calmly. "What will happen when you get the money?" He didn't give her time to answer. "You'll be able to throw it in Eric's face and prove once and for all that you're a better person than he is. That he wronged you, that he left you, but that you didn't need him. Will the money prove that to him? Will the money give you that kind of confidence?"

His words sounded awful to CeCe's ears, but they had been exactly what she was thinking. She'd apologize to Eric, all right, and after she did, he'd begin to feel guilty. He'd realize how badly he'd treated her, and then he'd realize he hadn't hurt her as much as he'd thought. She'd gotten over it and gone on with her life. And done very well—spiritually and financially—so well that she could forgive him and repay his money. "You're making it sound so . . ." She couldn't find the words.

"So what? Coldhearted? Calculated? Unchristian?" Again, he didn't give her time to answer. "I thought I knew you, CeCe. I thought that tough exterior of yours was just a façade. I thought that the real you was tenderhearted, kind, loving—all the traits that are valuable and worth cherishing. But the CeCe I'm seeing now is somebody else. This CeCe would rather hold on to her past, would rather plan for some outrageous revenge, than move on to her future with a clear heart. This new CeCe I don't understand. She's not the CeCe I fell in love with."

CeCe's heart broke with his last sentence, but she wasn't going to allow Nate to see how much his words had hurt her. "Maybe you never loved me, Nate. Not the real me."

Nate shook his head, and there was defeat in his eyes. "That's where you're wrong, CeCe." He gave a dry chuckle that held no humor. "I still love you, and I probably always will. But I don't see how we can build a future, a life together, on a foundation of unforgiveness and the presence of another man. I just don't see it. The problem for me is not that I don't love you. My problem is how do I deal with the love I feel for you when I know that nothing can ever come of it."

NINETEEN

"CeCe," B.B. called to her from the kitchen as she walked into the house. After a prayer that both of their hearts would be open to the Lord's leading, Nate had left her standing on the porch wondering what was going to happen to them. He loved her, but he couldn't make a life with her unless she forgave Eric, he'd told her. Why hadn't she been able to just forgive Eric? she asked herself. Then she tried to shake off the upsetting thoughts and paste on a happy face for B.B.'s sake.

"Nate gone already?" Miss Brinson asked. When CeCe nodded, the older woman pushed the mail across the counter to her. "For you."

CeCe picked up the envelopes. *Bills*, she thought. *Just more bills.* Then she came to the letter she knew B.B. wanted her to see. CeCe felt her friend's eyes on her. Would she ever get a break? First, Nate. Now, B.B.

"I wonder what they have to say this time," B.B. said. "Maybe they're apologizing for what happened in Alabama." She closed the door to the dishwasher and put away the last two plates.

CeCe put the letter aside. "I doubt it. They probably want to ask the same question again."

B.B. gave a deep sigh, causing CeCe to ask, "Are you all right?"

B.B. smiled. "Perfect. In fact, I have some good news."

CeCe put down the mail and gave B.B. her full attention. She could use some good news about now. "Well, tell me. Don't keep me in suspense."

B.B. took great care in folding a dish towel and placing it primly on the counter. Then she said, "Mr. Towers has asked me to marry him, and I've accepted."

CeCe ran around the counter and pulled her friend into her arms. "Oh, B.B., I'm so happy for you and Mr. Towers! I've suspected all along this would happen. I just thought Mr. Towers would move back here before he asked you." She pulled back and, heedless of her tears, asked, "When is he moving back?"

CeCe felt B.B.'s hand tighten on hers. "That's the thing, CeCe. He's not moving back here. At least, not right now. He loves it in Virginia, and he thinks I'll love it too."

CeCe dropped her hands to her side. "You're leaving?" *You can't go*, CeCe screamed inside. *What will I do without you?*

As B.B. nodded her assent that she was indeed leaving, CeCe realized that she was thinking only of herself. She had to let her friend go. "Forgive me, B.B. I'm being selfish. David and I are going to miss you a great deal. More than a great deal." She wiped at her eyes. "I'm just a watering hole these days," she said, using both hands to wipe her tears. "You're like family to me, B.B. You were my friend when I didn't have friends, and you were a mother when I felt I couldn't talk to my own mother. You've been a spiritual guide to me and a wonderful example of living a godly life. I'm going to miss you so much, but I know you'll be happy. I just know you will."

B.B. pulled CeCe close for a brief embrace. "I know I will too, but then so will you. Maybe you and Nate will start thinking about a wedding date soon. I couldn't have asked for a better life mate for you than Nate, CeCe. You're both blessed to have found each other."

CeCe decided not to put a damper on B.B.'s spirits by giving her the details of the status of her relationship with Nate.

"I know you're having problems now," B.B. went on, "but I believe you'll work them out."

CeCe wanted to believe her friend, but she didn't know if she could. "What makes you so sure about Nate and me?" she asked.

B.B. shook her head. "It's not Nate and you that I'm sure of, CeCe. It's God. He'll lead you back to each other. I know it."

CeCe didn't comment but instead changed the topic back to B.B.'s upcoming marriage. "So when's the date?" she asked.

"We're not getting any younger, so the sooner the better. Richard is coming to town next week, and we'll be married within the next month or so, either a Christmas or a New Year's wedding. We've already talked to the pastor. It'll be a small ceremony right after the morning worship. We just have to pick a Sunday."

"So soon," CeCe said, unable to douse the sadness she felt at the prospect of B.B.'s imminent departure. "Why didn't you tell me?" She had to sit down. She felt as though the earth had tilted on its axis. First, Nate and now, B.B. Her rocks. What was she going to do without them?

Miss Brinson sat next to her. "You've had a lot on your mind, and you've been really busy lately."

CeCe looked into B.B.'s eyes. "Not too busy for you. Never too busy for you." CeCe couldn't stop the second flow of tears. She wiped her eyes and tried to smile. "I'm sorry I'm crying. I'm happy for you, but I don't know what I'll do without you. What about our plans to open the day-care center?"

"You'll do just fine," B.B. said. She helped CeCe wipe her tears. "I'm going to miss you and David something fierce. You're my family and I love you, but I believe the Lord is ending our time together for a reason. We were there when we needed each other, but now it's time for us to part. The Lord has something special in store for both of us, and it's not a day-care center. I think we both know that, have known it for a while, in fact."

"Yeah," CeCe said. She knew Miss Brinson was right. A day-care center wasn't in either of their futures. She wondered if it ever had been. She'd wanted it more for B.B. than for herself, and now she realized that B.B. didn't really want it, had probably never wanted it. "You have Mr. Towers." *And now I don't have Nate,* she thought.

B.B. smiled. "And you have Nate, but that's not what I'm talking about. You'll know soon enough what I mean."

CeCe didn't understand her friend, but she didn't want to dwell on herself. This was B.B.'s time, and she'd do whatever she could to make it a happy one. "Well," she said, "we don't have much time, but I think we can plan a great reception. So will it have a Christmas or a New Year's theme?"

When Nate arrived home after his argument with CeCe, he was greeted by the familiar sight of Marvin stretched out on the couch in his family room watching television.

"Hey," Marvin called, his eyes still on the set. "You're home early again."

Something about Marvin's comment hit Nate the wrong way, or maybe the right way. As he looked at his friend now, allowing life to pass him by, Nate saw a male version of CeCe. Marvin was allowing the past to control his future as much as CeCe was. And Nate was helping him do it. He'd thought he was helping to save Marvin's marriage by giving his friend refuge, but now he understood he was only supporting his friend's habit. He couldn't save Marvin's marriage any more than he could make CeCe forgive Eric. He loved both of them, but he couldn't live their lives for them, no matter how much he wanted to. Without preamble, he said to Marvin, "It's time, my friend."

Marvin turned his eyes from the television to Nate. "Time for what?"

Nate would have lifted his shoulders, but they were too heavy tonight. "Time for you to go home—or somewhere. You can't stay here anymore."

"What's this all about, man?" Marvin asked, sitting up. Nate had his full attention now. "You have a fight with CeCe, and now you're putting me out?"

Nate shook his head. It, too, felt heavy. "It's just time. I'm your friend, Marvin, your brother, but I don't think I've been much help to you. You've got to get on with your life, and living here in this room is not going to help you."

"So now you know what I need? Nate, the answer man, strikes again," Marvin chided.

Nate gave a humorless, tired laugh. "You don't know how wrong you are, Marvin. I'm the last person you should refer to as the answer man. Sometimes I feel I don't have any answers. But what I do know is that I can't make you reconcile with Shay, and allowing you to stay here just keeps you from having to make the tough decisions. I've effectively put myself in the middle of your marriage, and now I want out. I guess, in a way, I felt that if I saved your marriage, it would make up for failing in mine. But you know what? Your marriage is between you and Shay and God. There is no place for me in it, so I'm getting out."

Marvin stared down at his sandwich and soda on the coffee table. "I'll leave," he said.

"All right. You can have a week to figure out what you're going to do, but no longer."

Marvin nodded. "No problem. I'll be out of here."

Nate looked at his friend, but he didn't say anything more. There was nothing else to say. He turned and went upstairs to his bedroom. He pulled out the engagement ring he'd never had a chance to give CeCe, and his heart ached because he knew he'd never give it to her. He was going to have to live without her. He was sure of it. "Why, Lord?" he asked. "Why did you bring her into my life and let me fall in love with her and David if I can't have a life with them? I did everything you wanted me to do. I didn't rush her. I waited patiently just as you wanted. So, why, Lord? I would have been much better off not knowing her. It hurts so much, Lord. I love her, and more than anything, I want to help her, but I can't. I feel so helpless. Help her, Lord. Please help her. Not just for me, but for her and for David, too."

Nate closed his eyes and remained silent for a few moments. When he opened them, he reached for his Bible.

CeCe was running late as usual. Shay, Anna Mae, and she had finished their last Saturday morning session of the year about fifteen minutes ago, and she'd headed off for work. Instead of their usual workshop, they'd held a preholiday celebration with their students, past and present, as the guests. She'd been halfway across town before she realized she'd forgotten her portfolio. She'd immediately called Margaret's office, told them of her delay, and headed back to the Center.

The past two weeks had been excessively busy for her—work, planning for B.B.'s wedding reception, more work, getting ready for the holidays, Genesis House, and more work. She welcomed the work because it helped keep her mind off her worries. With B.B. leaving, she was going to have to make some decisions. She couldn't keep working three jobs, that's for sure, and she had to find someone to keep David while she did work, even if she only worked one job. She had no idea how she was going to handle these problems. She couldn't even deal with them right now. If things were better between her and Nate, she could discuss all of this with him, but she knew right now wasn't the time.

She still saw Nate often because he continued to spend time with David despite the problems he had with her—again showing himself to be different from the other men she'd known—but things between them weren't the same. Neither had called a formal end to their relationship, but they both knew it was dying on the vine and neither one of them seemed able to save it. She thanked God they'd built their relationship on a foundation of friendship, and though it pained her to be around him still, she knew his friendship with David was important to both him and her son. And to her.

She found that what she missed most was talking to Nate. He'd come to be her best friend as well as the man she loved, and she missed his companionship. She wanted so much to tell him about an alternative financing idea that she wanted to present to Mr. Cronin. If implemented, she believed it would qualify more lower- and middle-income families to purchase quality Cronin homes. She would like to have Nate's support behind her when she presented her plan to Mr. Cronin. But she couldn't talk to Nate about the idea—or about much of anything else—because Eric stood in the middle of their relationship, as tangible as the two of them.

Nate would have believed in her and the idea, though—of that she had no doubt. He'd always believed in her, even when she didn't believe in herself. Like with this Eric business. In that, though, she'd let him down. Why couldn't she do what he wanted? she asked herself. All she had to do was pick up the phone and call. Why couldn't she do such a simple task? It wasn't that she didn't want to forgive Eric; it was that she didn't know how to forgive him. She'd carried her unforgiveness around for so long that it had become a part of her, and that now scared her. What scared her even more was that she was unable to pray about the situation. She knew that put her on dangerous ground.

She pushed these thoughts to the back of her mind as she pulled into the Rec Center parking lot and headed for the work- shop classroom. She found her portfolio on the shelf under the podium. As she turned to leave the room, a boy entered. He was a young man, really. A good six feet, 180 or 190 pounds, she'd guess. He looked vaguely familiar. She'd seen him around, but she couldn't immediately place him. "Can I help you?" she asked.

"I'm looking for Mrs. Wilson," the young man said, his eyes darting around the room. "I thought she came down here on Saturday mornings."

CeCe remembered the young man then. He was Danita's boy- friend. Anna Mae had pointed him out once or twice, and she'd seen him a couple of times when she'd gone to church with Nate, but she'd never been introduced to him. "You just missed her. We wrapped up around noon. Have you checked her house?"

The young man nodded. "Nobody's there."

CeCe detected an uneasiness about him. "Can I help you with something?" she asked again, even though she knew she didn't have time to get into a long discussion. She was already late for work.

"Uh, no, not really. I just need to talk to Mrs. Wilson. Do you know where I can find her? I really need to talk to her."

The boy's anxiety bothered CeCe. She wondered if the reason he needed to talk to Anna Mae concerned Danita. "Is Danita all right?" she asked. The boy looked at her with questioning eyes. "Mrs. Wilson told me that you were her daughter's friend," she said in response to his unasked question.

The boy's shoulders sagged, and CeCe thought she'd never seen anybody look so downtrodden. Her heart went out to the young man. "Then I guess she told you we broke up—Danita and me."

CeCe nodded. "She mentioned something about it," she answered honestly. "So is Danita all right?" she asked again, more concerned now about her friend's daughter.

"I guess," the boy said. "She's not talking to me, and she won't see me." His eyes clouded, and CeCe wondered if he was going to cry. Nonsense, she told herself. The young man would probably die before he cried in front of her. She needed to go, but—

"It's all my fault," the boy said.

Something in his tone made CeCe push her work to the back of her mind. She placed her portfolio on top of the podium. "Why don't you sit down a moment?" She pointed to a chair at the table next to the podium. "I'm sure it wasn't all your fault."

The boy dragged himself over to the table and slumped down in a chair. "But this was all my fault. I love Danita, you know. I love her so much, and now she hates me."

CeCe shook her head, still not sure what she was dealing with. The boy had said Danita was all right, and CeCe prayed he was telling the truth. "Have you seen her today?" she asked, trying to get more information.

"No, she's gone shopping in Commerce with a friend of hers." He peered over at CeCe. "I'm not following her. One of her friends told me." The boy leaned forward, his elbows on his knees, and rested his head in his hands. "I didn't mean to hurt her. I would never hurt her."

CeCe became alarmed again. "What do you mean you didn't mean to hurt her?" she asked.

"She said I broke her heart. That's what she said. She said I broke her heart. But I didn't mean to," he explained brokenly. "I loved her. I still love her."

CeCe sighed her relief. Danita was fine. Physically. She was pretty sure of that now. "Do you want to tell me what happened?"

The boy shook his head. "It won't help. Nothing will help now. If only she hadn't . . ."

"If only Danita hadn't what?" CeCe asked, wanting the boy to keep talking.

He shook his head again. "Not Danita. Patrice. Patrice shouldn't have told her. I told her not to tell her. I was going to tell her. I should have told her, not Patrice."

CeCe thought she was beginning to understand. Obviously, this young man had been seeing someone other than Danita. "So there was another girl, and the other girl told Danita?"

The boy nodded.

"And Danita broke up with you when she found out?"

The boy sighed, and his eyes skittered around the room again. "Sort of."

CeCe didn't say anything. The boy seemed to have calmed down a bit, and she was glad for that. She'd give him a few more minutes, and then she had to get to work. She knew they were expecting her to arrive any minute now.

"Do you think a person should spend his or her whole life paying for one stupid mistake?" he asked. His tone told CeCe he'd been thinking on the question for some time.

She wasn't sure how to answer him. "It depends," she said. "It depends on what the person did and what the law says about it. We do have to face the consequences of our actions." She had come to work at Genesis House to pay for her mistakes. But God had turned that sentence into a wonderful experience. For a time, anyway. "But many times in facing those consequences we gain a lot more than we pay."

"Like what?" he asked.

Recognizing his interest as genuine, CeCe told him about how she came to Genesis House, developed life friendships, fell in love with Nate, and grew in her relationship with Christ.

"How much do you love Nate?" the boy asked.

CeCe was surprised by the question. "I'm not sure what you mean."

"Is there anything he could do to make you stop loving him?" the boy clarified. "Do you love him so much that you'd love him regardless of what he did?"

CeCe thought seriously about the young man's question. "I'd like to think so."

The boy shook his head. "I don't think you would. I think if you found out about another woman, you wouldn't forgive him even if he told you he didn't love the other woman. Even if he told you it had been a mistake. I don't think you'd forgive him. Women never forgive you for that kind of stuff."

CeCe considered carefully before answering, and then she spoke slowly. "I would be hurt, true, and I would be angry, but I would like to think that one day I could forgive him."

"Do you think you could ever go back with him?"

"I don't know. It depends on so much. Every situation is different."

"This girl," he said. "Her name is Patrice. And I was, well, *seeing* her." His emphasis on *seeing* told CeCe that he and Patrice had done more than merely *see* each other. "Danita didn't know, and I only saw Patrice a couple of times and then I stopped because I knew I was wrong. What we were doing was wrong. And I knew Danita would be hurt if she found out."

"And you said she found out?"

"Yeah. Patrice told her. I wanted to tell her, but Patrice beat me to it. When I saw Danita, I knew Patrice had told her. She didn't yell or get mad or anything like that. She just cried."

CeCe felt the young man's pain, and she thought he might cry too. He was just a kid, regardless of his size, and he'd tried to play both ends against the middle and gotten caught. He'd realized his error, but he'd realized it too late. She believed he was sincere in his feelings for Danita, and she hoped one day the girl would believe him. She doubted she did now.

"I love her so much, but she'll never trust me now. She thinks I should marry Patrice."

That suggestion caught CeCe by surprise. "Marry her?"

The boy's eyes skittered away from her. "She's pregnant. That's what she told Danita. She told Danita she was pregnant and I was the father."

CeCe felt as though the wind had been knocked out of her. "Patrice is pregnant with your baby?" she asked.

The boy ignored her question. "I don't want to marry Patrice. I don't love her. I don't even know if I like her." He rested his head in his hands again. "How did my life get so messed up? I'm only nineteen years old. I shouldn't have to spend the rest of my life paying for one mistake."

The boy's shoulders were shaking now, and CeCe knew he was crying. She scooted her chair closer to his and pulled him against her side, which was awkward since he was so much bigger than she was. As she allowed his sobs to dampen her blouse, her own eyes filled with tears of sympathy for him, for Danita, and for Patrice. Three young people whose lives had been irrevocably changed by a youthful foray into territory where youth had no business venturing.

The boy had asked her if he should spend the rest of his life paying for his mistake, and CeCe had no answer for him. If the clocks were turned back, she'd be Patrice in this scenario, so her heart went out to the girl she didn't even know. But her heart also went out to this boy. Though he hadn't planned it, he was going to be a father. His reckless actions had resulted in the start of a new life, but what cost should he have to pay? Was the right answer for him to marry Patrice so they could try to make a life together for the sake of their baby? CeCe wasn't sure.

The boy pulled away from her suddenly, and CeCe knew he was embarrassed at having become so emotional. "Have you talked to your parents about this?" she asked after he'd regained his composure.

The boy shook his head. "I can't face them. My mom is going to be disappointed and start crying, and my dad is going to kill me."

CeCe bit back a smile. The man beside her was indeed still a child. "Don't sell your parents short," she said. "They may surprise you."

The boy cast a skeptical glance at her. "You don't know my parents like I do."

CeCe nodded. "You're right. I don't know your parents. But I have parents, and I know how my parents would react," she began.

Then she told him her story. For the first time, Eric wasn't the villain, and neither were her parents.

TWENTY

By the time CeCe and Ronald—she'd finally asked his name—left the Center, the young man had promised to tell his parents about Patrice. After giving him her home address and phone number, and telling him to get in touch if he needed to talk, she walked him to his car. Impulsively, she pulled him into an embrace. "It's going to be all right," she said. "You won't have to go through this alone."

When she pulled back, he gave her a half smile. She knew he didn't believe her yet, but he wanted to. She waited until he'd pulled out of the parking lot before going to her own car. Once settled inside, she put the key in the ignition. As she started to turn the key, her heart filled up and her eyes overflowed with tears. She was so overcome that she placed her forehead on the steering wheel and cried out the pain she'd stored inside for so long. She cried for Ronald, Patrice, and Danita and the challenges they were about to face. She cried for herself and Eric and the past they couldn't change. She cried for all the time and energy she'd wasted being angry with Eric. And she cried because she was no longer angry with him.

"Thank you, Lord," she murmured through her tears. "Thank you so much." When her eyes were again dry, she pulled out her cell phone and called Margaret's office. "I won't be in this afternoon," she told the office assistant.

When she hung up, she pulled out of the parking lot and

headed for a spot where she could be alone. She didn't go home because she knew Mr. Towers and B.B. would be there, and she didn't want to disturb them. She went to the first place that came to her mind.

Twenty-five minutes later, she was seated in Nate's favorite spot at Stone Mountain Park, the Bible she always had in the car resting on her lap. It was cool today so she wore a jacket. The tree that had shaded them during the summer no longer had its leaves. This was the first time she'd been here without Nate, and it felt right that she was. Today was about her and God, not her and Nate.

For more than an hour, CeCe cried, prayed, and cried some more. "Forgive me, Lord, for my unwillingness to forgive others. I know I've been wrong—so very wrong. Thank you for sending Ronald my way and allowing me to see how wrong I've been. I pray for him, Lord, and for Danita, and for Patrice. Guard their lives, Father. Direct their paths to you, and show them your love. Use me, Father. If there is any way I can help, just show me how. I've been so wrapped up in my own guilt and shame that I never realized you could use my story to help bring someone else along the way. Thank you for using Ronald to show me that today. Please keep me open and sensitive to other ways that I can help.

"And give me the courage and the strength to do the right thing about Eric, my parents, and Eric's parents. I've been so wrong, Father. Help me to show love to them the way you've shown love to me. And lastly, Lord, help me to do the right thing by Nate. I thank you for making him the man of God that he is. I thank you that he was willing to walk away from this relationship rather than pretend to be in agreement with my unforgiving attitude. I pray that he'll always show such strength and godliness in our relationship. And I pray that I can be the same way with him. Teach me to love him the way you want him loved. And if I can't do that, please send him a woman who can. It'll hurt me to lose him, but I'll be happy knowing that he's better off with somebody else."

CeCe was still in a prayerful mood when she left the park. She took 78 East to 285 South to 85 South. She was going home. She needed to see her parents. Instead of the dread she usually felt when making the trip to Alabama, this time she felt only excitement. Excitement at seeing her parents again, at having the opportunity to tell them how much she loved them.

She saw them before she pulled into their driveway. Her mother stood in the front door. Her father was working in the yard. Their surprise at seeing her was evident in their faces. Both of them met her at the car.

"Is something wrong?" her mother asked before CeCe could get all the way out of the car.

CeCe's heart hurt at her mother's question. Had she been such a negligent daughter that coming to visit her parents could only be a sign that something was wrong? She knew she had been. "No, Mama," she said, getting fully out of the car. "Everybody's fine. I just wanted to see my mama and daddy and tell them that I love them." She opened her arms and enclosed them both in a big embrace. When she pulled back, her parents' eyes were damp and so were hers.

"What happened, CeCe?" her mother asked. Her father remained quiet, which was his way. As a child she'd always taken comfort in his quiet strength, hidden as it was behind a gruff manner. She'd missed relying on it the last few years.

She put one of her arms in one of each of theirs and led them into the house. "Your daughter is finally growing up, Mama. Don't you think it's about time?"

Once her parents were seated on the couch in their living room, with CeCe in the wing chair across from them, CeCe asked for their forgiveness.

"You don't need forgive—," her mother began, but her father cut her off.

He covered his wife's hand with his. "We forgive you, daughter," he said, his voice gruff but full of love. "We're mighty glad to do it."

"Thank you, Daddy." She got up and gave him a hug. "And you

too, Mama." When she pulled back from her mother's embrace, she added, "I've been wrong about David, too. He needs to know his grandparents. I want you two to come visit us in Atlanta. Often. I can come pick you up if you don't want to drive, but I want you to be a part of our lives. I'll also bring David down here to stay with you sometime. Would you like that?"

Her mother couldn't answer for her tears.

Her father answered for both of them. "We'd like that a lot."

And that was that. Just a few words, and everything that had been wrong between her and her parents began to turn around. "I love you both very much," CeCe said again. "I don't want you to forget that. You've been good parents to me, better parents than I realized, but I was so bitter after Eric."

"We know, CeCe," her mother said. "We don't blame you. You were just a girl, and you had a lot to handle."

"Thanks, Mama, but there is something else that I need to tell you. I wasn't just upset with Eric all these years; I was also upset with myself. You see, there's something you don't know." CeCe took a deep breath and told her parents about blackmailing Eric.

"Oh, CeCe," her mother cried. "What a load you had to carry. I wish you could have told us."

CeCe shook her head. "I was too ashamed, Mama. I couldn't tell you. I couldn't tell anybody." *Until Nate.* "Now I have to make it right with Eric. I'm going to repay the money. First, I have to go see his parents and apologize to them. Hopefully they'll tell me how I can get in touch with him."

Her parents nodded.

"They're pretty bitter themselves, CeCe," her mother warned her. "Eric really hurt them. He doesn't call and he doesn't visit. He's abandoned his parents."

CeCe didn't feel any joy in that knowledge. She'd always assumed Eric had walked away from her and gone on to lead a carefree life. Maybe she'd been wrong.

"Do you want us to go with you when you talk to the Brad-shaws?" her father asked.

CeCe shook her head. "I love you for wanting to go, but I have to do this on my own." She looked from one parent to the other. "I'm still not ready for Eric's parents to be part of David's life. I'm not sure when I will be or when David will be. He's just a child, and I don't want to confuse him. Eric's parents will only bring up questions about Eric, and I'm not sure how to address those with David. The Bradshaws can't become part of his life until I know what to tell David. Can you both understand and accept my position?"

"But—," her mother began.

Again her father stopped her. "You are David's mother, CeCe. We'll trust you to do the right thing, and we'll respect your wishes."

Her mother nodded. "We will, CeCe. I'm sorry for what I did the last time you were here. I knew you didn't want the Bradshaws to be around David, but I also knew how they felt. He's my grandson too, and I know how much I miss him. It seemed so wrong to deny them a few minutes with him. I guess I was hoping they'd do the same for me if our situations were reversed. Can you forgive me?"

CeCe kissed her mother's cheek. "It's already forgiven. Maybe if I had explained myself better you wouldn't have been forced into that situation. Now I'd better get over to the Bradshaws. I didn't tell anybody I was leaving Atlanta, and I need to get back home before it's too late." She stood up. "I know this is short notice, but the holidays are fast approaching and I'd like you to spend them with us in Atlanta. Miss Brinson is getting married sometime between now and New Year's—the date's not set yet— and I'd like you both to come for the holidays and the wedding. I can pick you up the weekend before Christmas, and you can stay through New Year's. How does that sound?"

She thought her father was going to turn her down when he began moving his head back and forth, but he said, "I think I may be able to get up there on my own. Now that I know we're welcome."

CeCe smiled. "You're more than welcome, both of you." Then she jotted down directions and headed off to the Bradshaws.

CeCe drew in a deep breath and prayed a silent prayer as she rang the bell to the Bradshaws' home. Mrs. Bradshaw met her at the door. CeCe could read the hope in the older woman's eyes, and she felt compassion for her.

From the front door Mrs. Bradshaw called to her husband, "Harold, CeCe's here."

Mr. Bradshaw came from the kitchen. CeCe knew, because she'd been in this home many times when she was a child. "Hello, Mr. Bradshaw," she said, seeing the same hope in his eyes.

Mr. Bradshaw nodded. Mrs. Bradshaw invited CeCe in and pointed her to a seat in the upholstered rocking club chair. The two of them sat close together on the sofa, hands entwined, presenting a united front.

"I wanted to talk to you about David—," CeCe began.

But before she could finish her statement, Mr. Bradshaw jumped in as if he knew what she was about to say. "We want to see our grandson," he demanded, leaning toward her. "It's not right, your keeping him away from us."

CeCe understood the Bradshaws' frustration and their pain, and she knew there was little she could do to ease it. "This is not about rights, Mr. Bradshaw," she said, keeping her voice even and direct. "It's about a four-year-old boy whose biological father wants nothing to do with him. How will I explain to David that he has grandparents but that he has no father?"

"What do you tell him now?" Mr. Bradshaw asked.

She looked down and studied her fingers before speaking. "I tell him that his father can't be with him right now. And I teach him that he has a heavenly Father who's always there for him. That explanation has been enough so far, but if you start coming around, it won't be enough for long." She sighed. "I don't want to lie to David, but neither do I want to tell him that his father doesn't want anything to do with him. Not now. He's too young to understand."

Mrs. Bradshaw began to sob. "We are so ashamed, CeCe," she began between sniffles. "For Eric's actions and for our own. We should have been there for you even if Eric wasn't, but we tried to support our son. It seemed the right thing to do at the time."

Mr. Bradshaw patted his wife's knee. "Eric has been a big letdown for us," he said, his earlier defiance gone. "We haven't seen him but two or three times since he got married. When he comes in this direction with Yolanda, they stay with her folks over the state line in Columbus. Most of the time Eric doesn't even come home when Yolanda does. It's like he wants to forget he has a family, a hometown."

"Maybe it's more than that, Mr. Bradshaw," CeCe suggested.

Both Bradshaws looked at her, questions in their eyes.

"Don't be too hard on Eric," she found herself saying. "Maybe he's ashamed of everything that's happened. Maybe that's why he won't come home. I know my shame kept me away. I'd like to get in touch with Eric, if you'll tell me how to reach him." CeCe wasn't sure how much Eric had told them, and she didn't want to get into the blackmail again, so she settled for a simple, "I owe him some money that I want to repay."

"I'll get you his address and number," Mrs. Bradshaw said. She got up from her seat next to her husband and left the room.

"Do you really think it could be shame that's keeping Eric away?" Mr. Bradshaw asked, hope again in his eyes. CeCe knew the hope was that one day his son would be a part of his life again.

CeCe nodded. "I'm not sure, but it's a definite possibility, Mr. Bradshaw."

The older man inclined his head slightly. "You said you felt shame. You don't feel it anymore?"

CeCe shook her head. "Not anymore."

"Why?" Mr. Bradshaw asked.

She met and held Mr. Bradshaw's gaze with confidence. "Because the past is gone, and I can't change it. God has given me a present and hope for a future. I want to live both to the fullest. I can't do that by dwelling in the past. Eric and I were kids, Mr. Bradshaw. I was twenty-one and he was twenty-two, but we were still kids just learning what it meant to be adults. I'm still learning. Eric probably is still learning too."

Mr. Bradshaw nodded as Mrs. Bradshaw returned. "Here's his latest number," she said, handing CeCe a slip of paper. "Don't be surprised if you call and he's not home. He's never there when we call. At least that's what Yolanda says."

CeCe took the paper. "Thank you so much," she said. "I'm sorry about David, but for right now, it has to be this way."

Mr. Bradshaw nodded. "We don't blame you, CeCe. You have to do what's right for the boy. We just wanted to get to know him. We've lost so much. Our son and now our grandson."

CeCe's heart went out to the Bradshaws, and she wished she could give them the answer they wanted, but she couldn't. Not right now. Maybe after she talked to Eric, but not right now. "I'm sorry," she said again. Then she left.

"This sure looks good, Mrs. Murphy," Nate said to the widow whose front-porch steps he'd just repaired. While he'd been visiting, he'd noticed the warped board and decided to replace it for the elderly lady. "Your red velvet cake is the best I've ever eaten."

"Aw, go on, Nate," the older woman said, her voice full of fondness for him. "You'll eat anything that's not tied down. Don't you think I know that by now?"

Nate stabbed his fork into the cake and shoveled a large piece into his mouth. "Mmm, mmm, good," he said. "Will you marry me, Mrs. Murphy?"

"Hey, what are you doing, Nate?"

Nate turned around and saw Stuart strolling up Mrs. Murphy's walk, a big grin on his face.

"Only one woman to a man," Stuart said as he reached the porch. He pulled Mrs. Murphy into a big hug and said over her head, "You've got yours, so I get Mrs. Murphy."

Mrs. Murphy pulled out of Stuart's arms and propped her

fragile hands on her thin hips. "You're not foolin' anybody, Stuart Rogers. You just want a piece of my cake for yourself."

Stuart pressed his hand to his heart. "That's true, but it doesn't mean I don't want to marry you. What do you say? We could run off together and open a bakery."

Mrs. Murphy laughed, shaking her head. "Both of you sit down." She pointed a bony finger at Stuart. "I'll bring you a piece of cake, and both of you some milk." Then she left the two men on the porch, murmuring something about "growing boys."

"What are you doing down here?" Nate asked Stuart, sticking another piece of cake in his mouth, as both men seated themselves on Mrs. Murphy's top step. The December day was clear, and the air held only a slight chill that demanded no more than a jacket and long sleeves.

"Looking for you," Stuart said. "You had to be down here in Robinwood or over at CeCe's. Something told me that you weren't at CeCe's."

Before Nate could respond, Mrs. Murphy returned with a tray loaded with Stuart's cake and two glasses of milk. She was about to speak when her phone rang. "You two share this," she said. "I've got to get the phone."

Both men smiled as the elderly woman went back into the house. "She's a sweetheart, isn't she?" Stuart said, diving into his cake.

Nate took one of the glasses of milk and swigged down a gulp. "The best. So why were you looking for me?"

Stuart set down his plate and picked up his glass of milk. "Thanks to you, I have a houseguest."

"Marvin."

Stuart nodded.

"I guess I'm not surprised," Nate said. "How long are you going to let him stay?"

Stuart shook his head as if weary at the thought. "I don't know, man. I just don't know. What could I do when the brother showed up? This holiday season is an especially rough time for both him and Shay."

Nate pressed a fist against his forehead. "Oh, man, I didn't even think about the holidays. I don't know what I was thinking. I could have let him stay through the holidays. I'll have to apologize. What I did to him was cold."

Stuart was shaking his head. "No, you don't have to apologize, and what you did wasn't cold."

Nate stared at him. "You're kidding, right?"

Stuart shook his head. "Those were Marvin's words. Guess what? Now *he's* worried about *you!*"

"Me? Marvin's worried about *me?*" Nate couldn't keep the surprise and hope out of his voice.

"Yes, you," Stuart said. "I was surprised too. Surprised, but glad. You finally got the brother to think about somebody other than himself. There's hope for him yet."

Nate was dumbfounded. He'd kicked Marvin out when he was down, and now Marvin was worried about him. "Well, he ought to start worrying about Shay. Marvin needs to stop hiding and face his fears. Shay's right there waiting for him. Why can't he see it?"

"That's the same question Marvin asked about you." Stuart peered at his friend over his glass of milk. "Why can't you see how much CeCe loves you?"

Caught off guard, Nate almost spilled his milk. "What's this got to do with CeCe and me?"

"Everything. Nothing."

"What kind of answer is that?"

Stuart took another swallow of milk. "You tell me. What's up with you and CeCe? You've been down in the mouth for weeks now. Marvin commented on that, too, by the way. Are CeCe and her work still bothering you?"

When Nate didn't immediately answer, Stuart said, "I love you like a brother, Nate. So does Marvin. We want to help if we can."

Nate took a deep breath. He knew he'd been keeping his thoughts and feelings about his relationship with CeCe bottled up, and he realized now that wasn't a good idea. Not if it resulted in his treating badly the people he loved most. "It's rough, man. I love her and want to marry her, and she says she loves me and wants to be my wife, but . . ." Nate thought about CeCe's work, Eric, CeCe's relationship with her parents. So much seemed to stand between them.

"But what?"

"But sometimes love is not enough." Nate then proceeded to tell Stuart about Eric and the reason CeCe was working so much. "I can't get her to see that she's going about it all wrong. The simple solution to this whole matter is for her to call the guy, ask for forgiveness, and arrange some repayment schedule. Why can't she see that?"

Stuart didn't answer, and Nate watched as his friend took two more bites of his cake. "So you don't have anything to say?" Nate asked when he grew tired of waiting for a response.

"So you think CeCe is in love with this guy? You really think that?"

Nate searched his heart. Did he really think that? The way Stuart posed the question made it sound ridiculous. "Not really," he said, "but what if she does? She says she loves me and I believe her, but . . ."

"But Naomi said she loved you, too."

Nate nodded. How could a person really know what was in another person's heart? "I try not to think about that, try not to make the comparisons, but I can't seem to stop myself."

Stuart swallowed another bite of cake. "Let me ask you something, Nate. You're always talking about how God taught you a lot from your relationship with Naomi. What exactly did he teach you?"

Nate considered his friend's question. What had been the basic lesson? "To wait on God. To be sure of his voice and not go speeding off on my own."

"Have you done that with CeCe?"

Nate nodded. He thought he had. He'd certainly tried. If it were left up to him and his timing, his ring would be on CeCe's finger and they'd have a date set for the wedding.

"Then I don't see the problem."

Nate's cake lost its flavor, and he put down his plate and his fork. "I love her, and I'm losing her—that's the problem. Losing her to some guy from her past."

Stuart shook his head. "You're not losing her. Are you sure God has said 'no,' or has he just said 'not now'? There's a big difference in the two." He drained the last of his milk. "You used to be a fighter, Nate, but you've given up already. You already have you and CeCe apart for the rest of your natural lives. Maybe, just maybe, you're overreacting. CeCe is not Naomi. She's a sincere woman, growing in her faith every day. Right now, she's facing a challenge. She needs your support, not your anger. Instead of thinking about how your life is going to be affected if she doesn't get her act together, think about the pain she's going through as she faces her demons. She needs you now more than ever. Your support—not your demands or your disappointments."

Each of Stuart's words removed a few more scales from Nate's eyes. He had been focusing on himself—his needs, his hurts. It was so obvious now. Why hadn't it been obvious before? He'd been as blind to what he needed to do as he thought CeCe was to what she needed to do. The pain of his error burned deep in his heart. From the beginning, he'd told himself he wanted to be CeCe's friend, but when she'd really needed him, he hadn't been a friend to her. Not really.

"One thing I liked about your relationship with CeCe is that you appeared to be good friends," Stuart was saying. Nate found it difficult to focus on his friend's words because of the words his heart was speaking to him. "Now's the time to draw on that friendship. She's your sister in Christ first, Nate, and always will be. The wife part comes second."

Before Nate could respond, Stuart polished off the last of his cake, picked up his empty glass, and stood. "I think I need a refill." Then he turned and went into the house, leaving Nate alone with his thoughts.

Nate sat there thinking about all that had gone down between him and CeCe in the last few months. Did he really want to be a friend to CeCe, or did he only want to be in her life if he could be her husband? Did he really love her as a sister in the Lord? As he pondered these questions, he remembered his thoughts about CeCe's work schedule and its negative effect on her care of David. He heard himself as he questioned her love for him. He heard the impatience, disappointment, and disapproval in his response when she'd told him of her plan to deal with Eric. These memories together with many others were proof that he hadn't loved her as a sister. No, he'd been so hurt and angry over the possibility of losing her as a potential wife that he had totally forgotten his role as her brother in Christ.

"Oh, Lord," he murmured, his heart bowed low, "please forgive me. Forgive my self-righteous attitude in dealing with CeCe. Lord, I saw so clearly what she needed to do, but I didn't see at all what I needed to do. Forgive me for focusing on what I perceived as the negatives of the situation instead of praising you for the provisions you made. I thank you so much, Lord, for filling in the gap with David. Though in my heart I accused CeCe of shirking her parental responsibilities, I was wrong. You already had those covered. You gave CeCe support in the form of B.B. and me. You allowed us to stand in for her when the need arose, and you made that stand-in sufficient for David's needs. Thank you, Lord, for working in CeCe's life and for preparing her life situation so that she could learn the lessons you wanted her to learn without detriment to her child. Thank you for using me to make this way for her."

Nate felt tears moisten his cheeks, but he did nothing to wipe them away. His heart ached for the way he'd treated CeCe and Marvin. He knew now that God was working out his treatment of Marvin for his brother's good, and he prayed the same would happen with CeCe.

"I know, Lord, that I don't deserve a woman—a sister—like CeCe, but that doesn't change the fact that I love her as a man loves a woman. Show me how to love her through the challenges she's facing. I want to build her up in all ways. You've been patient and loving with her about this issue for five years, Lord, and I haven't been able to be patient and loving for six months.

Teach me your time schedule, Father, and your ways of loving. And, Lord, this is the hard part, but I want to pray it even though I don't feel it in my heart right now. If CeCe is better off without me, then show me how to settle for being her brother in Christ. Make that enough for me, for her, and for David. We all need your strength, Lord."

CeCe wasn't surprised to find Nate and David outside when she arrived home later that night. When she'd called from Alabama to tell B.B. she was going to be late, she'd spoken to both of them. No, she wasn't surprised to see Nate and David, but she *was* surprised to see Ronald. The three males were tossing a Frisbee in the front yard. The front-porch light was on, fighting off the coming of night. No doubt David was having the most fun.

Her son ran up to her as she got out of the car. "Mama, Mama," he called. "Ron's gonna teach me to play Frisbee football, right, Ron?" David looked over his shoulder at the young man.

Ronald palmed the boy's head, which CeCe was pleased to see was covered with a hat to ward off the early evening's chill. "That's right."

David looked back at his mom. "He's going to teach Mr. Nate, too."

CeCe glanced at Nate, smiled, then turned her attention to Ronald. "Thank you for teaching my son to play Frisbee football," she said.

"No problem."

"Come on, David," Nate called. "Let's get some practice in while Ron talks to your mother."

CeCe sent Nate an appreciative smile and noticed that Ronald did the same thing. "How are you?" she asked when Nate and David were out of earshot.

The boy nodded. Then he kicked the toe of his white sneakers against the concrete of the driveway. "I talked to my parents," he said.

"How was it?"

He looked up from staring at his feet. "My mom cried, and my dad yelled a lot, but afterwards we talked about it. My parents wanted to go talk to Patrice's parents, but when they called nobody was home."

"How do you feel about their talking to Patrice's parents?"

He shrugged. "All right, I guess. My dad says I have to take responsibility for my actions. That being a man means being responsible."

"He's right, you know." CeCe was so proud of the young man standing before her that she wanted to give him a big hug. She guessed he wouldn't appreciate it too much with Nate and David looking on.

The boy nodded. "I hadn't really thought much about Patrice until I talked to you today." He paused. "You have a good son."

CeCe nodded. "He's the best thing in my life."

"Patrice doesn't want the baby," he said. "She only told Danita she did to break us up. I think she's going to have an abortion."

CeCe tried to keep her features straight, but the thought of the young girl taking such a drastic step pained her. "How do you feel about that?" CeCe asked.

"At first, I didn't want to think about it." The boy's lowered gaze let CeCe know he was embarrassed by what he was telling her. "It would have made things much easier if she had done it instead of telling Danita."

"How do you feel now?"

He looked up at her. "I don't think she should have an abortion. Maybe she could give the baby up for adoption. Or maybe we could get married."

CeCe's heart went out to the boy. He had a lot of tough decisions to make for one so young. She was proud of him for facing his responsibilities, though. She'd have to tell his parents so when she met them. "Just take it a day at a time, Ronald. Listen to your parents. They sound like reasonable people, good people, and they love you. And don't forget you can talk to God. He'll listen and he'll help."

The boy nodded again. "I guess I'd better get back to the game. It'll be too dark to see the Frisbee in a while." He turned toward Nate and David. Then he turned back to CeCe. "You don't mind me just showing up here, do you? I didn't mean anything by it. I liked talking to you today. I felt like you understood me, you know. And you didn't judge me."

CeCe smiled from deep inside her heart. "It's more than all right. You're welcome to come by anytime. I think you've already won David over."

Ronald smiled his first real smile. "He's a great kid. So is Mr. Richardson."

"I'll have to tell Mr. Richardson you think he's a great kid."

"That's not—oh, you're teasing me."

CeCe laughed. "I'm trying to," she said. "Now get back to your game. I'll take a seat on the porch and watch."

TWENTY-ONE

It was some time later before Nate and CeCe were alone. Tonight they found themselves out back sitting on the deck. Mr. Towers was in town, and he and B.B. had taken their place on the front-porch swing. "I'm not sure if this is a good sign or a bad sign," Nate said.

CeCe didn't know if he was teasing. She sat in a wrought-iron chair next to his. "I don't think it's either. Just change. Maybe we needed one." When he didn't respond, she said, "Do you know that when I first met you at Genesis House I was prepared to dislike you?"

Nate shook his head. "You didn't even know me. Why were you prepared to dislike me?"

She smiled at the memory. "Because you had stood me up the week before. I had canceled two appointments to show houses in order to make the meeting, and then you didn't show up. I was very upset with you, Mr. Richardson. Very upset."

"You certainly fooled me," he said. "I had no idea you were upset."

"That's because that smile of yours disarmed me. I was lost the moment you smiled at me." She turned so she could see his face in the light from the deck lamp. "There was something about you, Nate. Something good and innocent. I knew when we were in the park that you were a man who could break my heart. I was right."

He cupped her jaw in his hand. "I've broken your heart?"

She shook her head. "But you could. You've burrowed yourself so deeply into my heart that you can surely break it."

"The same here, CeCe," he said, allowing his hand to fall away from her face. "I didn't know it that day, but I knew it soon after, and I know it now. You haven't broken my heart yet, but I'm so afraid that you will."

She took his hand in hers. "You've been right about so many things, Nate. I just haven't been able to see them. I don't have any other excuse." She sighed. "I'm so used to running that it's become my general reaction to things that I can't—or don't want to—handle. All those parking tickets are a perfect example. I let a small problem escalate into a major problem by refusing to deal with it when it was small. Maybe if I had paid the first ticket, I wouldn't have gotten the second. But once I started putting them off and not dealing with them, it became easier and easier to toss them into the glove compartment and forget about them. In a way, the tickets weren't real to me. Stuart made them real the day he sentenced me to a hundred and fifty hours of community service, though. I was so angry with that man that I could have spit."

She'd have to tell Stuart this story one day. A smile bubbled up inside her when she thought of his reaction to her news. "You know what?" she said, feeling the wonder of God's love and providence envelop her just as the darkness of night had overcome the day. "That sentence was one of the best things that's ever happened to me. I was forced to stop running. I had to deal with the consequences of my actions. The funny thing is, I always thought I was the most responsible person there was. Look at me, raising my son alone and doing a pretty good job of it. A part of me always considered the circumstances of David's birth as the consequences of Eric's actions rather than the consequences of mine. Every time I looked at the situation, Eric was more to blame than I was. Now I know I was just looking the wrong way." She shivered as she spoke those words, and she knew it wasn't the cool of the night that caused it. No, she shivered because she understood the jeopardy her faulty vision had placed her in, and she thanked God she'd finally been able to see the truth.

"Eric and I did what we did together, and now I know that we both suffered. Maybe Eric more than me because I had David to help me deal with my guilt and shame, and Eric had no one. He couldn't talk to his wife about it because she wasn't supposed to know. His parents say that he's cut them off. I did the same thing with my parents, but God was good and he gave me David and sent me to Miss Brinson. She showed me how to depend on God, how to have a living faith. I thought I had it mastered until I met you."

"Me?" he asked, squeezing the hand she'd placed in his.

She jabbed a finger in his chest. The cotton in his sweater felt soft to her touch. "Yes, you. You scared me to death. First of all, you made me want to stop running, while at the same time you made me know I had to keep running."

He grinned. "Huh?"

"I can't explain it. You made me want to believe that some-body could love me—really love me—and not use me. I was so scared to believe that was true. About as scared as I was to believe it wasn't."

"I do love you," Nate said.

"I know." She moved their joined hands to her heart for a brief moment and lowered her head. "My heart knows. But then once you loved me, I knew that if you knew what I'd done to Eric you wouldn't love me anymore."

He began shaking his head. "My love is tougher than your past, CeCe."

She lifted her head, looking straight into his dark eyes. "I know that now, Nate. I didn't then. Even though I was scared for you to know the details of my past, I wanted you to know. I wanted to believe you would love me if you knew, even though I was scared that you wouldn't. But you did."

Keeping their hands clasped, Nate placed his free one around her shoulder and leaned close to her. "And that scared you, too, I imagine."

"Well, not exactly," she said, wishing the wrought-iron chairs they sat in allowed them more closeness. "What scared me was when you started challenging how I was dealing with Eric. First, it was your response to the letters from his parents. You were more concerned about my anger than my decision. Then it was your response to my relationship with my parents. Then your response to my tale of blackmail." She shook her head at the memory of the day she'd told him her story at Stone Mountain. "You were more concerned about my feelings for Eric than you were about the blackmail. What I had found so shameful had not even registered with you."

He looked down at her. "But you called me on that last one. Fear of what I had experienced with Naomi did figure into my response."

She nodded her agreement. "I know, but that doesn't mean you weren't right. Not about any loving feelings between Eric and me but about the power I'd given him in my life because of my inability, or unwillingness, to forgive him. I couldn't forgive Eric because to forgive him would mean that I'd have to assume more responsibility for my role in our relationship. I wasn't ready to accept that responsibility."

"Do you think you'll ever be ready?"

"I got ready today." She paused, then told him about her talk with Ronald earlier. "He thinks that I helped him. Someday I'm going to have to tell him how much he helped me. Not now, but one day when he's ready to hear it."

"He thinks a lot of you. I could tell during the short time we spent together. I get the impression he's going to make himself familiar around here."

"Do you mind?"

Nate shook his head. "He's a good kid. You'll be a good influence. Do you mind?"

CeCe knew her smile split her face. "Not at all. In fact, I look forward to it. I have never felt like I did when I was talking to him today. When I was telling him my story, I found joy in what I had previously found only shame and guilt in. I began to see that by allowing God to take my shame and use it to help others, I was no longer ashamed. What happened is firmly in the past. I've been forgiven, and now I want to live in the fullness of that forgiveness. I have nothing to be ashamed of but a great deal to be happy about, thankful for, and proud of."

"Sounds like you've had a life-changing day."

She heard the joy in his voice and was happy to have him to share her challenges and victories. "That's not the half of it. You know what? I think this is what God had in mind when he first sent me to Genesis House. Do you remember that first day when you gave me the option of doing the teen pregnancy workshops or the employment workshops?"

"Of course I remember."

"Well, I chose the employment workshops because I wasn't ready to deal with my own issues around teen pregnancy. I'm thinking now that I really should have taken on the teen pregnancy. I believe that's where God wants to use me."

"Does that mean you're now volunteering for the job?" he asked, unable to keep the pleasure she knew he felt from his voice. "Your hours are up, you know."

CeCe waved away any concern about hours. She knew this was work she had to do. "That's exactly what it means. I want to get started next week." She was already planning to get in touch with Patrice. She knew the girl would need all the support she could get to make it through her pregnancy with her dignity and her heart intact, and she wanted to be there for her.

"I don't want to put a damper on your plans," Nate said, "but how are you going to fit one more thing into your already full schedule?"

"By taking something off, of course."

"Something like what?"

She gave him a huge grin. "Either my day job or the job with Margaret or both. I have a couple of ideas that I think Mr. Cronin may find interesting. Maybe we can talk about them and my jobs next week, and you can help me decide what I should do."

Nate's silence told CeCe that she had surprised him. When he squeezed her shoulders, she felt his joy deep in her bones. "What about repaying Eric's money?" he asked a little later.

"I got his number from his parents and tried to call him today, but I didn't get him. I'll try again, and if I don't get him, I'll write him a letter. I'm sure we can make arrangements for me to repay him over time."

"You're ready to leave the past behind, aren't you?"

She lifted her hands in pure joy, wanting to shout the freedom she felt. "Oh, Nate, I'm just so sorry I waited so long. I think Eric needs to hear from me. His parents are so worried about him. They hinted that his marriage is in trouble. If I had contacted him sooner, maybe I could have saved all of us—his parents, my parents, Eric and me—a lot of unnecessary pain."

Nate's hoot of laughter surprised her. "Why are you laughing?" she asked.

"Because I'm so proud of you. Because I'm so happy." He smiled into her eyes. "And because I love you so much."

CeCe basked in his words. "I love you too, Nate," she told him. "And I want a future with you if that's what you still want."

He nodded. "It's what I want more than anything."

"But," CeCe began slowly, unsure of Nate's reaction to her next words, "I'm going to need some time. I want to get to know my parents again. I've invited them to spend the holidays here, and I'm hoping I can convince them to move in after B.B. leaves. Then I want to get started with the teen pregnancy program. I have no idea where that's going to lead, but I want to be able to go with the flow. If Ronald is any indication, I have a feeling this house is going to become a teen hangout."

Nate rubbed her hand with his. "Sounds like you have a lot that you want to do, and it could take a long time."

CeCe nodded. "Too long for you to wait?" she asked.

Nate tilted her chin up. "Forever wouldn't be too long for me to wait for you, Ms. Williams. I love you, CeCe, more today than I did yesterday, and I didn't even think that was possible. I'm willing to wait until you're ready. I *want* to wait until you're ready. I don't want to rush ahead of the Lord, so taking some time is probably a good thing for us." He brushed at the tears that were falling down her cheeks. "I can wait because I trust you and your love for me, and I trust God to direct our relationship."

"Oh, Nate—," CeCe said, knowing that the past was truly in the past. There were no longer any ghosts in their relationship, and they both knew it.

He pulled her close, allowing her tears to dampen his sweater. "You aren't the only one who's been learning something about herself lately. I've been doing some learning myself."

When he said nothing more, CeCe asked over her tears, "So aren't you going to tell me?"

He sighed a contented sigh. "Sometimes I think I can do the Lord's job for him, CeCe. Of course, I can't, so I usually end up frustrated about all the things I can't fix. I think I've done some of that with us. The Lord has been doing a great work in your life recently, and I just wish I had been more supportive of what you were going through. I want us to always support each other in our faith—the victories and the challenges."

She pressed her hand to his chest and looked deep into his eyes. "You have supported me, Nate. You've supported me and challenged me. How can you think otherwise?"

He pressed a soft kiss to her brow. "I'm glad you think so, sweetheart, but I know I could have done better. I admit to being afraid of losing you and allowing that fear to color my reactions to what you were going through. But no more. I trust you, and I trust us."

"Oh, Nate," CeCe said, crying in earnest.

Nate pulled her into a close embrace and just held her. She knew he cherished the new level they'd reached in their faith and in their relationship just as she did. A short while later, he placed a finger on her chin and tilted her face up to his. "You're going to have to stop crying and kiss me. I have a feeling we won't be doing as much of that after your father moves in. I only *thought* B.B. had a shotgun, but I *know* your father does."

CeCe's laughter was cut short by Nate's firm lips as they pressed against hers.

A Note from the Author

Dear Friend,

I'm so happy that you decided to pick up a copy of my book. Awakening Mercy is a story that's close to my heart for a couple of reasons. First, because it's my first CBA novel, and I consider it an honor to write for the Christian market. And second, because in many ways, CeCe's story is my story.

When I sat down to write this book, I wanted to tell about a person's journey back to right relationship with God. Instead, Awakening Mercy became a story that illustrates how God forgives us, but in order for us to walk in that forgiveness, we have to forgive ourselves and those who have wronged us.

The word forgiveness is very easy to say. But many times it's difficult for us to live out because, like CeCe, we focus so much on our personal hurt that we fail to realize and accept the role we played in bringing pain into our lives. I pray that reading Awakening Mercy will encourage you about the love and care that God has for you, and that it will spur you to seek forgiveness in your own life, if you need to do so.

I love to hear from readers, so if you're inclined to drop me a line, please do. Awakening Mercy is the first book in the Genesis House series, so I hope we'll meet again. The second book is scheduled for publication early in 2001.

Until then, I leave you in God's care.

Angela

About the Author

Angela Benson is a native of Alabama and now lives in Georgia. She is a graduate of Spelman College and Georgia Tech. She holds master's degrees in operations research and human resources development from Georgia Tech and Georgia State University, respectively, and she is currently a doctoral candidate in instructional technology at the University of Georgia.

Angela's first book was published in 1994. Since then, she has published seven novels, one novella, and a nonfiction book on writing. Her books have appeared on regional and local best-seller lists, and she has won several writing awards, including Best Multicultural Romance from *Romantic Times* magazine and Best Contemporary Ethnic Romance from *Affaire de Coeur* magazine.

Angela welcomes letters written to her in care of Tyndale House Author Relations, P.O. Box 80, Wheaton, IL 60189-0080. You can also send her E-mail at GenesisHouse@BensonInk.com.

Visit www.HeartQuest.com for lots of info on
HeartQuest books and authors and more!

www.HeartQuest.com

Current HeartQuest Releases

- *Magnolia*, Ginny Aiken
- *Lark*, Ginny Aiken
- *Camellia*, Ginny Aiken

- *Sweet Delights*, Terri Blackstock, Ranee McCollum, and Elizabeth White

- *Awakening Mercy*, Angela Benson
- *Abiding Hope*, Angela Benson

- *Freedom's Promise*, Dianna Crawford
- *Freedom's Hope*, Dianna Crawford
- *Freedom's Belle*, Dianna Crawford

- *Faith*, Lori Copeland
- *Hope*, Lori Copeland
- *June*, Lori Copeland
- *Glory*, Lori Copeland

- *Prairie Rose*, Catherine Palmer
- *Prairie Fire*, Catherine Palmer
- *Prairie Storm*, Catherine Palmer
- *Prairie Christmas*, Catherine Palmer, Elizabeth White, and Peggy Stoks

- *Finders Keepers*, Catherine Palmer
- *Hide and Seek*, Catherine Palmer
- *A Kiss of Adventure*, Catherine Palmer (original title: *The Treasure of Timbuktu*)
- *A Whisper of Danger*, Catherine Palmer (original title: *The Treasure of Zanzibar*)
- *A Touch of Betrayal*, Catherine Palmer
- *A Victorian Christmas Cottage*, Catherine Palmer, Debra White Smith, Jeri Odell, and Peggy Stoks
- *A Victorian Christmas Quilt*, Catherine Palmer, Debra White Smith, Ginny Aiken, and Peggy Stoks
- *A Victorian Christmas Tea*, Catherine Palmer, Dianna Crawford, Peggy Stoks, and Katherine Chute

- *Olivia's Touch*, Peggy Stoks
- *Romy's Walk*, Peggy Stoks

Coming Soon (Fall 2001)

- *A Victorian Christmas Keepsake*, Catherine Palmer, Kristin Billerbeck, Ginny Aiken

Other Great Tyndale House Fiction

- *Jenny's Story*, Judy Baer
- *Libby's Story*, Judy Baer

- *Out of the Shadows*, Sigmund Brouwer

- *Ashes and Lace*, B. J. Hoff
- *Cloth of Heaven*, B. J. Hoff

- *The Price*, Jim and Terri Kraus
- *The Treasure*, Jim and Terri Kraus
- *The Promise*, Jim and Terri Kraus

- *Winter Passing*, Cindy McCormick Martinusen

- *Rift in Time*, Michael Phillips
- *Hidden in Time*, Michael Phillips

- *Unveiled*, Francine Rivers
- *Unashamed*, Francine Rivers
- *Unshaken*, Francine Rivers
- *A Voice in the Wind*, Francine Rivers
- *An Echo in the Darkness*, Francine Rivers
- *As Sure As the Dawn*, Francine Rivers
- *The Last Sin Eater*, Francine Rivers
- *Leota's Garden*, Francine Rivers
- *The Scarlet Thread*, Francine Rivers
- *The Atonement Child*, Francine Rivers

- *The Promise Remains*, Travis Thrasher